SALT CITY BLUES

SALT CITY BLUES

Barbara Block

This first world edition published in Great Britain 2004 by
SEVERN HOUSE PUBLISHERS LTD of
9–15 High Street, Sutton, Surrey SM1 1DF.
This first world edition published in the USA 2005 by
SEVERN HOUSE PUBLISHERS INC of
595 Madison Avenue, New York, N.Y. 10022.

British Library Cataloguing in Publication Data

Block, Barbara
    Salt city blues. - (A Robin Light thriller)
    1. Light, Robin (Fictitious character) - Fiction
    2. Murder - Investigation - New York (State) - Syracuse - Fiction
    3. Women private investigators - New York (State) - Syracuse - Fiction
    4. Pet shop owners - New York (State) - Syracuse - Fiction
    5. Syracuse (New York) - Fiction
    6. Detective and mystery stories
    I. Title
    813.5'4 [F]

    ISBN 0-7278-6153-0

Typeset by Palimpsest Book Production Ltd.,
Polmont, Stirlingshire, Scotland.
Printed and bound in Great Britain by
MPG Books Ltd., Bodmin, Cornwall.

To DJM. Thanks for lending your karma to me, as well as for being, funny, charming, and smart

One

I took the photograph of the dead man the detective was holding out to me and held it up to the light so I could get a better view. The guy, whoever he was, didn't look real good, but then no one does when they're dead, especially before the make-up artist gets done with them.

'Bummer,' I told the detective as I handed the picture back to him.

'For him absolutely. Do you know who this man is?'

I shook my head. 'Haven't a clue. Did he come with the breathing tube in his mouth?'

The detective ignored my question and passed the photo in front of my face again. 'You're sure?'

'Well, he hasn't come into the bar when I've been working here. Why are you asking?'

'Because some kid found him lying in a snow bank down the street early this morning when he went to school. Guy probably froze to death. We're trying to put a name to him.' The detective looked at me for a moment. His eyes got all squinty, then he said, 'Hey, aren't you Robin Light? George's friend. Don't you own the pet shop?' He snapped his fingers. 'What's it called?'

'Noah's Ark.'

'So why are you doing this?' I took 'this' to mean working behind the bar at Shamus's.

It was a good question. I'd been asking myself the exact same one for the last two hours. 'I'm helping Ian out.' Ian Yates was the man who owned Shamus's. I was also not coincidentally helping myself out, since the money I was making here was going to pay the store's utility bill. 'Hey, you should come into Noah's Ark and check out the tropical fish,' I told the detective. If there's one thing I've learned from being in retail it's that you have to get in there and sell, sell, sell whenever an opportunity presents itself. 'I'm giving a twenty percent discount to police and firemen.' Which wasn't true, but would be from now on.

'Maybe I will,' he replied, but I could see from the expression on his face that he was just being polite. 'Mind if I talk to the other denizens of this place?'

There were ten of them hunched over the bar, intently eyeing the TV. All of them had been here when I arrived, which meant they'd been here for at least four hours. Some of them had been here for considerably longer. The expression "rooted to the spot" came to mind when I looked at them.

'Be my guest.' Like I was going to say no. But it never hurts to be courteous. Especially to the powers that be.

'Where's your dog?' The detective asked.

'Zsa Zsa? She's home,' I lied.

Actually she was in the back room sleeping next to the heating vent, but I wasn't going to tell him that, because having a canine in here was a violation of the health code, not that he was going to cite me. He had other things on his mind right now.

Now that I thought about it, the detective did look familiar. He and George used to go to the SU games together up at the Dome. What the hell was his name? He'd shown me his badge but Ian kept the place so dark I couldn't read it and I didn't feel like asking him.

'Well, tell George I said hello,' the detective said.

'Will do,' I told him.

The detective nodded. As he went down the line of customers I remembered his name. Noel Conrad. He was divorced and had a little girl. Funny thing but no one at the bar seemed eager to see the photo. Maybe because they figured that guy could be them. Everyone took a quick glance, shook their heads, and went back to their beers. Except for Carmen that is. She insisted on holding the photograph this way and that before she finally allowed as how she didn't know who it was

2

either, but then at this point in her life I don't think Carmen could ID her own kid.

'Guess that guy won't be having a good Christmas,' Bill observed as he motioned for me to bring him another PBR after the detective left.

'Not unless you believe in heaven.' I popped the top of the can and slid the beer over to him. Years of working outside had left Bill's face looking like a walnut shell.

'I like Christmas,' his girlfriend Shelley declared. She waved her hand around the place. Even in this light you could see the veins in her hands stuck out like lines on a roadmap. 'You should do something in here to make it more festive-like.'

'I'll relay your message to Ian,' I told her before retiring to the other end of the bar to light a cigarette. According to Ian, Shelley and Bill had been sitting at the bar since twelve o'clock. Since it was now nine o'clock at night I figured they were going for their personal best.

Not that I was going to tell Ian what Shelley had said, even if I thought he'd listen. Anyway the place was decorated – kinda. Ian had put a scraggly tree in the corner near the pool table and wrapped a couple of strands of white lights around it – the tree not the pool table. I figured that he figured, given the nature of the place, that that was all the festiveness the clientele at Shamus's could handle, and maybe he was right.

Of course I wasn't one to point a finger in the beautification department. The holiday decorations I'd come up with at Noah's Ark left something to be desired as well. They consisted of cutout snowmen on the windowpanes, a statue of a dog and a cat dressed up in Santa Claus suits, and some colored holiday lights strung around the perimeters of the windows.

Manuel, the kid who works for me, had pronounced my efforts pathetic, but he hadn't been willing to come up with anything better when I told him I'd give him a free hand to do whatever he wanted. On a personal note, I'm not a big Christmas fan. However, when you're in retail Christmas is your friend. My place makes about thirty percent of the entire year's sales during the period between Thanksgiving and Christmas.

This year we weren't doing well – at least not so far, although I was trying to remain optimistic. What is it they say about it not being over until the fat lady sings? Well, according to my accountant she's better start belting it out pretty friggin' soon.

All it would take would be one good week saleswise and I'd be out of the woods. Unfortunately I don't see that happening any time soon. For openers, the economy in Syracuse sucks. All the jobs that are left are moving to Southeast Asia. The weather isn't helping either. Funny thing but people don't like to go out when it's minus ten, they stay home, and we'd had two solid weeks of this weather. I was thinking it was probably warmer in Juneau, Alaska, than it was here when Bill started talking to me.

'Hey,' he said. 'You do this detectin' stuff, right?'

'Once in a while I do favors for people,' I said cautiously. One way or another I'd been involved in several criminal cases over the years. These days, though, I'm trying to keep a low profile. Besides, I don't have a license.

'So why don't you find out who that dead guy is? Maybe he's from around here.'

'No ... no ... no ... he isn't,' a guy everyone called Stuttering Sam chimed in.

'How do you know that?' Bill demanded of him.

'B ... b ... because I would have recognized him,' Stuttering Sam told him.

'So you say,' Bill replied.

'Ye ... ye ... ye ... yeah. I do,' Stuttering Sam stammered.

Then he blurted out a string of words that I couldn't understand, although I think I caught a fuck or two in there. But it was hard to tell. This I've learned since I've been working at the bar is a good indication that Stuttering Sam is getting upset. I got another beer for him and calmed him down.

Bill took a gulp of his PBR and banged the can down on the counter. 'Well, I still think Robin should investigate.'

'Really?' I said.

The picture on the TV went out and I went over and gave the set a couple of good whacks with the side of my hand.

4

Then I proceeded to tick off the reasons on my fingers why I wasn't planning on getting involved.

'One. Because the police seem to have the matter in hand. Two. Because no one has asked me to. Three. Because I don't have the time.'

'You should do it anyway,' Bill's girlfriend Shelley observed.

'Why should she do that?' Carmen demanded belligerently. She was sitting towards the door and raised her voice to be heard. 'It's none of Robin's business. She should stick to what she does and let the police do what they do.'

'No one asked you,' Shelley said. She took a sip of beer. Then she had another thought, which I've learned is never a good thing with her. 'Hey,' she said nodding towards Carmen. 'Maybe you know who that guy is. Maybe that's why you don't want Robin to do nuthin'.'

Carmen's jaw trembled. She started to get up off her stool. Since she and Shelley had what they liked to call a history, I decided now might be a good time to intervene.

'Shelley is just teasing you, Carmen. Right, Shelley?'

Shelley clamped her lips together and studied her can of PBR.

'Right, Shelley?' I repeated more forcefully.

'Right,' Shelley said grudgingly after a moment had gone by.

'Good,' I said.

'I feel as if I'm a kindergarten teacher,' I'd complained to George after the first week I'd worked at Shamus's.

'Yeah, but little kids are cute,' George had replied. 'These people aren't.'

George was right I thought as I put my hands on my hips and looked around the room. 'Everyone happy now?' I asked.

I could just see myself having to explain to Ian how I let two seventy-year-old women fight with each other. That just wasn't going to happen. Especially since Ian hadn't wanted to give me this job in the first place and I'd badgered him into it. How hard could this be? I'd asked him.

He'd just raised his eyebrows. I do well with people, I'd

continued. I have a good memory. And it isn't as if I've never set foot in a bar. I know what goes on. Ian had crossed his arms over his chest and given me an amused smile.

But I figured, hey, if I could deal with a fifteen-foot boa constrictor I could deal with whatever came up at Shamus's easy. Well, after two weeks of doing this I've decided it's a lot harder than it looks, especially when the bar is busy. And while I don't mind working, putting in two sixteen-hour days twice a week is a bitch. I'm definitely getting tired of working my tush off.

'I'm going home,' Carmen announced, getting up.

'Good riddance,' Bill muttered as Carmen stumbled out the front door on to the sidewalk.

Fortunately Carmen only lived two houses down. I went and peeked outside anyway to make sure she made it. We didn't need two dead people in one night. That would be bad for business.

'She likes to make trouble,' Shelley told me as she took another sip of her beer.

Then she proceeded to regale me – for what had to be the nine hundredth time – with how she'd discovered Carmen in bed with her second husband – or possibly her third. It's hard to keep track. I nodded and made uh-hunh noises and tried to keep from yawning in her face while I kept one eye on the bar and the other on the television. Shelley kept talking. I was wondering how often one person could repeat the same story – maybe she had short-term memory problems brought on by a lifetime of drinking – when the door swung open. I expected it to be the detective coming back if I was lucky, Carmen if I wasn't, but it was some kid.

From where I was standing I could see he wasn't dressed even remotely warmly enough for the weather outside, which the weather announcer on TV was telling me was minus one. The kid had a knit cap pulled down to his eyebrows and a hoodie pulled up over that. No gloves. No scarf. No jacket. Obviously he was a hardier soul than I was. Either that or he was crazy and inhabiting his own little corner of the universe.

'Hey,' he said to me.

6

'Hey,' I said back. 'How old are you?'

'I got some cool stuff to sell.'

'That's not what I asked you.'

The kid rubbed his nose with his right hand. 'I'm not drinking anything,' he told me, his voice going all petulant.

'You seen the sign when you came through the door? You got an ID to show me?'

The kid shifted his weight from one leg to another and hitched up his pants. 'This is America, man.'

'It's also a private place of business.'

He rubbed his nose again. 'I already told you I don't want to do no drinking,' he whined.

I couldn't help thinking he sounded like George's eight-year-old nephew when I'd told him he had to stop drinking soda and he'd told me he didn't have to, because he was drinking Pepsi not soda – so there.

'Hey, don't give the kid a hard time. Let him show us what he's got,' the guy who was sitting next to Stammering Sam and who'd given me his name variously as Hector, Ulysses, and Roberto in the last couple of hours called out.

Bill raised his can. 'Yeah. He comes in here all the time.'

'Damn right I do,' the kid said. He pointed to the Christmas tree in the corner. 'I sold Ian that tree and the lights for five bucks and I got more stuff from the house I'm cleaning out down the block. I'm helping the people move.'

'At nine thirty at night?' I replied. 'Boy, they're lucky to have such a diligent worker.'

The kid retracted his head into his hoodie. 'You got no cause to say something nasty to me.'

'I didn't.'

'You said I was diligent.'

'I meant you're a hard worker.'

'Oh.' The kid scratched his arm. 'Yeah. I am.'

And maybe he was in his own unique way, just not in the way society had in mind. I and the rest of the world would probably give a name other than 'cleaning out a house' to what he was doing – something more along the lines of fencing stolen property – but then I decided what the hell. It was late, none of the customers seemed to care, and, anyway, the kid looked as if he could use a couple of bucks.

'You got a name?' I asked him.

I could see his face working as he thought about the answer. 'Jimmy,' he finally said. 'It's Jimmy Slade.'

Right. And I was going off to St Barts in my Lear jet tomorrow, but then I figured that if the customers knew who the kid was Ian did too and that was all that mattered.

'Okay, Jimmy. What have you got?'

He gestured to the street. 'I got a headboard on a handcart outside. I'll sell it for twenty dollars.'

'A headboard? For a bed?'

'Yeah.'

Why would anyone steal something like that? Talk about being conspicuous. Talk about being unclear on the concept.

'Anyone need a headboard?' I asked the assembled crew.

'You got a woman to go with it,' Hector/Ulysses/Roberto yelled out while everyone else shook their heads.

'Ten then,' the kid who was calling himself Jimmy Slade wheedled. A note of desperation was creeping into his voice. 'I'll give it to you for ten. The thing's real nice. Solid wood. Its got mirrors and drawers and everything.' He took a step towards the door. 'Come out and take a look.'

No one sitting at the bar moved. Out of curiosity I decided to take a quick peek. When I stepped outside there was the headboard sitting outside on a dolly just like Jimmy had said. I have to say it was one of the ugliest ones I've ever seen, plus the thing looked as if it weighed a ton. I can't imagine how Jimmy got it out onto the street.

'You like it?' Jimmy asked hovering around me anxiously.

'No.'

'Maybe one of your friends would like it.'

'Very doubtful.'

'Call them up and ask them,' he whined.

'No.' Now he was getting on my nerves.

Jimmy gestured towards a cardboard box wedged into the headboard. 'I got other things.'

I stamped my feet to keep them warm. 'Why don't you

bring them inside?' I told him as I started back towards the bar. Jimmy was right behind me.

He set the cardboard box on the table. I decided he reminded me of one of the kids down in Mexico City who follow you around trying to sell you cigarettes, gum, a coke, a lighter, a key chain, whatever. Eventually you give them money just to get rid of them.

'See,' Jimmy said as he held up a WaterPik. 'I got a nice electric toothbrush here. I'm selling it for five bucks.'

'Like I'm going to buy a used toothbrush,' Hector/Ulysses/Roberto told him. 'It's probably been in some crack whore's mouth . . .'

'Or Carmen's you-know-what,' Shelley cried out.

Lovely image.

Bill put his hand on Shelley's arm and shushed her before I could say anything. 'What else you got?' Bill asked the kid.

Jimmy rummaged through the box and came up with a Monopoly game and the kind of mobile that you attach to a baby's crib. No one was interested.

'I'll give 'em both to you for four dollars,' Jim offered as he wound up the mobile. The sounds of 'Rock a Bye Baby' floated through the bar.

'See. It works real good. Don't any of you got any grand-children?' he whined.

'Ga . . . Ga . . . Got a lamp?' Stuttering Sam asked.

Jimmy searched around in the box and came out with a picture frame, a wound up length of cable cord, and a pocket size tape recorder. 'No. But I got these. Or what about some shoes. I got shoes.' And he held up a pair of men's black shoes. The aroma of dirty feet wafted out into the air.

'Put those away,' I told him.

By now everyone was turning their attention back to the television set. Jimmy wound up the mobile again.

'I'll give it to you for a buck,' he said.

'Maybe it's time you left,' I suggested.

'I got other things,' Jimmy insisted.

As I watched him rub his nose and dance from one foot to the other, I decided that I'd made a mistake letting him in.

.

'One more thing and that's it,' I told him.

'Anyone here got a dog?' he asked.

'I do,' I said. 'Why?'

'Because I got this great stuff. You're gonna love it.'

Somehow I doubted it. 'And after you show it to me you're going to leave, correct?' I told him.

'Correct,' he said.

Suddenly Shelley piped up with, 'Ask him about the dead guy.'

'Will you stop already with the dead guy,' Bill told her.

Shelley glared at Bill. 'Maybe he knows something. There's nothing wrong with asking.'

'What dead guy?' Jimmy demanded.

'The guy that some kid found in a snow bank,' I replied. 'There was a cop in here showing his picture around, trying to come up with an ID. You didn't have anything to do with that, right?' I asked hoping to hurry Jimmy out.

Jimmy nodded his head up and down so rapidly I thought he was going to injure something in his neck.

'Good. Then you don't have to concern yourself with it. Now show me what you have.'

'Sure. Sure. Sure thing.' And Jimmy dove into the box and rummaged around in it. A moment later he pulled out five dog collars and held them out to me. 'I'll give them to you for ten bucks each or twenty bucks for all of them.'

Considering that they sold retail for seventy-five to one hundred bucks each Jimmy was offering me quite a bargain, and I should know because I sold them in my store. To my knowledge my shop was the only one in Syracuse that carried this particular merchandise line.

And there wasn't much chance of mistaking these collars for something else, either, because no one else made faux jewel collars, pale pink leather ones with spikes, and orange and pink braided ones with matching leashes other than Adorable Dogs. And to add insult to injury, as the expression goes, I'd gotten them in the store four days ago and I'd seen them when I'd closed up shop this evening. Which meant Jimmy had just stolen them.

'Exactly where did you get these from?' I demanded.

'I already said,' Jimmy whined. 'I got them from this house I was cleaning out.'

'I don't think so,' I told him. 'I think you got them from my store, Noah's Ark.'

Jimmy turned and ran out the door. I went after him.

Two

I'd just reached the outside door when it swung open and Jimmy reentered. Ian was right behind him, towering over him.

'He probably got the collars off the dead guy,' Shelley informed everyone, blaring the information out, as Jimmy kept saying, 'I didn't do nuthin. I didn't do nuthin,' over and over again.

Ian clapped a hand on Jimmy's shoulder and gave a slight squeeze. A look of pain crossed Jimmy's face and he suddenly shut up.

'Now,' Ian said to me, 'You want to tell me what's going on here?'

His expression was perfectly pleasant and his tone was quiet but I had a feeling – no, I knew – that he'd look and sound like that if he was breaking someone's arm.

So I explained about the dead guy and Jimmy coming in trying to sell stuff and about my recognizing my collars and about how I was pretty sure he'd just broken into my shop

'These collars?' Ian asked me, pointing to the ones Jimmy had in his hand.

I nodded.

He looked down at Jimmy. Jimmy looked up at him.

'I didn't . . .' Jimmy began but Ian put his hand on Jimmy's shoulder again and Jimmy got quiet.

'The collars better be all he took,' I said to Ian.

Three weeks ago I'd caught someone trying to stuff a ball python into his jacket and the week before that someone had tried to sneak out with two lovebirds stashed in their backpack.

'Did you take anything else?' Ian asked Jimmy.

Jimmy looked down at the floor. 'No,' he said sullenly.

'How'd you get in?' I asked him.

'Through the back window,' he muttered.

At least that was an easy fix. I could cut up one of the shipping cartons and duct-tape a square of cardboard in there until tomorrow when I could fix it.

'Good.' Ian took the collars out of Jimmy's hand. Then he walked over and looked in the box. 'Does the tape recorder work?'

Jimmy nodded.

'I'll give you a dollar for it and Robin will give you five bucks for the collars. How's that?'

'What? Are you nuts?' I said to Ian before Jimmy could answer. 'I'm not giving him a dime.'

Ian kept his attention focused on the kid. 'And I don't want to see you in here again for a while,' he told him.

It was as if I wasn't there.

Jimmy nodded again.

'Give him the five bucks,' Ian told me as he reached in his pocket, took out a dollar bill, handed it to Jimmy, and took the tape recorder out of the box and slipped it in his breast pocket. 'You never know when something like this is going to come in handy,' he explained to me.

'So let me get this right,' I asked Ian. 'This kid breaks into my store and steals something from me and I'm giving him money for it?'

'Essentially, yes.'

'Forget it.'

'It would be a mistake not to,' Ian said.

Normally I would have refused but something in Ian's tone made me dig into my pocket and come out with five one-dollar bills.

'My neighbor's kid,' Ian explained to me as he handed my money to Jimmy and gave the collars to me. 'And get that dolly out of here,' he yelled at Jimmy as Jimmy exited the place.

Ian looked around the bar to see that everyone had what they needed in terms of drinks. Then he took off his black leather jacket, carefully hung it over the corner of the bar, and beckoned me over to the corner.

'I don't get it,' I said.

'What's to get,' Ian said. He rebuttoned the top button of his flannel shirt. 'The kid's a crack head. Crack heads steal things. It's what they do.'

'I understand that. I don't understand why you didn't call the cops or why you insisted I give him five dollars. Is it because Jimmy's your neighbor's kid?'

Ian filled a stein with water, stuck it in the microwave, and pressed the button. 'No. I didn't call the cops because any time the cops are called the bar loses business.' He must have seen the blank look on my face because he continued explaining. 'People don't like to come into places where there's trouble. They come here to relax and have a good time. Plus, from your point of view, if they did arrest Jimmy they'd hold the collars as evidence and it would be six months before you'd get them back.'

Which was true. I hadn't thought of that.

'And then there's the fact that if you report the theft to your insurance company your rates will go up.'

Also true.

The microwave beeped. Ian took out the glass, and added two tablespoons of hot-chocolate mix to the water and stirred. Then he rinsed the spoon off and carefully laid it on top of the can of hot-chocolate mix.

'I'll take over if you want to check on your store.'

'Thanks.'

I went in the back room and got my cocker spaniel, Zsa Zsa. Now that she's going deaf it's amazing what she can sleep through.

'You know if I get cited for that dog you're paying the fine.' Ian told me.

'So you've said.'

'Just so we're clear on that.'

When I left the bar Ian was listening to Bill ranting on about how the Syracuse University chancellor was electrocuting pigeons on top of the Upstate Medical Building. It was one of his favorite conspiracies.

The streets were quiet as I drove over to Noah's Ark. With the temperature at minus fifteen with the wind chill factored in, it was too cold to be out. No one was around, not even the boys who are usually doing business on the corners.

I called George on my way. I wanted to tell him what had just happened, but he didn't pick up the phone. I tried his cell next, but he didn't answer that, either, which was odd considering that he'd told me he was going to be home grading papers all night. Maybe he'd gone to bed, although he usually didn't turn off the lights until twelve. So be it, I thought as I pulled up in front of Noah's Ark. At that moment I had other things to worry about.

I studied the window decorations. They didn't look so awful. They weren't brilliant, but they did the job. I got out and walked up to the store. The streetlight showed footprints in the snow. Jimmy's, I presumed. They were going away from the store and down the street.

Now that I was closer I could see that the door was open a crack. Ergo, Jimmy had come in through the back and left through the front. A piece of brilliant detective work if I did say so myself. At least he could have shut the door behind him I thought as Zsa Zsa scooted in ahead of me. Like her mistress, she's not a big fan of the cold. I flicked on the lights and inhaled the familiar pet store odor, half cedar bedding, half water from the tanks.

The place was so peaceful at night. The lights on top of the fish tanks made them pop out in the dark. I stood there for a few moments and watched the neon tetras swimming around. Next month I was going to get some tanks with salt-water fish up and going. Plus I was getting some genetically engineered boas in from a dealer down in Florida this week. The snakes

14

were gorgeous. Their scales showed iridescent in the light. When you're not a chain you have to have unique merchandise, which is why I carried Adorable Dog's fancy collars.

I would really miss this place if I didn't have it. Miss it a lot. Yes, it was ridiculous to take a second job to keep this place going. Yes, it was ridiculous to go from month to month never knowing whether I could pay my utility bill, whether I could pay my sales tax, or my suppliers. Yes, it was extremely stressful. Yes, sometimes that was all I thought about. Especially when, like today, I'd taken in sixty-eight dollars and fifty-two cents, which wasn't even enough to pay my operating costs. And if George got a job at a university outside of Syracuse, what then?

It was a question George kept asking. What are you going to do then? Are you going to go with me or stay? I kept on trying to explain to him that the problem was I wasn't only selling pet foods and cages, I was selling livestock as well. I knew I could sell the fish and the reptiles and the small mammals to other shops. But what about Bertie, the cockatiel, and Ernie, the macaw, that I got from an old woman because she couldn't take care of them anymore; or the African Gray parrot I promised the old man who was going into a nursing home that I'd look out for, or the two abused ferrets. What about them?

'What about them?' George had said when I'd asked him. 'They're not your responsibility.'

Okay, maybe George was right about that, too. Maybe I shouldn't be running an orphanage for old and abandoned animals. Maybe it was time I, as George kept on saying, moved on with my life, but he couldn't seem to understand that this place had been my life for so long. It was the only link I had left to Murphy. And even though he'd been dead for years and he'd been a real pain in the ass, what with his drinking and dealing and tomcatting around, there was a part of me that still didn't want to say goodbye.

Perhaps things would work out. Perhaps I'd have a good Christmas season. Perhaps the genetically engineered snakes would do the trick. Or perhaps I could convince Ian to put

15

a large fish tank in his bar. That's how I'd met him. I'd gone into Shamus's to try and drum up some business. He'd said no, but that didn't mean I couldn't ask him again. I'd proposed a tank with an Oscar in it. They're big nasty fish, and the bar patrons could toss in feeder fish into the tank for a dollar a shot. It would be like reality TV only in real life.

'Sounds pretty violent to me,' Ian had said.

'Then we can do something else. Maybe tropicals. Consider it,' I'd urged. 'I'll put it in for free.'

My thinking was that if I could get a tank in Shamus's and it was a draw then the other bar owners would want one too. I'd make money maintaining the tanks, which is a twice a month deal, plus I could have my business cards on display, which would generate even more business.

I bit the cuticle on my right thumb, realized what I was doing, and stopped. I lit another cigarette – I was trying to keep it down to five a day; this was my third – and looked around. At first glance it seemed as if Jimmy had been telling the truth. Nothing looked as if it had been disturbed, except for the display where the collars had been.

What had made him take those particular items I wondered as I walked around the store. It's true I cleaned out the register every night so there was no money. But why take those particular collars? If he had taken the other ones, the ones that every pet store has, I never would have recognized them.

And speaking of thinking clearly, I still couldn't believe I'd paid Jimmy, or whatever the hell his name was, to get the collars back. Even if it was only five dollars. The idea still rankled. But Ian had a way getting people to do what he wanted. Just amazing. I put the collars back on the display and went around and checked on all the animals.

Everything looked good. I peeked in the bird room. They were all asleep. So were the reptiles. I checked the thermometers on their tanks just to make sure the temperatures were all right. Then I stopped at the gerbils' cage. All ten of them were massed together in a heap. The Peruvian guinea pigs squeaked when I went by. I stopped and petted them.

They looked so silly. With all the hair they had it was hard to tell their fronts from their rears.

Finally I went into the back. As soon as I opened my office door a blast of cold air hit me. I didn't want to think about the amount of heat I was losing through the broken window, but at least Jimmy had closed the office door.

I spent the next ten minutes cutting up cardboard and duct-taping a double layer of it over the broken pane. Then I checked out my office to make sure nothing else was missing. Nothing was. I called Ian.

I could hear the sounds of the jukebox and the television going in the background.

'Why don't you go home,' he said when I told him I was heading back to his place. 'I'll finish up here.'

Which, since I was too tired to argue, is exactly what I did.

Three

We'd already had almost four feet of snow since winter began and there was going to be more to come. The *Farmer's Almanac* had predicted an especially cold and brutal winter. Unfortunately it looked as if they were going to be right.

At least I'd learned one thing this year. My high school science teacher was wrong. It can snow when it gets down into the single digits! As I nosed my car into my driveway I couldn't help wondering where we were going to put the rest of the winter's accumulation. We had as much snow on either side of the driveway now as we had last year in March.

George's Subaru wasn't there and judging by the amount of snow in the driveway hadn't been for some time. He's

17

probably gone out to get a beer with one of his friends, I was thinking as I pressed down the handle of my car door. The door didn't open. Great. This was the last thing I needed. Usually this happened in the morning. Most people's locks freeze from the outside. Mine, for some obscure reason, freeze from the inside, which meant I was locked in my vehicle.

I tried lowering the window. It was frozen as well. Even better. I couldn't even reach out and open the door from the outside. I kicked the door. The frame didn't like it, but what the hell – the car was heading for the junkyard anyway. After four kicks the door yielded. Zsa Zsa jumped over me, scampered out of the car, and raced ahead. I followed her cursing under my breath. I opened the door to the house and Zsa Zsa scurried in and barked at my cat, James, who as per usual ignored the cocker spaniel.

'How ya doin', big guy?' I asked him as he wound himself around my feet.

I bent down and petted him. He purred, a throaty rumble that always seems to start deep in his chest and work its way up.

After a minute or so, I threw my coat over the back of the sofa and went into the kitchen, poured myself a shot of Scotch, and took a sip. I don't drink when I'm behind the bar – Ian's rule – a good rule I think. After all, bartending is a job not a night out on the town. I could feel the liquor sliding down my throat. Some of the tension I'd been carrying around the back of my neck seemed to dissipate.

I checked the messages on the answering machine to see if George had phoned in. He hadn't. Fair enough. I went back into the living room and sat down on the sofa. James jumped into my lap. I petted him for a few more minutes then reached for the remote and switched on the TV. I was just settling in with *The Attack of the Killer Clowns* when George came through the front door. He poked his head into the living room.

'Hi. You're home early.' Weather announcers had more enthusiasm than he did.

I explained what had happened.

'Oh,' he said. 'And here I thought you'd come to your

senses.' And he went and hung his jacket up in the closet.

Nice. I decided to ignore the comment.

'So what did the police say?' he asked when he came back in.

'Nothing.' I took another sip of my drink and held the Scotch on my tongue for a moment. I could taste the peat. 'I didn't file a police report.'

'That wasn't very smart.'

Well what had I expected him to say with him being an ex-cop, a straight-arrow one at that? I switched to CNN.

'Was that Ian's idea?' George asked.

'So where were you?' I asked, changing the subject.

'What do you mean?'

Patches of light glanced off his ebony cheekbones.

'I thought you were going to be home grading papers.'

'I was. Natalie called.'

Natalie was the mother of George's daughter, Benecia. Natalie was blonde. George was black. Ebony and ivory. They made a stunning couple. In the old days they would have been dead.

George had been carrying on with Natalie for six months at the same time he'd been seeing me. Then he'd knocked her up, at which point he told me, and I'm quoting here, that he had 'to do the right thing and marry Natalie.' Of course, doing the right thing by me didn't come into it.

I was devastated. Being shot wasn't as painful as this was. We separated. Then we'd had this big tearful reunion scene. George loved me so much he couldn't do without me, blah, blah, blah. It was very heartwarming. He was going to support the kid but not live with the mother and I said fine. At which point he moved into my house. Everything was going to be hunky-dory because our love could overcome anything. Right.

I must have been out of my mind, because it wasn't fine. If I'd had my head screwed on straight I would have known that it couldn't be. Natalie called all the time, and George went running. Never underestimate the power of fatherhood. Or maybe it was the power of a size D cup. But when I said something along those lines to George he'd give me 'the look' and I'd back down.

'She needed some milk,' George told me.

Sure she did. I took another sip of Scotch. 'How is she?'

'All right.' He pointed to the drink in my hand. 'I would have thought you'd have had enough of that.'

'Meaning?'

'Working at the bar.'

'This is the first one I've had all day.'

'Oh that's right. I forgot. You can't drink when you're bartending. Ian's rule.' He gave Ian's name a sarcastic twist. George didn't like him. At all. I couldn't figure out if he didn't like him because I was working for him or if there was some sort of guy thing going on that I wasn't getting.

'That's right,' I said evenly. 'I can't. How come you didn't answer your cell?'

'I guess I forgot to turn it on.' George never forgot to turn it on. 'I'm going to bed,' he told me and he turned and walked out of the room.

As I heard him climb the steps it occurred to me that he hadn't asked me if I was coming to bed and then it occurred to me that I didn't care that he hadn't because the truth was that I'd rather sit downstairs, finish my drink, and watch CNN than go to bed with him. It had been four, no five months since we'd had sex.

I took another sip of my Scotch, upped the volume, and leaned back and watched the news of the day with James on one side of me and Zsa Zsa on the other. I knew the authors of the book I was reading about relationships would suggest that I go upstairs and talk to George about my feelings. But I stayed where I was.

There was nothing I could tell George that he didn't already know. I was tired of talking about Natalie with him, of trying to be understanding.

All in all, I decided as I listened to the weather forecaster tell me that we were due for anywhere between six inches and a foot of snow tomorrow, it had been a really crummy day.

Four

M anuel's girlfriend, Bethany, looked at the donut I was
consuming, looked at me, and said, 'At least eat a
protein bar for breakfast.'

Sixteen and already an expert on life. It must be nice. I
gave the last piece to Zsa Zsa and wiped the crumbs off the
counter top.

'I don't like protein bars. I like chocolate peanut donuts.'

We'd had this discussion before. Several times in fact.

Bethany sighed and slid the package with the glass windowpanes over to me. 'Here,' she said. 'Manuel will be in in a
minute. He's talking with his mom. She drove us today because
her car died last night.'

I glanced at the clock on the shop wall. 'I thought you guys
were going to be here at nine to help me open.'

It was now a little after ten. In the last hour I'd shoveled
and salted the sidewalk in front of the store, washed the floor,
cleaned the bird cages, and fed the small mammals.

Bethany shrugged. 'The car doors were frozen. We had
trouble getting them opened.'

'You and everyone else in this town that doesn't have a
garage to put their car in.'

Of course, I had one. Unfortunately it was unusable in
the winter because the doors on it were from the horse and
buggy days. They slid open. Meaning they froze in the
winter. I needed to get new garage doors. The modern
kind. The last estimate I'd gotten was for fifteen hundred
dollars.

I was wondering if there was any way I could possibly
afford that when I became aware of Bethany scrutinizing me.

21

Here comes the lecture on caffeine consumption I thought as I put down my cup.

'What?' I asked.

'Did you have another fight with George?'

I wasn't used to having someone around who could read me. Normally I thought of myself as invisible, and it unnerved me.

'No. I didn't.'

Bethany shook her finger at me. 'Don't lie to me.'

'It wasn't a fight. It was more like a glacial event.'

Bethany reached over and took a sip of my coffee. 'This George thing is not working out for you.'

No kidding. 'It's fine.'

'Sure it is. And, by the way, you look like crap.'

'Thanks for the ego boost.'

'Well. It's true.'

Even if it was I didn't like to hear it. Who would? So I got defensive. 'I'm tired,' I told her. 'I've been working two jobs.'

Bethany rolled her eyes.

That gesture used to drive her father nuts. That guy is such a prick. Trust a psychologist to think he knows it all. Bethany had run away from home and after I'd found her her father had wanted to go to court and have a PINS taken out on her, which translates to Person In Need Of Supervision, or have her committed to some school for troubled children out in Colorado.

I'd managed to convince Bethany's dad to let her live in the city with Manuel and his mom. Thinking about it I realize he probably said yes because he was glad to have her off his hands. So now Bethany feels as if she owes me. She doesn't. But I can't seem to get the message across. What is it they say about no good deed goes unpunished?

'You know what you need?' Bethany continued.

'Some sales?'

'A new boyfriend.'

'And you're going to find me one?'

'You should go on Match.com. The mother of one of my friends did and she hooked up with this great guy.'

'Bethany, I don't have time for that.'

'Sure, you do.'

'No. I don't.'

'You should make time.'

I was contemplating what to say to that when Manuel came in, trailing Shelley behind him. She was wearing a faded tweed men's coat that was at least five sizes too big for her, a grayish scarf that I was willing to wager had once been white wrapped around her neck, and a bright orange men's watch cap pulled down to her ears. I could smell her as she got closer. She smelled stale.

She banged on the counter with her palm. 'You're the detective?' she demanded.

'I wouldn't go that far,' I told her.

She dug her hands down into her coat pocket and came out with two crumpled five-dollar bills and threw them on the counter.

'You know Bill?'

'Your Bill? The one you always come into Shamus's with?'

Shelley nodded. 'I think he's going to have me thrown out of my house and sell it.'

'Okay.' I waited to see what was coming next.

She leaned forward. I could smell the beer on her breath. 'I want you to find out what he's up to. I think he and my son are in it together.'

I pushed her money back towards her. The last thing I was going to do was get in the middle of something between her and Bill.

'What's the matter?' Shelley said. 'You don't think I can afford to hire you? I got tons of money.'

'I know you do.' And maybe she did, hidden in a mattress somewhere, although I seriously doubted it.

If she ever had any she'd given it all to Budweiser. Five minutes with Shelley and you knew that she was crazy. The only thing I couldn't figure out was whether she was crazy because she drank or she drank because she was crazy.

'He's talking to people.'

'Who's talking to people?' With Shelley it always pays to clarify.

'Bill. Who else?'

'Maybe the people he's talking are his friends.'

'They're wearing suits and ties,' Shelley spat out. 'And they're related to the dead man.'

'What dead man?' Manuel asked.

I explained about the dead man they'd found on the street down from the bar.

'Hey, I saw that on TV.'

Shelley whacked the counter again to get Manuel's and my attention. We both shut up.

Shelley continued. 'I own that house and two on West Onondaga and one on Shonnard. They're worth lots and lots of money. Millions.'

Even if Shelley did own them, which was extremely doubtful, I'd be surprised if altogether they'd bring in more than thirty to forty thousand dollars. You couldn't give property away on this side of town.

'Maybe you should sell them to Bill,' I suggested.

Shelley coughed. 'I can't do that. Bill wants them all so he can raise pigeons in them. I don't want pigeons pooping everything up. There are grand pianos in there. I used to play in the symphony, you know.'

I glanced at the clock. This had gone on long enough. Besides, hopefully I'd have customers coming in soon and I didn't want Shelley chasing them out. 'I don't think I can help you.' I pushed Shelley's two fives back across the counter. 'Maybe you should go talk to the police.'

She wiped her mouth with the back of her hand. 'I already talked to the police. They think I'm some crazy lady. But I'm not.' She was going to say something else when Ernie the macaw started squawking. A few seconds later Bertie joined him. The noise was deafening. Shelley stared at me for a moment then she said, 'I didn't know you had birds in here. I hate birds.' And she turned and started running out the door.

'Hey. Take your money,' I called after her, but she didn't answer. I really didn't want to go after her and stuff her money in her coat pocket. I didn't want to get that close. Returning it to her at the bar would be good enough.

'She's a real wack job,' Manuel said while I put the money in my wallet. 'Who is she?'

'One of Shamus's customers. A regular.'

'No wonder George doesn't want you working there.'

'How about starting to clean out the fish tanks instead of commenting on my personal life?' I told Manuel.

'There's no need to give me attitude. I was just making an observation.'

'Well, you've made it. Now, could you please go to work.'

'Actually, as long you're asking . . .'

'I wasn't.'

Manuel hitched up his pants and retreated. He spent the next hour cleaning out the fish tanks, while I fed the reptiles, did orders, called to see when my genetically engineered boas were coming in, and waited on customers. Bethany spent the time sitting in my office reading a romance novel and playing with Zsa Zsa.

I was just explaining to her why Zsa Zsa didn't need to eat even more dog biscuits then she already did and that the vet had told me she had to lose five pounds – can we say the words doggy treadmill – when Ian walked through the door. I was surprised to see him since it was ten thirty and the bar opened up at eleven.

'Changed your mind about the fish tank?' I asked.

'Not exactly.'

'Hey, this is a great opportunity. You can be the first bar in Syracuse with a real fish tank. I'll give you a good deal.'

He kinda smiled but didn't reply. It occurred to me as he came towards me that even though we were on the minus side of the temperature equation I'd never seen him wear gloves or a hat or zip up the black leather jacket he always wore. He brushed his hair off his forehead – he was one of those one-haircut-a-year-whether-I need-it-or-not kind of guys.

'Remember Jimmy Slade?' he asked. 'The kid that came into the bar last night with the headboard? The one that stole your collars?'

'Of course I remember him,' I replied as I watched Manuel stop working so he could listen to the conversation. 'What did he do now? Steal a washing machine from someone's basement?'

'He didn't do anything. He's dead.' Ian's face was expressionless. He did expressionless well.

'You're kidding.'

'Was that the kid they found in the house?' Manuel asked Ian. 'The kid that someone shot?' He put down his broom and came over to where we were standing. 'That was on the morning news, too.'

Two homicides in one day. Not bad for a city of one hundred fifty thousand, I thought.

'When did this happen?'

Ian took out a cough drop, unwrapped it, and popped it in his mouth. 'About two hours after he left the bar.'

'Great.' You think you're doing someone a favor and it turns out like this. 'We shouldn't have let him go. We should have called the police on him.'

'Why did you let him go?' Manuel demanded.

Ian continued as if he hadn't spoken. 'Well it would have been better for him if we had,' Ian agreed. He glanced at his watch. I knew he had to go soon. Shelley was probably waiting for him to open up right now.

'Where was the house?'

'On Shonnard Street,' Manuel answered before Ian could.

That was about five blocks away from the bar. There'd been two fires on that block in the past month, as well as three shootings, one of which had proved fatal. I reached over to take a sip of my coffee and realized Bethany had finished it. She always did that to me.

'How old was he?' I asked.

'Fifteen.'

Bethany's age, I couldn't help thinking. She was in the process of turning her life around, but he wasn't going to have the chance to do that, unless you believed in reincarnation – which I didn't. Poor Jimmy Slade. He could have gone into rehab, gone back to school, maybe become a famous artist.

Okay, he probably would have ended up in jail like all the other miscreants in the area. But it was still sad.

'So what happened?'

'According to the police it was a gang thing,' Ian said.

That made sense given what he'd looked like, as well as the prevalence of gangs on the west side.

Ian moved the cough drop around his mouth. 'But Freddy's mom doesn't think so.'

'Freddy?' I said momentarily confused. 'Who's Freddy?'

'Freddy Sanchez. The kid who stole the collars from the store. Jimmy Slade was his street name.'

I turned to Manuel. 'Do . . . did . . . you know him?' I asked. Manuel pretty much knew everyone within a certain age range.

Manuel tugged his pants up. 'I went to elementary school with his cousin. He used to babysit him when his ma ran errands. Freddy was always a pain in the ass. He'd scream bloody murder if his French fries touched his Big Mac. Stuff like that.'

I looked at Ian. He had eyes that always made him look as if he were half asleep, which was very deceptive because he never missed anything. Ever. 'I was just over at her house,' he continued. 'Bea's very upset.'

'Well, she isn't going to be happy, that's for sure.'

Ian covered his mouth with his hand and coughed. 'To calm her down I told her I'd ask you to look into things. See what you could find out.'

'Thanks for volunteering me.'

He gave a little nod. 'You're welcome.'

I tried again. 'From what you've told me it doesn't seem as if there is anything to find out.'

Ian glanced at his watch. I could see that he was tapping the fingers of his right hand against the side of his leg. 'Probably, but she's a good customer of mine . . .'

'I thought she was your neighbor.'

'That too, and I'd like to keep her happy.'

'Being a full service bar and all.'

Ian smiled for the first time. 'That's right. It's all about keeping the clientele happy.'

'Have I seen her?' I asked him. I didn't remember waiting on a Bea Sanchez.

'You wouldn't have. She comes in the afternoons. Maybe once, twice a week.'

'Listen, if you're feeling guilty about—'

Ian stopped me before I could say anything else. 'The kid was a crack head, and the way he was going he was going to get himself killed sooner or later. I don't think this is going to be a big deal. Just asking a couple of questions to make her feel better.' He looked at his watch again. 'So what do you want me to tell Bea?'

I thought for a moment. I didn't want to do this. On the other hand, I didn't want to piss Ian off. Especially because I needed to continue working at his place.

Ian drummed his fingers on the counter. 'Well?' he asked.

Suddenly I had a flash of inspiration. Looking into Freddy's death might actually work out well for me.

'Okay,' I said. 'How about this.'

Ian cocked his head and folded his arms across his chest. 'I'm listening.'

'If I do this you let me put the fish tank we've been talking about in your bar and you let me put my business card on the tank as well as on the counter.'

Ian's face was deadpan as he thought. Finally he said, 'I think it's a waste of time but I'll let you do it for two weeks. But,' he went on. 'I won't assume any liability for anything that happens to it.'

'Agreed. But forget about the two weeks. It'll take a week just to get it working right. I'm thinkin' more like six months.'

'Six months,' Ian scoffed. 'I'll let you keep it in there for a month.

'Five,' I countered.

'Three,' Ian said.

'Done,' I agreed.

'And we do tropicals,' Ian said. 'I don't want anyone saying I encouraged violence in my bar.'

'Tropicals it is.'

'So you'll go and talk to her today?' Ian asked.

'This afternoon.'

All in all, I decided as Ian pushed a piece of paper containing Freddy's mom's address and phone number across the counter, this was turning out to be a good morning after all.

After he left I turned to Manuel. 'Do you think you can see what you can find out about Freddy these days?'

'Am I getting paid?' he asked me.

'Am I?' I replied.

'No,' he said.

'Then the answer to your question should be self-evident.'

'Forget it,' Manuel said as Bethany came up behind him. 'Anything I do, I get paid for.'

'He'll do it,' she told me.

Manuel turned to face her. 'No. I won't,' he said to her.

Bethany cocked her head to one side and opened her eyes wide. 'Please,' she said, stringing out the word.

'Why should I?' Manuel asked.

But I could see the scowl he was wearing was softening even though he was trying hard to maintain it.

'Because Robin needs your help.' And Bethany gave Manuel a big smile.

Manuel tried to keep looking tough, but he couldn't. He smiled back at Bethany. 'Oh, all right,' he grumbled. 'I'll see what I can come up with. But just this once.'

'You are such a sweetie,' she said.

Sometimes I have to say that I love that girl.

Five

The weatherman proved to be right again. Unfortunately. It had been snowing when I got up and it was still snowing in the middle of the afternoon. We were supposed to get between a foot and a foot and a half by the time the storm was over. Big, fat flakes drifted down. It was pretty, but the road crews couldn't keep up and I slipped and slid up West Onondaga Street on my way to Bea Sanchez's house.

I inched my car up the hill. Normally I don't care about being out in bad weather, after all if you live in Syracuse you'd better get used to it or you'd never go out of your house, but I didn't trust my car any longer.

The transmission was going, some of the engine mounts had rusted out, I was going to need front brakes soon, and my snow tires had no tread left on them. And did I mention the door freezing on the inside? That had to be the most annoying thing of all. Aside from that it was fine. George kept telling me the Taurus wasn't safe to drive. Like I didn't know this. The problem was I couldn't afford a new car. Hell, I can't afford a new used car. On the other hand, I couldn't afford not to buy another vehicle. The last time I'd been at the garage my mechanic had looked at me and said, 'You are getting a new car soon aren't you?'

'How soon?' I asked.

'Let me put it this way. I wouldn't drive it more than thirty miles an hour if I were you.'

How's that for a heads up. As I changed the radio station so I wouldn't have to hear another rendition of 'Frosty the Snowman' I remembered Ray. Big Ray. He was a retired Onondaga sheriff who ran a used car lot. Maybe I'd talk to him and see if we could work out a straight trade. A used car for a python. Not everyone's cup of tea but this guy had had big snakes when he'd lived down in Florida. Maybe he wanted another one.

Hopefully he would, because it just so happened – what a coincidence – that I had a beautiful twenty-foot long Burmese python named Matilda in my shop that I would love to get out of there. I'd taken her in as a favor for someone five months ago and she was still there, there not being a big market for reptiles on that scale, unless of course you're a stripper or a drug dealer. Something that large can be intimidating if you don't know what you're doing, although I have

30

to say that Matilda is pretty mellow, and I keep her that way by handling her every day and taking her out of her cage to feed her.

I was selling Matilda for a little over eight hundred bucks. On a straight trade that should buy me a Junker that would get me through another year.

I pulled up in front of Bea Sanchez's house. The sound of rap music flowed into the car. Welcome to the hood. When I opened the door of my Taurus and stepped into the street I could feel the bass reverberate through the soles of my feet. The noise was coming from a couple of kids sitting in a Jeep Cherokee that was parked in the driveway across the street. For sure they'd be deaf before the age of twenty if they kept playing their music at that decibel level.

Like most of Syracuse, Skunk City, as the area used to be called, has seen better days. West Onondaga is wide enough to be called an avenue, but the houses on either side of the street butt up against each other as if they'd been designed for a narrower street. Visually the mix is jarring. At one time the people living here were mostly Irish, but now they're a mix of Latinos, Native Americans, and African-Americans.

Driving through Bea Sanchez's block, you wouldn't have said West Onondaga looked like a bad area, but the crime blotter in the local paper told a different story, what with the robberies, stabbings, home invasions, and arrests for drug possession.

According to my friend Calli, who'd done a series of articles on this neighborhood for the local paper, some of the people living here were trying to turn the area around, or at least halt its downward slide. They'd formed a community neighborhood group called SNAC, Syracuse Neighbors Against Crime. Maybe what this group was doing was actually helping things for a change. Maybe they weren't in some politician's pocket. West Onondaga wasn't like Shonnard and Gifford Streets where the roofs of the houses bowed in and the wood on them was turning pulpy with rot.

Bea Sanchez's home exemplified the neighborhood building stock. It was a small two-story gray-shingled house with white trim. The two front windows were draped with a couple of strings of colored lights and decorated with the white stuff that comes out of a can. A white wreath with blue lights hung on the door.

In my neighborhood lots of the yards are filled with wire reindeer with white lights that slowly turn their heads from one side to another. I didn't see any here. But then I wouldn't. The reindeer are expensive, eighty to ninety dollars a pop, and the people that live on West Onondaga don't have money like that to spare – or if they do have it they don't want to advertise the fact.

The wind whipped snowflakes in my face as I got out of the car. Zsa Zsa ran in front of me as I trudged through the unshoveled path to Bea Sanchez's front door. I'd been going to leave Zsa Zsa in the store with Manuel but when I'd reached for my jacket she'd given me 'the look' and I'd weakened. As per usual. Then I thought I'd leave her in the car – she has a quilt in the back seat she can curl up on – but that didn't happen either because she'd slipped out as soon as I'd opened the door.

At that point I figured the hell with it. The worse that could happen was that Mrs. Sanchez would object, in which case I'd put Zsa Zsa back in the car. At best Zsa Zsa might serve as a distraction. When I saw the rope looped over the top of the handrail – a dead giveaway that there was another dog in residence – I reconsidered my plan. But it was already too late to put Zsa Zsa back in the car because by then I'd rung the bell and Mrs. Sanchez had opened the door.

When I looked at her I couldn't imagine her in Ian's bar hanging out with the likes of Shelley and Bill and Stuttering Sam. She looked like someone who was trying very hard to distance herself from people like them. But Ian said she was a regular. She must be the one Ian got the wine for because I certainly couldn't see her drinking PBRs out of a can.

Bea was a small woman who I put in her early- to mid-forties. She was wearing black pants, a gray knit jacket, and boots with small heels. Her hair was perfectly done and she'd applied a full complement of make-up. It made her face look as if she'd dipped it in Shellac.

But her make-up couldn't hide the red rims around her eyes or the circles under them. Her face had that slightly puffy appearance crying gives it. Only she wasn't crying now. She was angry. Furious from the looks of her. Studying her I couldn't help thinking that some people let themselves fall into grief and other people pull themselves back from it.

As I told her who I was a small dog raced out the door. It had black curly hair, long ears, and a funny kink in its tail, which it was wagging as hard as it could. Definitely not a watchdog.

'That's Freddy's dog, True,' Bea told me as she scooped him up in her arms and motioned for Zsa Zsa and me to come inside.

'True. That's a nice name,' I observed.

'Freddy said it was to remind him to be true to himself. He was a present from a friend of Freddy's. That's the kind of person my Freddy was.'

'What kind was that?'

'Someone people always gave things to.'

Right. And I was buying a BMW tomorrow.

'What kind of dog is he?' I asked as Bea took my jacket with her free hand and hung it in the hall closet.

He looked familiar, but I couldn't identify exactly what he was. A cockerpoo maybe? But there was something about it that didn't quite fit. I couldn't put my finger on what it was though.

Bea shrugged. 'Freddy told me but I forgot.'

I noted there wasn't a trace of a Spanish accent in her voice. When I asked her about that she told me that even though she'd been born in the Dominican Republic she'd lived here since she was six.

'But we still have land there.' She pointed to a badly painted oil hanging on the wall. It was of a beach surrounded by palm trees. A small cottage sat a hundred feet or so back from the ocean. 'Freddy loved that place. We try to go every year. I'm only glad my mother isn't alive to see this. She'd never have survived his funeral.'

And with that she led me into the living room and set True

down on the floor. He and Zsa Zsa immediately started chasing each other. I kept one eye on them while I took in the room's furnishings. The walls were painted white. They were bare except for a Dominican flag that was tacked to the far wall and several photographs hanging above the sofa. The windows, which overlooked West Onondaga, were hung with heavy satin drapes that looped down and over the valances above the windows.

The room was too small for the scale of furniture that was crammed into it, not that that stopped Zsa Zsa and True from racing around. For a second I thought they were going to knock over the white tinselly Christmas tree covered with angels that stood in the left-hand corner of the room.

I pointed to Zsa Zsa. 'Do you want me to put her in the car?'

'No. Now that Freddy is gone she needs someone to play with.'

Worked for me. I went back to looking around the room. A large-screen TV sat near the tree. An enormous leather sofa faced it. Two leather recliners flanked the sofa. A glass and metal coffee table sat nestled between them. On the other wall were a stereo system and a desk with a computer on it. Lots of expensive stuff. I wondered if it was rented or bought or possibly had fallen off the back of someone's truck, although given Bea Sanchez's demeanor I'd go with rented.

'Nice sofa,' I commented as I watched a car pull up in front of the house across the street.

One of the kids in the Jeep Cherokee jumped out, ran over to the other car, leaned in the window, then went back to the Jeep Cherokee, while the other car zoomed off. The whole episode must have taken all of thirty seconds.

'They're trash,' Bea said as she followed my glance with her eyes. 'People like that give us all a bad name. Not like my Freddy.' Ignoring the dogs that were now practically sitting on her feet she leaned over the sofa, took down one of the photos hanging on the wall above it, and handed it to me. 'This is Freddy,' she said.

I stared at the picture of the boy. It didn't look anything

like the kid that had wandered into the bar last night. This kid had a sweet face, with delicate almost feminine features. His eyes were large, his lashes incredibly long. He was thin, almost too much so. He was wearing navy slacks, a white shirt, and a red-striped tie that was snugged up to his collar.

'How old was he when this was taken?' I asked.

'Fourteen.'

One year. It's amazing how fast someone could go down hill. I motioned to a family shot on the wall. 'How old are his brother and sister?'

'Seventeen and nineteen. They're working,' Bea Sanchez said before I could say anything else. 'They wanted to stay home but I told them no. I told them they must be responsible.' And she glared at me as if daring me to disagree.

I nodded politely, and asked where Mr. Sanchez was. My questions were strictly pro forma, anyway.

Bea Sanchez turned her head away slightly and focused on a point on the wall. 'Mr. Sanchez is on vacation,' she announced.

Around here being on vacation was a euphemism for being in jail. Judging from Bea Sanchez's frosty tone, Mr. Sanchez sure wasn't going to be getting a loving welcome when he came home. I wondered what he had done and where he was serving his time as I looked at the other photos. Most was family stuff, but there were several of Bea Sanchez with groups of other people.

When she pointed to one of herself and three women and two men her expression softened. 'See,' she said. 'This is me and the other members of SNAC. They had an article about us the other day in the neighborhood section. Freddy was going to join.'

Her tone made me feel that she was angry that her son had had the bad taste to go and get himself killed in such an unseemly way.

'When I saw your son . . .' I paused for a few seconds trying to find a tactful way of telling her that her son had been trying to sell stuff he'd stolen from my store to buy crack, but I

35

couldn't. I don't think there is a way to say that. So I just told her straight out.

She looked at me for a moment before replying. 'Freddy had allergies,' she finally said. Her tone dared me to contradict her. 'Very bad allergies to everything. When he was little he took shots and those seemed to help. But recently the allergies came back. Nothing helped. That's why his nose ran like that. Ask his doctor.' And she gave me his name. 'Why aren't you writing it down?' She demanded of me. 'Don't you believe me?'

What was I going to tell her? Lady get a grip. Your kid was inhabiting his own little corner of hell.

Instead I got my pad and pencil out of my backpack and dutifully scribbled the name Bea had given me down on a blank page. I wasn't going to talk to Freddy's doctor. It wasn't worth my time. But if it made his mom feel better to see me writing the name down then fine. It was my charitable act for the day.

Bea stared out the window at the kids sitting in the Cherokee across the street. I waited for her to continue. Finally she said, 'He wasn't like those ones over there. He never ran with a gang. He never did anything wrong. My Freddy got good grades. He went to church.'

I wondered what the kids sitting in the car would say about Freddy if I went over and asked them. Plenty, I was willing to bet. They'd probably helped him along his path. I decided I'd try and speak to them when I was through here, although it wouldn't surprise me if Bea Sanchez came running out the door when she saw me with them. They were probably the last people she wanted me to talk to.

'Then why are the police saying what they're saying about your son?' I asked Bea.

She whirled around to face me. In the light streaming through the window I could see the acne scars she was trying to cover up with her make-up. 'I'll tell you why. The police are saying this because they don't like that I'm a member of Syracuse Neighbors Against Crime. They don't like the fact that we're cleaning this place up when they can't. They don't like the fact that we're talking to City Hall. Ian said you would understand. He said you were a smart lady, that you know what's going on here, but if you can't get what I'm telling you then I don't want you in my house.'

For an instant I almost said, 'Fine. I'm leaving.' But I'd given my word to Ian so I made soothing noises instead. 'You've misunderstood, Mrs. Sanchez,' I said. 'Of course I'm going to help you.'

She finally quieted down and started talking again – but she kept on saying the same thing over and over as she fingered the small diamond drop that hung around her neck. She kept telling me that her Freddy was a good boy. That he didn't do drugs. That he'd been a sickly child since birth. Finally I persuaded her to let me have a look at his room. Zsa Zsa and True raced ahead of us as we climbed the stairs.

'Did you straighten up this place?' I asked when we were standing in the doorway of Freddy's room.

Bea Sanchez shook her head. 'He always kept it like this.'

It was neater then any teenager's room I'd ever seen. It was neater than mine, but then that's not saying much. I stepped inside. The posters on the wall – all sports related – were carefully aligned with each other instead of just hung any which way. A shelf across from Freddy's bed held neatly arranged model cars, trucks, and airplanes. Freddy's desk was bare except for a history book and three notebooks and a slick-looking laptop. I went over and took a closer look. It had a seventeen-inch screen, a DVD player, and a CD burner. Not bad.

'Nice machine,' I commented

Bea fingered the diamond drop again. Or maybe it was zirconium. I'm not good with gems.

'Freddy found it in the garbage on Lancaster,' Bea Sanchez told me.

I raised an eyebrow.

'You know how those college kids always throw things out,' she continued.

Not something like this they didn't, but I let it pass.

I pointed to his desk. 'What school did Freddy go to?'

'Fowler,' Bea replied. 'He was a good student. You can ask any of his teachers.'

At this point she was standing so close to me I could smell the cough drops on her breath and the sour smell coming from her body.

I opened a desk drawer. Everything in it was neatly arranged. 'He didn't have CDs?' I asked. 'A stereo? A Discman?'

Bea shook her head. 'He had one of those IPod things.'

Another expensive toy. He'd been selling stuff on the street and yet he'd had these things in his house. Very strange. Why hadn't he sold his laptop, for example? I went over to his closet and opened the door. I could have been looking in an army locker. All his clothes were hung half an inch apart from each other.

Either this kid was OCD, had a split personality, was identical twins, or his mom had totally cleaned out his room, because what I was seeing here did not jibe with the kid I'd seen in the bar. I had another thought as I closed the closet door. Maybe Freddy didn't live here anymore. Maybe he'd been living on the street and his mother couldn't bear to admit that.

'You know,' I told her, 'I can't help you if you don't tell me the truth.'

'You think I'm lying,' she cried. 'Why would I lie?'

'I've just never seen a teenager's room that looked like this.'

'Well, that's the way Freddy was.'

For a moment I thought she was going to cry, but she didn't. She picked up True and we walked down the stairs together. When I got outside the kids across the street had left. I'd have to talk to them another day.

As I brushed the snow off the Taurus's windows it occurred to me that I didn't know much more about Freddy Sanchez now then I did when I went into his house. I was just thinking that I hoped Manuel could come up with something, when he called me on my cell.

'I was just thinking about you.'

'You'd better come back here quick,' he said.

I recognized the tone. 'Why? What's the matter?'

'Matilda is out.'

This was not good. On the other hand it could be worse – at least I'd fed her yesterday.

Six

I jumped in the Taurus, started her up, and sped down the street. How the hell had Matilda gotten out? I was always careful to lock the cage. Manuel must have taken her out and forgotten to close the cage up properly. I stepped down on the gas. He was a dead person.

And then as I skidded onto South Geddes, I remembered. It wasn't Manuel. It was me. I'd forgotten to refasten the padlock on her cage after I'd fed her yesterday afternoon. I couldn't believe I'd done that. But I had. Ian had called right when I'd been going to do it, and instead of putting the padlock through the clasp before I answered the phone I'd put it down and dug my cell out of my jeans. I'd talked to Ian. After I'd clicked off a customer had walked in and I'd helped him buy a Christmas present for his girlfriend's two cats, and after that I'd gone into the back to straighten out an order with one of the vendors. The padlock had gone clean out of my mind. I'd never refastened it.

I felt like kicking myself. How could I have been so friggin' careless? Maybe Calli was right. Maybe people actually do need seven hours of sleep a night. Obviously operating on four hours shut-eye wasn't doing it for me. Or maybe I needed to increase the nicotine levels in my blood. Studies are now saying it helps you think – something I clearly needed to do more of.

When I got to Noah's Ark I made Zsa Zsa stay in the car.

She objected, but that was too bad. She wasn't going to be Matilda's afternoon snack if I had anything to say about it. Manuel and Bethany ran up to me as I came through the door.

'She's over there,' Manuel said pointing to the aquarium on the shop's far wall that held tetras, tiger barbs and gouramis.

It took me a moment to spot Matilda, which is pretty amazing. You'd think that something that large would jump out at you. The fact that she didn't is a pretty good testament to her camouflage abilities. Imagine what she'd be like in her native habitat. Gives one a new respect for the species.

As I approached I could see that she had wrapped herself around the bottom of the aquarium stand, which made sense because that's where the heat vent was. She seemed quite happy. Dislodging her was going to be a bitch. Every inch on her is muscle. There is no excess flab on a constrictor. It took the combined efforts of Manuel, Bethany, and myself to pry her loose from the aquarium stand and carry her back to her cage.

'At least Matilda didn't eat any customers while she was out,' I observed.

Manuel readjusted the brimmed white knit cap he'd taken to wearing recently. 'Yeah. That would suck,' he deadpanned. 'Especially since we need all the ones we've got.'

Bethany's eye got wider. 'Could Matilda really eat someone?'

'Not an adult,' I answered. 'She could kill them, but she couldn't eat them. She couldn't swallow anything that large. Now a baby or a small child on the other hand . . .'

Bethany began to look distinctly ill. I decided it was time to drop the subject, but either Manuel didn't notice Bethany's expression or he didn't care.

'How about if you hacked someone up into small pieces?' Manuel asked. 'Would that work?'

'Don't say things like that,' Bethany remonstrated.

'Why not?' Manuel did indignant. 'I'm not doing it. I just want to know.' And he turned towards me. 'Well?' he asked.

I stopped biting my cuticle and considered the question. 'I don't think it would work,' I told him after a moment had gone by. 'Constrictors aren't like pigs. Pigs eat anything. If you have something you want to get rid of put it in the pigpen. Constrictors like their food live.'

'Yeah, but we use those frozen pinkies for the baby snakes,' Manuel said.

Pinkies are dead baby mice. We get packages of them from a place in Texas, defrost them, and warm them up on top of the heat lamps.

'That's true.' I thought for a moment. 'It might work if the snake was raised eating warmed prey. It's an interesting question.'

By now Bethany was edging away from Manuel and me as fast as she could. I can't imagine why.

'Maybe we could do an experiment with Shelley and find out?' Manuel suggested.

'I agree that a world without Shelley would certainly be a more agreeable place, however I have a feeling that Ian might object to that, Shelley being his customer and all. And speaking of customers, did we have any while I was out?'

Manuel held up two fingers.

'That's it?' I said. 'Just two.'

Manuel nodded. 'One came in to buy a tin of fish food and the other bought a rawhide bone for $3.23.'

Wonderful. I went over and checked the register. We'd made thirty-eight dollars and twenty-three cents today. That wasn't even enough to cover out operating expenses. Maybe we'd have a stampede of crazed Christmas shoppers right before we closed, but somehow I doubted it. And the weather certainly wasn't helping any. I took fifteen dollars out of the register and handed it to Manuel.

'Do me a favor and go across the street to the Chinese restaurant and get us something to eat.'

'Like what?' Manuel asked.

'Your choice. And get Zsa Zsa out of the car. Oh. And make sure Ling doesn't put any MSG in the food.'

'Anything else?'

I took a cigarette out of my backpack and lit it. The next thing I knew I wouldn't be able to smoke here, either, never mind the fact that this was my store. God save me from people wanting to save me. 'Yeah. When you're done eating, try and see what you can find out about Freddy.'

Manuel's forehead creased. 'Now? My mom dropped me off, remember?'

Bethany whipped out her cell phone. 'I'll take care of it,' she said as she walked into the back. She returned a few minutes later. 'Your mom will be here in twenty minutes,' she announced.

'But what about work?' Manuel demanded.

'What about it?'

'You're going to pay me for the rest of my hours, right?'

'That's correct,' I told him.

At least that way Manuel would be doing something productive instead of standing around talking on his cell. I wanted to get the Freddy thing wrapped up as quickly as possible. Maybe if I was lucky I could get the fish tank into Shamus's before Christmas.

After Manuel and Bethany left to go in search of Freddy's cousin I changed the bedding in the small mammals cages and fed Bertie and Ernie each a treat and then returned to standing behind the register. No wonder my feet hurt at the end of the day. I was on them enough. I lit another cigarette – I was now over my five a day limit – and took a drag. On the surface the Freddy thing looked like an open and shut event. My best guess was that Freddy had done something to piss someone off and whoever it was had shot him. Simple. Happened at least once or twice a month on the west side of town. Only . . . I knocked the ash off my cigarette and watched it fall into the empty soda can I was using as an ashtray. Only something didn't feel right.

I tried to work out what it was. I could explain the laptop in Freddy's room – he'd either stolen it or gotten it from one of his hood rat friends. Same was true of the IPod. And I could explain his mother's attitude. Maybe she couldn't control him when he was alive, but she was damned if she wasn't going to at least control his image when he was dead. That would even explain why his room looked the way it did.

And then there was Freddy's dog. I was thinking about True as Zsa Zsa came out of the back room. She wagged her rump at me, her sign that she wanted to be petted. As I bent down to scratch her behind her ears I tried to figure out what it was about True that was bothering me. I'd seen a dog like that before. In a magazine? On the news? I tried to figure out where but the thought wouldn't come.

After a couple of moments of doing that I knocked the ash off my cigarette, went into the back, got my AKC dog book off my desk, and thumbed through it. There was no breed in it that even looked remotely like True. She was probably a mutt. But I didn't believe that. I closed the book, and then I closed my eyes, and tried to think of what I was looking for. It was the tail and the way the ears sat on the dog's head that seemed significant.

I laid the AKC book back on my desk and went out to the front and pulled a coffee-table book about dogs off one of the shelves. I'd gotten the books on consignment – a good thing too because they weren't selling very well, but they had great pictures in them.

I started thumbing through it. On page seventy I saw a picture of the dog I'd seen at Bea Sanchez's house. According to the copy, True was a mini Labradoodle, a new breed of dog that was a cross between a poodle and a Labrador retriever. The copy went on to say that it was a 'designer' dog. Up until recently it would have been called a mutt, but we'll let that go. I don't know why I hadn't thought of doing this. The hell with the fish tanks, this could solve all my money problems. I looked at Zsa Zsa. Maybe I could breed her to a Pomeranian and she'd be a Cockerian. According to the book, *Dogs of the World*, there were just one hundred and fifty mini Labradoodles in the country.

So, I thought as I slowly closed the book, the question was: What would Freddy Sanchez be doing with a dog like that? If that's what is was. Where had he gotten something like that from? I called Ian up and asked him.

'Simple answer,' Ian said over the noise of the jukebox. 'He stole it.'

'But—'

43

'Fine,' Ian interrupted. 'Then one of his buddies stole it and gave it to him. Happy now?'

'Not really.' I raised my voice over the yelling I was hearing in the background. 'What's going on?'

'Nothing I can't handle,' Ian told me. 'Later.' And he clicked off.

Probability said Ian's assessment was correct, but my gut was telling me something different. I put my cell on the counter, stubbed out my cigarette, and went for another one. Of course, if the health inspector came in and caught me smoking I'd get a fine – thanks to New York State's most recent law I couldn't even smoke in my own store. But the inspector certainly wasn't going to be out in weather like this so I was safe for the day. I inhaled and considered True.

I'm sure if I asked George he'd say True was an anomaly. And then he'd say that anomalies happen all the time and by definition don't count because they are aberrations and aberrations don't illuminate anything. But I don't agree. I think aberrations can be the canary in the coal mine. They shed light on different possible realities.

I couldn't write off the fact that Freddy had a dog that probably cost a good deal of money, money that neither Freddy nor his mother had, a dog that didn't belong in the world that Freddy lived in. The fact bothered me precisely because I couldn't explain it. I was still thinking about True when I closed up the store and went home.

Seven

George was sitting at the dining room table grading papers when I walked through the door. I hung up my jacket, kicked off my boots, and went over to him.

He glanced up briefly then returned to his work. 'I got a telephone interview from a community college in Bismarck, North Dakota,' he announced.

'You're not actually going to take it are you?'

'No. But I am going to do the one in Fresno.'

Now that George had finally gotten his PhD he was in the middle of applying for various teaching positions Some of these were tenure-track, others were fellowships, still others one-year positions, but none of them was around Syracuse. We'd had lots of discussions about my going along but considering the way things were going between us I couldn't see how I could say yes. And even if I wanted to there was still the question of what I would do with the animals at Noah's Ark? Whenever I asked George that he'd just shrug and tell me it was time for me to move on.

Impulsively I put my arms around him and gave him a hug. I could feel him stiffen and pull away.

'You smell of smoke,' he informed me, his eyes still fastened to the pile of papers in front of him.

Screw you too, I thought as I straightened up and moved back a step.

'That's because I was smoking,' I replied as I noticed the plate with the crusts of a pizza on it sitting in front of him. 'I thought we were going to go out for dinner together tonight.' It had been almost two weeks since we'd eaten together.

George kept his eyes on his papers. 'I thought you were working at Shamus's tonight.'

'No. We talked about it this morning, remember?'

'Obviously not.' He raised his pencil and made a red mark on the paper in front of him.

I felt like taking the pencil and ramming it through his skull.

'Hey,' he told me. 'Don't make such a big deal out of it.' I could tell he was annoyed – as if somehow this was all my fault.

'I'm just disappointed.'

I watched him make another mark on the page, then put the page on the pile on his left, and reach for another one.

'How about if we go out anyway,' I suggested. 'You can keep me company while I get a hamburger.'

George shook his head. 'Sorry. Maybe another time. I have too much to do.'

I looked at the back of George's neck. I used to love to kiss it and now, now I didn't know what I felt. I took a deep breath and tried to stay positive.

'You have any pizza left?'

George shook his head again. 'I ate it all. You wouldn't have liked it anyway. I got it from Dominick's.'

'Dominick's?' Dominick's was an interesting choice. The restaurant was on the way from Natalie's house to mine.

'Yes. Is that a problem?'

'Did you see Natalie this afternoon?'

George slapped his pencil down. 'What does that have to do with anything?'

'I'd like an answer.'

He made an exasperated noise. 'Yes. If you must know. I did. So what?'

'What do you mean so what?'

'You always have to make such a big deal out of everything.'

'Right.' I took another deep breath and said, 'You know it makes me feel bad when you do that,' just like all the advice books said instead of saying what I really wanted to say, which was more along the lines of, 'You know, you're a real scum-sucking piece of shit.'

George half turned and looked up at me. 'Then that's your problem not mine,' he said.

I should have called him what I'd wanted to.

George's voice was cold, the expression on his face colder. 'I will continue to see Natalie and my child however you feel about it.'

'Your child is not the problem and you know it.'

'You're paranoid.'

'And you don't even have the guts to tell the truth.'

I turned on my heels, grabbed my jacket, and headed out the door. Otherwise I would have smashed a plate over

George's head, which would have been satisfying but messy. It wasn't until I was driving down my street that I realized that it was my house I'd just left and if anyone was going to leave it should be Saint George.

But I didn't want to go back. For openers I was afraid I'd break down and cry in front of George and I was damned if I'd let him see me do that. I drove around for a little while trying to decide where to go. Finally I headed over to South Geddes and Shamus's. I wanted to speak to Ian anyway and maybe a couple of beers would calm me down. At least it had stopped snowing.

I kept looking at my cell phone as I drove, hoping that George would call and apologize. Only he didn't. For a brief moment I thought about calling him and then I said to myself, Robin, are you crazy? You're going to apologize . . . why? For what? At least have a little self-respect. Then I told myself maybe George was right. Maybe I was imagining he and Natalie were back together again. Maybe I was just jealous of the baby. But in my gut I knew I was right.

I read in some psychology book that the definition of neurotic is a person that keeps on doing the same thing over and over again without getting the result that he wants. But he keeps going anyway, hoping against hope that this time things will work out. That certainly describes me. And it isn't as if George hasn't stepped out on me before either. Heaven knows the man has trouble keeping his dick in his pants. Everyone said I should never have taken George back. And they were right. But I didn't listen, because – let's be honest here – I never listen to anyone. I always think I know it all, that I'm smarter then everyone else.

Yup.

Shoulda, woulda, coulda.

Could be the anthem for my life.

Okay. So I was having a pity party. The words could describe almost everyone else's lives, too.

But that didn't make me feel any better.

I lit a cigarette as I drove down East Fayette. The streets were silent. Everyone was in for the night.

*　　*　　*

The air was hazy with a cigarette smoke when I walked into Shamus's. The health inspector would have had a field day with ticketing here. But if Ian didn't let people smoke they wouldn't come into the bar so the choice was pretty clear.

The Dixie Chicks were playing on the jukebox and a basketball game was playing on the television. I counted ten people sitting at the bar and two people playing pool, a respectable crowd for a weekday night. Half were regulars and half were people that came in occasionally.

Shelley was sitting with her boyfriend, Bill, on one side of her and Carmen on the other, an arrangement that was bound to cause trouble because when Shelley got drunk – or should I say drunker – she always accused Carmen of lusting after Bill.

Stuttering Sam was near the door. He was talking to three men. Two of them I'd served last week. One of them was a taxi driver, the other was on disability, and the third one was a parking garage attendant. Those were the 'old' folks.

The rest of the crowd were in their twenties. Four of them were Mohawk, one Onondaga, and the other Oneida. Unlike the old people, who practically lived at the bar, they came in occasionally to shoot a game of pool and have a few beers.

'Hey,' Shelley yelled when I stepped inside. 'It's the detective.'

Everyone turned to face me. Just what I wanted.

'You found out about the dead guy yet?' she demanded at the same time Carmen told her to pipe down.

'Not yet.' I said.

'Why not?' Shelley asked.

Carmen put her hand on Shelley's shoulder and Shelley slapped it away. 'I know what you want,' she hissed at her.

'I don't want Bill,' Carmen hissed back. 'I never have. He's all yours. His dick's too small anyway.'

'That's because you've got such a big twot.'

'Hey,' Ian yelled, pointing a finger at Shelley and Carmen. 'You two keep it nice down there or I'm going to have to ask you to leave.'

'I wasn't saying anything,' Shelley replied as she snuggled

up to Bill. 'He's my sweetie,' she told me. 'Aren't you?' She asked him.

'Sure I am,' Bill told her. 'That's why we're living together.'

Shelley's expression changed. She straightened up and poked him in the shoulder with the tip of her finger. 'You want to sell my house. He wants to take my house away from me,' she told me.

'Come on, Shelley,' Bill pleaded. 'I've already explained about that. They were just people asking directions.'

'Men in suits.'

'That's what businessmen wear.'

'Not on Geddes Street they don't.'

'Doesn't do no good explaining anything to her,' Carmen said to me. 'She never remembers what you tell her anyway. You might as well be talking down a well.'

Shelley leaned over, took my hand in hers, and pulled me towards her. 'She's just telling you that because she's jealous of me and my money. You know I have a house on Ontario.'

'She doesn't care about your house,' Bill said to her.

Shelley ignored him and pulled me closer to her. 'He wants that, too.'

'I don't want it,' Bill said. 'And even if I did it's gone. They took it away because you didn't pay your taxes.'

'They stole it from me.' She gestured to Bill and then stage whispered to me, 'You find out what I asked you to?' When I told her I hadn't she let go of my hand. 'You're not very good, are you?'

'That seems to be the general consensus. Which reminds me. Here.' I reached in my pocket and got out the ten dollars I'd been saving to return to Shelley. 'You can have this back.'

She pushed my hand away. 'I don't want it. I have lots of money. Use it to find out who the dead guy is.'

'Sh . . . Sh . . . Shelley,' Stuttering Sam said, 'they kn . . . kn . . . know who kill . . . kill . . . killed the dead guy.'

'No. They know who the dead guy is.' Bill corrected. He raised his can and took another gulp of his PBR. 'Juan . . . Juan . . . Something.'

'Sanchez,' Ian said as he set another can of beer down in front of Carmen. 'It's Juan Sanchez.'

'Whatever,' Bill said and redirected his attention to the game on TV.

'Are he and Freddy related?' I asked Ian.

One of the kids who was shooting pool piped up with the answer. 'Yeah,' he said. 'He's some distant cousin on his father's side. A carpenter or something like that. My mom said he always drank too much.'

'Interesting,' I mused. 'Two deaths in one family within a twenty-four-hour span. No. Make that less than twenty-four hours. What are the odds of that?'

'It's probably a random event,' Ian commented as he went over to the soak sink and dropped a disinfecting tablet into the water. He waited for it to dissolve then started washing the glasses.

'You know that for a fact?' I asked.

Ian looked up. 'Well, according to the cop who was just in here the two deaths aren't related.'

I took a seat towards the end of the bar and asked Ian for a Guinness. 'How do the police figure that?'

'Because Juan Sanchez froze to death. He slipped on the ice, hit his head, passed out, and froze to death. And that as they say was that.'

'Does he live around here?'

Ian shrugged. 'Don't have a clue. The cop didn't say.'

'Interesting.'

'You keep saying that.'

'You don't think it is?'

'When I was a kid I had two dogs, mutts. We used to let them run loose. In those days you didn't have to worry about that kind of thing. One day I came home from school my mom was at the door. Both had been killed within an hour of each other. One hit by a car in front of the house, the other run down by a tractor.'

'I get the point.'

'The kid was a crack head. What possible connection could he have to the old guy?'

'Possibly none, but it doesn't hurt to ask.'

'Who do you want to speak to?'

'Bea Sanchez comes to mind.'

'You should leave her alone. She has enough on her plate right now.'

I took my cell out of my backpack and put it down on the floor next to my seat. 'I wouldn't think she'd object. In fact, I'd think she'd be happy to answer my questions given the circumstances. After all, she's the one that wants me to look into this, right?'

'Right,' Ian said.

'So what's the problem?'

'There isn't one. I was just trying to be a nice guy and save you some time.'

'Considering the deal we have going that's generous of you.'

'I'm a generous kind of guy.'

From the corner of my eye I could see Carmen and Shelley starting to argue again. Carmen picked up her coat and slammed out of the bar. Oh well. At least it would be quieter. I turned back to Ian

'What do you know about Bea Sanchez?' I asked him. Because try as I might I couldn't see her in here on a regular basis.

Ian shrugged. 'Not too much. She's a good customer.' He motioned to the bottles of wine standing in back of the bar. 'She drinks one of those a week. That's about it.'

'I thought you had those bottles up there for show,' I told him.

'One or two of my customers drink that stuff. Anything else?'

'What is her husband in jail for?'

'Armed robbery. Murder two. Tried to take down a drug dealer.'

'It's hard to see Bea Sanchez with someone like that.'

Ian shrugged. 'People screw up. It happens all the time.'

Mr. Informative. 'So how well do you know her?' I asked.

Ian laughed and wiped the counter off in front of me. 'What do you want to drink?'

51

'Is she your girlfriend?' I insisted. Given the circumstances, that was the only thing that made sense to me.

Ian put his hands on the counter and leaned forward. 'Listen. I don't fuck my customers and I don't fuck my help, okay? It makes for bad business.'

'How about your neighbors?'

'You just don't give up do you?'

'Not usually.'

'Well neither do I.' He put the bottle of Guinness I'd asked for down in front of me and twisted off the top. 'That'll be three dollars, please.'

I pushed a five-dollar bill across the counter towards him. 'You really are touchy.'

'I'm not touchy. I just don't like discussing my private life.'

'Why?'

Ian shook his head and moved down the bar to get Shelley another beer. She usually averaged about two or three an hour. Not bad for a woman her size. For a little while I watched the pool players sinking their shots. There were four balls left on the table when the player closest to me scratched.

'Son of a bitch,' he said as he took a quarter out of his pocket and put it in the slot.

When I turned back Ian was talking to someone who must have just come in. I hadn't seen the kid before, but then I only work here two nights a week. From the looks of him I figured him to be a Native American. Maybe Mohawk. He was on the chunky side and the gangsta clothes he was wearing made him look even heavier than he was, which was probably the idea. Out on the street thinness is not considered a virtue. You want to be as big as you can be.

He and Ian were halfway down the bar and I couldn't hear what they were saying to each other but judging from the body language it wasn't cordial. Ian leaned towards him and said something. I don't know what it was but the kid went all stiff then he backed away and left. Ian kept his eyes on the door for a moment as if he expected him to be back, before he surveyed the room again.

'What was that all about?' I asked when he came back in my direction.

'Nothing,' Ian said. 'Just one of the local hoodlums. I told him to get the hell out of here. The last thing I need is for him to be selling in here. I have enough problems as it is.'

'How did you know that's what he was going to do?' I hadn't seen him go up to anyone.

'Because he wanted to sell some stuff to me,' Ian told me.

I was about to ask him what when my cell rang. It was Manuel. He'd found Freddy's cousin. Or rather he'd found someone who knew Freddy's cousin. Close enough.

Eight

The people who live in my neighborhood wouldn't be caught dead driving down Seymour Street at 10:30 at night. They think they're going to get robbed or shot. Well maybe, but that can happen in good neighborhoods, too. It's all a matter of timing and luck.

I figure I mind my business and don't bother anyone and the odds are they won't bother me. It worked when I lived in the southeast Bronx, and Syracuse's west side isn't any worse then that – even though people get off telling you how tough this place is. Besides, people know me from the store and anyway who's going to be out on a night when the temperature is hovering around minus nine degrees? No one, that's who.

I spotted Manuel's car out in front of the house, with Manuel waiting in it – just like he said he would. Which was good because most of the numbers on the houses on this block are either absent or unreadable and I wasn't in the mood to figure them out. He got out as soon as I pulled up behind him and came over to the Taurus. I opened the door since my window was frozen shut. Manuel leaned down and pointed to a house recessed back from the street. No Christmas decorations on this baby. The windows on the bottom floor were dark, but I could see a Jeep parked in the driveway.

'The guy you want to speak to is in there,' he told me.

I followed his finger. In the dark it was hard to tell what the house looked like – especially since the streetlight wasn't working.

'So what happened to Freddy Sanchez's cousin?' I asked as I got out of my vehicle. It was so cold the tips of my fingers were burning despite the fact that I had gloves on. I flexed them to get the circulation going.

'The Feds are after him,' Manuel replied.

'That's impressive. What did he do?' I asked as we started walking towards the thin sliver of a path leading toward the house.

'He's a member of the K Street Boys. Or at least that's what they're saying.'

'Who are they?'

'The prosecutors.'

'Ah.'

Manuel jammed his hands into his jacket pockets. 'My mom said it was in the papers. They had a list.'

I remembered the story. The K Street Boys had attracted the attention of the Feds – unhappily for them – and were being scooped up and prosecuted under the RICO Act for everything from murder, drug dealing, gun running, and extortion to spitting on the sidewalk and perjury.

Bar talk said the locals had called in the DEA because the K Street Boys weren't paying the people they were supposed to, but then these were the same people that were convinced that the reason Onondaga Lake was as polluted as it was was because the county wanted to drain it and use the land to enlarge the mall next to it. Not very likely. But this I do know. Using the RICO statute, a law intended for organized crime, to go after a local gang sets up a bad precedent.

I skirted a chair shedding its filling. 'So I guess I won't be talking to him.'

'I guess not.'

'Okay. So to whom am I talking to?'

'A kid called Jose Flores.'

'How'd you find him?'

'He went to school with my brother.'

I shivered and picked up the pace. I couldn't wait to get inside.

'And he's agreed to talk to me – why?'

'Out of the goodness of his heart.'

'Right. Try again.'

'Because you're a friend of mine.'

'And . . .'

'I promised him one of the baby iguanas if he'd talk to you.'

At least they weren't expensive.

'Well I had to promise him something, didn't I?' Manuel said defensively.

No one does anything for nothing around here, but then that's true everywhere. It's a bottom-line kinda world.

'Yes you did, but it would have been nice if you'd consulted me first. Has he been in the store?'

I didn't remember a Jose Flores and I try to make it a point to recall all of my customers' names and faces. It just makes good business sense.

'He's come in a couple of times but you weren't there. He bought some dog food.'

'What kind of dog does he have?'

'A pit.'

Why had I even bothered to ask? They were pretty much the only kind of dog people owned around here. They were good dogs, too, when they were treated properly.

As Manuel unlatched the gate to the chain-link fence he pointed to the house and said, 'Smile. You're on camera.'

For a few seconds I couldn't see what he was pointing at, then the motion-detector lights came on and I noticed the two video cameras suspended from either side of the porch roof.

'I guess he doesn't like surprises,' I observed.

'You could say that. He can see everything that goes on

out on the street and he's got three more cams in the back,' Manuel informed me.

I wondered if this guy had constructed a safe room in his house as well.

'It wouldn't surprised me if he had,' Manuel replied when I asked him.

It occurred to me that I was about to talk to someone who was really paranoid or a serious hoodlum. Not that one precluded the other – in fact, they usually went together for good reason. Or maybe he was just scared of home invasions, which were taking place with increasing frequency in this area.

As we walked up the path to Flores's house I could hear his pit bull barking. She'd been barking ever since Manuel had opened the gate and she was getting louder as we got closer. It wasn't a comforting noise.

I could feel the steps giving under my feet as I went up the porch. Manuel was slightly ahead of me. He lifted up his hand and knocked on the door. The dog went ballistic. I could hear her throwing herself against the door.

'Down, Frieda,' a voice on the other side of the door said.

The barking and snarling stopped. I heard the locks being pulled back. A moment later the door opened. The kid who was standing against the light was slender. He could have been anywhere from early twenties to early thirties. It was hard to tell.

He had a watch cap pulled down almost to his eyes and plugs in his ears and a large silver ball right below his lip. He was wearing a white tee-shirt, an oversized red hoodie, and a pair of gray sweat pants. Frieda was standing in front of him, waiting for anyone to lift a hand so she could chomp it off. Well it wasn't going to be mine that was for sure.

He and Manuel bumped fists and we went inside. The house was cold. Not as cold as outside, but cold enough. I noticed blankets hung on the windows.

'To keep the drafts out,' Jose explained when he saw me looking at them. 'The friggin' landlord don't do shit.'

He didn't offer to take my coat, which was okay with me

because I wouldn't have given it to him anyway. It was too chilly.

'Don't worry,' he told me as he led us through the living room. 'I got a special place all set up for Chita.'

'Chita?' I repeated.

'The baby iguana you be giving me. I'll show you.' And he took Manuel and me down the hallway, opened a door, and stepped inside. 'See,' he said as we followed him inside.

It was like walking into a little piece of the islands. I felt as if I should put my sunglasses on. The temperature must have been in the eighties. The lighting was full spectrum. Tree branches decorated all four walls. There was one of those recirculating water fountains in the middle of the room.

'Wow,' I said. 'I'm impressed. You could sell tickets.'

Jose grinned. 'Good, isn't it? I done some research on the Internet.'

'It's excellent.' I unzipped my jacket and took off my gloves. I think I could have stayed in here forever. Or at least until it got warmer outside.

'Manuel says you got some good stuff in that store of yours.'

'I hope so.'

'If Chita works out I'm going to get me one of those lizards that look like dinosaurs next . . .'

'Monitors.'

'Exactly.' Jose grinned again.

'So,' I said to him, 'what can you tell me about Freddy Sanchez?'

Jose grinned for the third time. 'He was a friend of my cousin.'

It seemed as if everyone here was a friend of someone's cousin.

'And?'

'He was a good kid.'

'Did he run with a gang?'

Jose made a dismissive noise. 'This gang stuff is such a load of shit. Kids get together, hang out, people call them a gang. Don't matter though. Freddy, he didn't hang out with no one. He was a loner. No one had it in for Freddy.'

'Then why are the cops saying it's a gang-related killing?'

Jose sawed the air with his finger. 'You should ask them.'

'I can't. That's why I'm asking you.'

'They just want to put this on us.'

'They? Us?' I asked.

'Yeah. Us. Me and my guys.'

'Do you and your guys have a name?'

'Nah.'

Why didn't I think that was the case?

'Can you tell me anything else about Freddy?'

Jose thought for a moment.

I felt a trickle of sweat working its way down the front of my turtleneck.

'He started acting weird.'

'Weird as in how?'

'Like he was wacko.'

'Wacko?'

'Crazy-like.'

'How crazy?'

'Like weird.'

I gave up and tried another tack. 'When did this start?'

'Six months. No. A year ago. Something like that. I mean I didn't see Freddy all that much. His mom didn't like me coming around.'

'Why?'

'Guess she thought I was a bad influence or something like that.'

At which point Jose stepped out of the room and we followed. It almost felt comfortable in the hallway now.

'Can I have the names of some of his friends?' I asked him.

'Ain't you been listen' to me? I just tole you he didn't have none.'

I apologized. 'That's right. You did. Then is there anyone I can talk to who used to be his friend?'

Jose thought for a moment. Then he gave me two names. 'But they'll tell you the same thing I am.'

I nodded. 'That's okay. Maybe they can add another piece of information or two that might be helpful. Do you know where can I find them?'

'Try the strip mall down from Fowler High School around three or so. They work in the convenience store.'

I thanked him

'So you'll let me know what you find out, right?'

'Right,' I said. 'Absolutely.' I didn't know whether I would or not, but this didn't seem the time to argue the point.

Jose smiled at me again. I smiled back at him. Manuel smiled at both of us. Good feelings all around.

'I think we should go,' Manuel said.

As we were walking towards the door I spotted several cartons with Apple labels on them stacked up against the far living-room wall.

'I'm storing them for a friend of mine,' Jose said, following my glance.

'Nice of you to do him a favor,' I replied.

'He's moving and he needed to leave them with me for a month or so.'

I nodded. In truth I really didn't care.

'If you're in the market I can get him to give you a good price. Three instead of twenty-one hundred.'

Now that's what I call deep discount. Jose went on with his sales pitch.

'They're notebooks with seventeen-inch screens, DVD, CD burners, weigh about three and a half pounds. Or if you want something else we can get that for you, too.'

I thought about the laptop I'd seen in Freddy's room. 'Did Freddy get his from you?'

Jose laughed. 'Nah. He got that for free. Guess you can't beat that.'

'Who'd he get it from?' I wondered if it was the same person that had given Freddy the Labradoodle and, if so, what that was about.

Jose shook his head. 'Couldn't tell you.' He pointed his finger at me. 'Like I said, you need something good, you come and see me. I'll fix you up right. Or ask my man Manuel and he'll get back to me and my friend. We've been doing real well with this stuff. Right, Manuel?'

'Right,' Manuel repeated, looking at the wall, at the floor, in short everywhere but at me.

'So,' I said to him when we were outside, 'you know Jose how?'

'I already told you.'

'You're his man?'

'It's a figure of speech.' Manuel stamped his feet on the street. 'Come on, Robin. I gotta go. It's too cold to be standing out here gabbin'.'

'You'd better not be doing anything with him.'

'Bethany and I want to get out of my mom's house and get our own place. We need cash.'

'You can get it other ways.'

'How? By working at McDonalds?'

'Point made. But you're an adult now. The penalties are different if you get caught.'

Manuel gave me a how-stupid-do-you-think-I-am look. 'I'm not going to get scooped up.' And he started walking to his car.

I caught up with him as he was opening the door to his vehicle. 'I'm serious,' I told him.

'So am I.' He looked at me for a moment then said, 'You're going to fire me, right?'

'No. But I will if I find any of this spilling over into the store.'

Manuel hugged himself and stamped his feet. He must have been freezing in the jacket he was wearing. With his face in the shadows it was hard to read his expression.

'Come on, Robin. You know I have more respect for you then that.'

Up until fifteen minutes ago I would have agreed with him. Now I wasn't so sure. I watched Manuel get in his car.

'Don't worry,' he said before he closed the door. 'I've been taking care of myself since I was ten.'

And not doing a very good job of it in my opinion – not that I was being asked.

He rolled down his window and stuck his head out. 'Hey,' he called out to me. 'Promise you won't tell Bethany.'

'I'm not promising anything,' I told him.

'Please.'

I relented and told him I'd think about it even though I was really pissed at him for putting me in this position.

As Manuel rode off, I wished I could ask George what he thought I should do – he always had good suggestions – but we'd have to be speaking to each other for that. And we weren't.

At least Zsa Zsa was glad to see me. So was the cat. Unlike George, who didn't even look up when I came through the door, so I pretended he wasn't there either. Childish, I know, but then I never pretended I was mature.

I gave James his late-night snack and took Zsa Zsa out for a short walk. I'd wanted to watch TV, but that would have meant sitting in the living room, which was right next to the dining room, so I didn't. Instead I downed a couple of shots of Black Label, smoked a cigarette, and went up to bed. I read for a half an hour with Zsa Zsa curled up beside me, then I turned out the light. But I couldn't fall asleep.

For a while I watched the telephone wires swaying in the wind and listened to the laughter that was coming from the TV. I wanted to yell to George to turn the sound down but I couldn't because that would have meant talking to him – which I wasn't prepared to do yet. I wanted to figure out what I wanted to say to him first.

Finally I drifted off to sleep thinking about Manuel and Jose Flores and where he'd gotten the computers and wondering how bad it would be if I actually got one from Jose, because the one I had in the store was definitely on its last legs. I knew that I shouldn't – I'd lose all credibility with Manuel if I did – but boy it sure was tempting. I've always wanted a Mac.

Nine

'So,' Manuel said, looking over my shoulder at the computer screen. 'Have you decided what you're going to do yet?'

'In regard to what?'

'Telling Bethany.'

'I haven't even thought about it.'

Which was true. I'd gotten up late this morning, therefore I was late opening up the store – not that it really mattered. It wasn't as if there was a line of customers waiting to get in. But if you aren't open when the sign says you are and someone is there, odds are they won't be coming back. After I'd done the necessaries I'd gone in the back and hopped online so I could look up Labradoodle breeders, and I was still doing that when Manuel walked through the door.

I'd expected maybe twenty sites, but there were over seven thousand. The dog, which originated in Australia, was more popular than I'd thought, and cheaper, too. Most of them went for anywhere from 2,000 to 650 dollars. But they were still unusual enough to call attention to themselves. Now I might not have been surprised if a five-thousand-dollar fighting pit bull had ended up in Freddy Sanchez's home, but a Labradoodle? A soft dog, in Manuel's words. It made me want to know a little bit more.

There were no Labradoodle breeders in Syracuse so I chose fifteen of the biggest ones from New York State, Pennsylvania, Connecticut, and Canada, reasoning that whoever had originally bought the dog had stayed relatively close to home, and emailed them. I told them who I was and explained that I was interested in finding out more about the breed and that I'd love to see one in the flesh.

I lived in Syracuse, I continued, and would like to know if anyone had placed puppies in the central New York area. Usually breeders are happy to share that kind of information with prospective buyers. If nothing came of that then I'd contact a new bunch of breeders and/or get in touch with the local vets and see what they could tell me.

'About Bethany,' Manuel reiterated.

I swung my chair away from my desk and looked at the clock on the wall, then looked back at Manuel.

'You're late,' I told him.

He hitched his pants up. 'It wasn't my fault.'

'It never is.'

'The alarm didn't go off.'

'Maybe you should invest in a new one. Under the circumstances I'd think that you'd at least try and be on time.'

Manuel did a good imitation of looking contrite. 'I've been thinking,' he said.

'About what? Finding another way to make some extra cash?'

'You could use a new computer,' he went on, disregarding my last statement. 'This one,' he pointed at the one on my desk, 'is a dinosaur.'

For a fraction of a second I almost said yes. But I knew I couldn't. Sometimes upholding standards is a real pain in the ass. 'Don't even go there, Manuel,' I warned him. 'And take off your hat. You shouldn't be waiting on customers looking like that.'

'I didn't get a chance to wash my hair,' he protested.

And who said women are vain?

'Okay,' I conceded. 'But tomorrow I want to see you here on time, hair washed, and combed.' I mean really. Was that too much to ask?

Manuel turned to go. I logged off the computer and took a sip of my coffee. Zsa Zsa came out from under my desk and nudged my hand with her nose. I was feeding her a piece of my donut when I noticed something sticking out of the corner of Manuel's back pocket.

'Excuse me,' I said.

Manuel turned around.

'Is that a blade I see in your back pocket?'

Manuel shrugged. 'It's not a big deal. Everyone on the west side has one.'

'Wrong answer.' I made a come here gesture. Manuel approached me reluctantly. I put out my hand. 'Let me see.'

'Robin . . .'

'Now . . .'

He took the knife out and slowly handed it to me. It was a five-inch jack knife with a locking blade.

'Why are you carrying this?' I asked him.

'To cut down cartons and stuff like that.'

Right.

'You want to tell me what's going on?'

Manuel did sullen. 'Nothing's going on.'

'Let's see – you've been straight for the last couple of years and you've never carried a weapon—'

'I told you it's not a weapon it's a tool—'

'And now you're selling boosted stuff . . .'

'It isn't boosted,' Manuel protested.

I ignored him and went on. 'And you're carrying a blade. Do we see a connection here? What else are you selling for Flores? Weed?'

'I shoulda never hooked you up with Flores,' Manuel complained.

'Are you going to use the no-good-deed-goes-unpunished line? Because if you are – don't.'

Manuel gave me a blank stare. 'I don't know what you're talking about. All I'm sayin' is I was trying to do you a favor and look at what happened.'

'Yeah. I get to talk some sense into you.'

'That's not what I meant.'

'I'm aware of that,' I told Manuel as I opened my desk drawer and put the knife in it.

'Hey,' he protested. 'That costs good money.'

'As opposed to bad money?' I shut the drawer. 'Now go clean the fish tanks.'

Manuel opened his mouth. I waited for him to say something. Finally it came out.

'I just began, you know.'

'Good. Now you can stop.'

'It isn't that easy.' And he started for the door. I called him back.

'Yeah,' Manuel said.

'I find you carrying anything similar on your person again and I *will* tell Bethany. You can depend on it.'

Manuel bobbed his head up and down. 'Thanks. And, Robin – I'm serious about the computer.'

I pointed to the door. 'Out,' I ordered.

After Manuel was gone I took out the knife I'd just confiscated from him and balanced it in the palm of my hand. It was a cheap blade with lousy balance. Probably made in China. The blade still wobbled when you locked it. But that didn't mean you couldn't hurt someone with it.

I sighed. If Manuel ever put half the effort into school that he did trying to hustle people he would be a straight 'A' student and wouldn't be needing this. Then I put the blade back in the drawer and called Calli at the newspaper and asked her to find out what she could about Juan Sanchez's death.

I didn't think it had any relation to Freddy's – I believed what Ian had told me – but it never hurt to check. As I stretched I caught a glimpse of the time. It was almost eleven o'clock. I had to hustle if I wanted to talk to the two kids Jose had told me about, because I had a lot to do at the store before I could leave. I was just about to start checking on my pet food orders when the phone rang. It was George.

'We have to talk,' he said.

'I know.' I could feel a lump growing in my throat. 'Tonight?' I asked.

'I'll be back at the house around nine,' he told me.

'See you then.'

After George hung up I realized that he had said 'back at the house' instead of 'at home'. Calli says I tend to over think things, and maybe I do – but not in this case. Man, I wasn't looking forward to tonight. Fortunately I had enough to do to keep me distracted until then.

*   *   *

65

The day turned out to be full of phone calls – most of them annoying. I was just on my way out the door to look for the kids Jose Flores had told me about when I got another call. It was Bea Sanchez asking me to meet her at a SNAC meeting at six thirty. There were some people there she wanted me to talk to about Freddy. I told her I was pretty sure I could make it. Then I asked her about John Philips and Tony Shepard, the two names Flores had given me. Her sniff was audible.

'They're no good. Either of them. They haven't been any good since the fourth grade. They threw a smoke bomb into my house. I had to call the police. I used to have to wait at the bus stop with Freddy when he was in second grade so they wouldn't beat him up.'

'The kids used to pick on him?'

'Just those two.'

'People change.'

'Not these.'

'So they weren't friends with Freddy?' I asked.

'He'd never have anything to do with people like that.'

'Jose Flores said they were.'

'Another bad one. Why talk to someone like him?'

'Maybe Freddy saw them and didn't tell you,' I suggested.

'Freddy always told me everything,' Bea retorted. 'Everything.'

I didn't point out to her that if he had her son would have come to a different end.

'Why do you want to speak to them anyway?' Bea continued. When I told her she said, 'Don't waste your time with them. Come to the meeting tonight and I'll introduce you to some good people.' She emphasized the word good. 'Then you'll see what kind of child my Freddy was.'

I snugged the phone against my chin while I dug in my pocket for my car keys. 'Let me ask you something.'

'What?' Bea replied. Her voice sounded tinny. I heard a beep beep and looked at my phone. It was telling me I needed to recharge it.

'It sounds as if you're a hundred percent positive that Freddy didn't run with anyone.'

'I am,' Bea Sanchez said.

'So if that's the case,' I asked her, 'why do you need me to make these inquiries?'

I caught the words 'city' and 'character' before the phone line went dead. I waited for her to call back but when she didn't I got my jacket off the back of my chair and put it on. As I zipped up I wondered if she were thinking of suing the city for defamation of character regarding her son. Usually things like that were announced in the newspaper, and I hadn't seen a mention of it there. However, that didn't mean anything. You had a year to file a motion of intent to sue.

I couldn't imagine Bea winning. Defamation of character is a pretty flimsy charge to level. Especially since as far as I could see Freddy didn't have a moral character left to impugn. But then again these days you never know how law cases like that are going to turn out. Maybe the city would settle and Bea would get ten thousand out of the deal. Or maybe I just heard her wrong. I made a mental note to myself to ask her when I got in contact with her again. Then I said goodbye to Zsa Zsa and Manuel and left the store.

Ten

It had started snowing again – I had the feeling the snow was going to fall forever. When I got out on the road I realized it was greasy. I could see skid marks from where cars had tried to stop and failed.

As I drove down South Geddes I thought about what the city had been like. An inscription on one of the buildings proclaimed it the Street of Shoppes. And in 1895 it had been. Then came the city's long, slow decline into what it is today, a place the young leave instead of go to.

I kept going by the bakery that had been built in 1919 and the boarded-up brick bank until I got to the strip mall Jose had talked about. The main building was a long, low rectangle that had been divided into five stores. Slapped together out of vinyl siding and concrete blocks, I'd be surprised if it lasted twenty years – but considering how ugly it was maybe that was a good thing.

The parking lot was crowded with high school students. Two patrol cars were parked along each side of the lot to make sure that no one got out of hand. They'd been there keeping an eye on things since the fight in October that had sent two kids to the hospital. As I nosed my vehicle through the kids I realized that I'd picked a bad time to come talk to John Philips and Tony Shepard. They'd be too busy waiting on people to be able to talk to me.

I could have gone back to Noah's Ark, but as long as I was here I decided I might as well go in and see what was what. I found an empty parking space near the car wash, locked my car, and shouldered my way through the group of high school kids hanging out by the entrance to the All The Time convenience store. They made way reluctantly.

I didn't recognize the man behind the counter. I knew the owner – he was one of the few Irish convenience store owners in Syracuse. Most of the others were of Middle Eastern extraction.

'Where's Sean?' I asked.

'Gone to Queens to see his sister-in-law,' the guy told me. He touched the skin under his left eye. It was pulsing up and down. He looked as if he was having a meltdown. 'I'm his cousin.' Then he turned to deal with a deliveryman with a dolly full of cases of soda.

A kid by the register was busy counting out change for someone. He was the kid that Ian had been having a disagreement with at the bar the other night, or at least I thought he was. I wasn't one hundred percent sure.

'Can I help you?' he asked.

I bought a pack of gum and slid it across the counter. 'Is your name John Philips or Tony Shepard?'

The kid's face became expressionless. 'Why?'

'I'm interested in some information about Freddy Sanchez. Jose Flores said you might be able to help me.'

'Yeah?' the kid said, still trying to figure out what it was that I wanted from him.

I handed him a five-dollar bill. Ordinarily, given the circumstances, I would have handed him a twenty and told him to keep the change. But that was when I was collecting expenses.

'Yeah, John.' He gave an involuntary start and I knew I'd guessed his name right. 'You know,' I continued, 'I can always go over to Sean and ask him what you're called.'

He shrugged. 'Do what you want.'

'Look. All I want is some info on Freddy Sanchez.'

'I don't know why Jose told you to talk to me.'

'He said you were the closest thing to a friend Freddy had.'

'That was in fifth grade.'

'Maybe I could speak to Tony. Tony Shepard?'

'He's not here now.'

'When will he be here?'

'Couldn't tell you.'

'Do you have his home address?'

The kid gave me my change. 'He moved. Now if you don't mind.' And he nodded to Sean's cousin, who was watching us. 'Jimmy doesn't like me chatting with the customers when I'm working.'

'Just one last question.'

'What?' The kid sounded impatient.

'You were at Shamus's last night, weren't you?'

'And your point is?'

'Nothing. My point is nothing. I was just curious.'

He grunted and motioned for the person in back of me to step forward. I watched him for a moment. If I had any doubts before I was positive now that he had been the one Ian had thrown out for trying to deal. So maybe Bea Sanchez had been right about this one after all. Philips looked at me again.

'Are you buying anything else?'

I told him I wasn't and left.

Well, this little excursion had certainly been a waste of

time, I thought, as I made my way towards my vehicle, which was now blocked by a Jeep Cherokee with two kids with corn-rows sitting in it and one, strung with enough gold jewelry to fill a display case, leaning into the window talking to them.

'You think you could let me get out?' I asked them.

All three of them stopped their conversation and gave me dirty looks. I just smiled and waited. When I was younger I might have said something impolite, but I've gotten more patient in my old age. Or more chicken. After a few more moments they deigned to slowly move out of my way. Yes, I wanted to say to them. I get the point. You own the streets. For now.

As I maneuvered my car out I wondered if the Shepard kid would be a little chattier than his buddy. Once I was on the street I got out my cell. I was going to call Manuel and ask him to look up the name Shepard in the phone book but then I realized that would be a waste of time. I didn't know the name of the kid's parents, for openers, and there were a fair number of Shepards in the book. He might not even be living with his parents and he probably had a cell instead of a land-line. So I called Manuel and asked him for Jose Flores's number.

'Are you going to give Jose a rough time?' Manuel demanded.

'Hardly.' And I explained why I wanted it.

'Oh.' There was a moment of silence then Manuel said, 'I thought maybe you wanted to talk to him about me.'

'No. I wouldn't do that.'

'Okay then.' And he gave me the number.

I called Flores and got Tony Shepard's number. However, when I dialed it I got a girl's voicemail. I hung up. Tony had obviously changed his number. I had several options open to me at this juncture, but the easiest one was to return to the convenience store. Either Philips or Sean's cousin would have it. The question was, would they give it to me?

John Philips did not look happy to see me when I walked in the store. I'd been hoping to talk to Jimmy, but since he was nowhere in sight I took what I could get.

70

'What do you want now?' Philips said when he'd finished waiting on the kid in front of me.

'I need Tony Shepard's phone number and address,' I told him.

'I already told you I don't have it.' And he began to motion to the person behind me.

'Jose Flores said you'd help me.'

He shrugged. 'I don't know it.'

'I just need to talk to him.'

'Bummer,' Philips said.

'For you it is.' And I leaned towards him and lowered my voice. 'You know what you were trying to do in Shamus's?' I asked him.

'I don't know what you're talkin' about,' Philips replied.

'Well, I'm betting you're doing some of it here.' I pointed to the cop car outside. 'How about if I go have a chat with them?'

Philips didn't answer. I could see he was thinking about whether I would follow through on my threat or not.

'I will do what I say,' I told him. 'And though I'm sure you'll be out on the street again real quick, do you need the hassle? Is this the way you want to spend your day?'

'Okay.' Philips scratched his cheek. 'Sure. Why should I care? He's being weird these days anyhow.' There was that word again. 'Tony don't have no phone right now,' Philips said. 'It's shut off until he pays the bill. But he's living here.' And he gave me the address.

'Thanks.'

Once I got back to the car I checked in with Manuel again.

'How's everything going?' I asked him.

'Quiet,' Manuel said. 'Oh, by the way,' he added, 'George called. He said he forgot he had to go to a faculty thing and wouldn't be back at the house until after twelve so he'd like to postpone your talk until tomorrow. What talk?'

'Never mind.'

'Talks are never good.'

I didn't say anything.

'Hey, Robin.'

'Yes, Manuel.'

'I'm here if you need me.'

'Thanks. I know.'

I could feel my eyes misting over as I clicked off my cell.

Why is it that when people are nice to me it makes me want to cry? And Manuel could be so sweet. Somehow he'd managed to escape that hardness that John Philips carried around with him. I guess that was one of the reasons I let him get away with as much as I did.

As I waited for a break in traffic so I could pull out of my parking spot onto Geddes Street I thought about George's message. Must be a hell of a faculty thing – but maybe I was being unfair. Or, as George would say, I was overreacting. That was his favorite descriptive word for me whenever I got upset. I wanted to scream, 'You want dramatic. I'll give you dramatic,' and hurl a plate at his head. But I didn't. At least I hadn't yet.

If you hire a private investigator and you ask him to find out whether or not your mate is fooling around, if he's reputable he'll always ask you if you want to know the truth. Because when it comes right down to it most people don't. They want to keep their illusions intact. Witness Bea Sanchez. She wants me to reconfirm her view of her child, not tell her what I find.

Well, I think I was at the point with George where I needed to know what was going on. I could hire someone to look into it or I could look into it myself. Since I didn't have any money the choice was obvious.

I fished my cigarettes out of my bag and lit one. Now that I'd made a decision I felt better.

I've never done well in limbo. I'm one of those people who needs a plan.

Eleven

The guy I'd nearly sideswiped leaned on his horn. Then he pulled ahead of me and gave me the finger. Yeah, yeah. Like he'd never done anything like that before. Accidents happen, buddy. That's why they're called accidents. Live with it.

Okay, so maybe I should pull over and clear off my rear window and side-view mirrors instead of doing the New York City driving thing – which was just look straight ahead and go and trust that everyone else will get out of the way. I guess you could say that between George and Manuel I was not in the best of moods.

But when you think about it who needs to see what's going on to the side and the rear of you anyway? That's for wusses. Of course if I had a new vehicle I might feel differently, but I don't care what happens to the Taurus. In fact, if someone hits me – or better yet steals the car – it'll be a blessing.

The roads were getting worse fast so it was a good thing that Tony Shepard's house was nearby. Where were the salt trucks when you needed them? I avoided a car that was skidding into my lane as I turned onto Daisy Lane. Daisy Lane is a small street that runs almost parallel to Fowler High School. It's edged on both sides with one- and two-family colonials. Two months ago it had been the site of another fight that had made the papers.

The street was still crowded with groups of shrieking kids laughing and throwing snowballs at each other as they headed home. I slowly made my way through them and parked in front of number two ninety-seven.

It was an unremarkable two-family green colonial with white

trim. There was a child's drawing of Santa Claus, plus a few random strings of multicolored Christmas lights strung across the windows of the upper-floor flat – nothing on the bottom. A Honda Civic was parked at the bottom of the driveway, a small Ford truck above that. I got out, slogged through the snow up to the porch, and rang the bell.

The kid that answered the door was wearing the uniform of the moment: a watch cap pulled down to his eyebrows and a hoodie and pants that were at least four sizes too big for him. He was 5'7" at the most and was carrying fifty extra pounds on him.

I could hear the TV blaring in the background and the sounds of children fighting.

'If you want to see my mom she went to the doctor's,' he informed me. 'You'll have to come back later.'

He began closing the door. I took a step inside so that he couldn't, and he stuck his face in mine to show me what he thought of my action.

'What the . . . ?' he said.

I gave him Jose Flores's name before things got out of hand, and he calmed down. I was now standing in the hallway. The linoleum on the floor was curling up where the wall and the floor intersected. The wallpaper had been torn and patched over with other pieces of differently patterned wallpaper. The effect was quilt-like and not unpleasant, although I'm sure that aesthetics was the last thing on the mind of the person who had done it.

A jumble of coats, hats, and gloves was overflowing off a small table onto the floor. Underneath the table a pile of boots lay jumbled together. A large picture of Jesus surrounded by tiny red blinking lights had pride of place in the middle of the near wall. To the left I could see a corner of the living room. A scooter was leaning against a La-Z-Boy recliner.

'Are you Tony Shepard?' I asked. No answer. Okay. I could go with that. 'Because if you are Jose Flores said you'd be able to help me out with Freddy Sanchez.'

'Why?' he asked. 'He's dead.'

'So you *are* Tony Shepard?'

74

Sometimes I surprise myself with my perspicacity.

'Why do you care?'

'I don't. But Flores said you were his friend and you'd be able to fill me in on him.'

'Freddy?' Tony sneered. 'I don't know why Flores told you that. He wasn't ever no friend of mine.'

'You went to the same school. Lived on the same block.'

'So what? Lots of people live on West Onondaga.'

This was an unarguable fact. I moved my fingers to keep the blood flowing.

'Maybe you should close the door,' I gently suggested. 'All the heat is going out of the house.'

He did so grudgingly. Even with the door closed I could feel the draft coming through the crack underneath it.

'Why you care anyway?' Tony demanded.

I decided to employ a different strategy than the one I'd used with his friend. 'His mom is very upset about what the paper said.'

Tony puffed himself up. 'Hey. I didn't have anything to do with what happened to him. Don't come trying to lay this on me.'

'I didn't say you did.'

Tony didn't seem to hear me. 'You know,' he went on, 'his mom called the cops on me when I was six years old. Six.' His mouth twisted down. Over ten years had gone by and he still hadn't forgotten. 'My mom went over and popped her one right in the jaw for that. Had the cops over and everything.'

'That was the smoke-bomb thing, right?'

'The Sanchez bitch told you?'

'Yeah, she did.'

'Did she tell you it was purple smoke? She said she thought it was a fire. Give me a break.' Tony almost rolled his eyes.

'So then I guess you guys weren't the best of neighbors.'

'Yeah, yeah. You could say that.' He pulled at his crotch. 'Freddy's mom always was saying to my mom and John's that we was,' Tony made his voice go falsetto, 'a bad influence on Freddy.'

75

'So you and Freddy never did things together.'

'I already told you that. He did fag stuff.'

'Fag stuff?'

'What? You deaf or something?'

'Like what?'

'What do you mean like what?'

'I don't know. Did Freddy go out with guys? Did he belong to the Lesbian and Gay Choir? Give blow jobs in the back of the adult book stores?'

Tony looked at me as if I'd lost my mind. 'That's sick, man. Really sick. I don't like to even talk about stuff like that.'

'Fine. Then tell me what you meant.'

'Faggy. He cried if you pushed him down. Stuff like that. He was always playing some board game or reading some book.'

'Board game?'

'One of those things with pieces.'

This was not a helpful description.

'Go? Parchesi? Chess?'

'Yeah.' Tony snapped his fingers. 'That's it. Chess.'

'Are you sure?' Somehow I couldn't see the kid I'd seen in the bar playing chess.

'Yeah. He used to carry this stupid set with him. Always asking people if they wanted to learn how to play.'

'Was he playing last year?'

'How the fuck should I know?'

'Is there anyone who would?'

Tony gave me another blank look.

I explained. 'Did he have any friends? Anyone he hung out with? Played chess with?'

'He played by himself. The board beeped and the numbers lit up and showed him where to move.'

Freddy was using an electronic chessboard. Now that was interesting. It wasn't a piece of equipment I expected to see around this part of town. Around the university absolutely. But not here. A gift maybe? Like the Labradoodle and possibly the laptop. For one thing an electric chessboard is expensive.

I could always ask Freddy's mom, but she'd probably say he'd gotten it off the street. And maybe he had. Maybe he'd found a really good load of trash. When the university students go away for the summer they've been known to throw out working TVs and other electronic devices because they don't want to bother taking them home.

But still. Most people who played chess liked to play with someone. There was a group that gathered at the Food Court at Carousel Mall on Monday nights from seven to nine to play. Maybe Freddy played over there. It would certainly be worth going and talking to whoever was there. While I was thinking about that the noise in the next room got louder.

'Stupid kids,' Tony said. 'I'll be right back.'

He marched inside. I heard a shriek and the sound of something falling.

A kid yelled, 'I'm going to tell Ma on you.'

'You do and I'm going to tell her what you've been watching.' Then Tony came back out. 'Listen,' he said. 'I have to go take care of these brats.'

'Just a couple more questions.'

'I already told you I don't know anything.' He glanced into the living room and started tapping his fingers against his thighs. He was anxious to go.

'Okay. One last thing. Why do you think the police are saying his killing was gang related?'

Tony sniffed. 'That's simple.'

'Enlighten me.'

'They want to put it on us so they can get us on a RICO beef like they did the K Street guys.'

'Us?'

'Me and my buds.'

'And why would they want to do that?'

''Cause they want to put us all away so developers can come in here and buy everything up and resell it and make lots of money.'

Right. Now there was a statement you could file under the category of wishful thinking. With a few exceptions most of

77

the houses in this area were going for ten thousand, maybe thirty thousand dollars max.

'Where'd you hear that?'

'From my mom.'

We were deadending here. I got back to my original question.

'So why do you think Freddy Sanchez got killed?'

Tony shrugged. The tapping of his fingers increased. 'Because he pissed someone off.'

'Any idea who?'

'No. He was weird.'

As if weird explained everything. I tried one last time. 'Freddy have any friends that I could talk to?'

Tony shook his head. And that was that.

I looked at my watch again. It was after four. Which left me two and a half hours before I had to be at the SNAC meeting, time enough to go back to Noah's Ark and get on the phone and find out why my pet food supplier was insisting I hadn't paid last month's bill.

Even though Bea Sanchez had told me to be at the SNAC meeting at 6:30, it didn't actually start until a little after seven. They were giving people extra time to get here because of the weather, Bea explained to me when I arrived.

It would have been nice if she'd called me up and told me they were going to be starting late I thought as I took off my jacket and hung it on the coat rack outside the door. I could have used the extra half-hour to get some more of my paperwork done.

The meeting was being held in a small room off the main hallway of the Third Baptist Harmony Church. Someone had tried to introduce a note of cheer into the place by taping a large rainbow to the rear wall. It wasn't working. All it did was call attention to the room's dowdiness. As I watched people trickling in and getting themselves settled I tried to keep my eyes open. Which was hard because they kept trying to close of their own accord.

Maybe it was coming from the cold into a room that must

have been eighty-five degrees that was making me feel this way. Or it could have been the stale air, or the fact that I'd gotten four hours sleep the night before. I kept on not being able to fall asleep. Perhaps tonight I'd take one of the sleeping pills Calli had given me. This being tired all the time sucked. And then I'd be asleep when George came home instead of watching the clock, waiting to see when he came in.

I realized I should have picked up some coffee on the way over as I watched the police officer standing in front of the room, next to the podium, trying hard to stifle a yawn. Bea had introduced me to him to me when I first came in. Officer Driscoll was the community liaison between the Syracuse police force and the community and attended all the meetings. He looked as bored as I felt.

Now that I was here I regretted my decision to come. I had so much to do and this looked like a waste of time. Plus the folding chair I was sitting on was uncomfortable and the air in the room smelled of too many tuna noodle casseroles. But it's hard to say no to a woman that's just lost her youngest child. As I was wondering how long I had to remain here before I could make my excuses and leave Bea Sanchez brought over a woman for me to meet.

'This is Dora,' she told me.

Dora pumped my hand.

'Dora was Freddy's kindergarten teacher. She's the person I was telling you about,' Bea explained.

At which point Dora started enumerating all of Freddy's multiple virtues while Bea stood there beaming. Freddy knew the alphabet, Freddy could tie his shoes, and Freddy could count to twenty when he started kindergarten. Not only that but he was already reading. Plus Freddy's scissoring skills were excellent and he could color within the lines. Also Freddy played well with others.

I didn't know whether to laugh or cry.

Bea looked at me when Dora finished. 'So you can see that my Freddy was a good boy.'

Was this the best Bea could do? Give me a reference from his kindergarten teacher? How sad.

'Do you think there's . . .' I paused, trying to find the right word. When I had I started over. 'Do you think there's someone more current I could speak with about Freddy?'

Bea nodded. 'Of course.'

'Belle,' Dora put in.

'Belle was Freddy's fifth-grade teacher,' Bea said.

'How nice,' I replied. 'How about someone he played chess with?'

Bea shook her head as she scanned the crowd.

'I take it that's a no.'

'That's right.' She looked at her watch and frowned.

'Do you know where he got his electric chessboard?'

'No.' Bea's gaze was riveted on the doorway. 'He came home with it one day.'

The place was starting to fill up. People were eddying around us. There were more people around than I'd thought there'd be. A few I recognized from the bar, but most I didn't.

'Where is he?' Bea wondered out loud.

'Who?' I asked

As Dora leaned towards me she bumped me with her ample bosom. 'Tonight's speaker,' she told me.

Bea bit her lip. Then she looked at her watch again. 'The roads are so bad. I hope he hasn't gotten into an accident.'

A moment later her face lit up as a man walked through the door. Bea excused herself and hurried towards him. I was about to ask Dora if that was the speaker when my cell rang. It was Manuel. He wasn't feeling well and he wanted to go home. I had to go.

Twelve

Manuel moaned and groaned and clutched at his stomach while he told me he was at death's door. I might even have believed him if he hadn't kept looking at the wall clock. I sent him home anyway. I was guessing that one of his friends had called and told him there was a party going on. So be it. At least someone should be having fun around here, because I certainly wasn't.

'You'd better be on time tomorrow,' I yelled at Manuel's back as he went out the door. Not that he would be, but I felt obligated to say it anyway. Just to be on the record.

Judging from the amount of money we'd taken in since I'd left I could certainly manage the store on my own. The hordes of crazed Christmas shoppers still hadn't trampled down the door. It would happen tomorrow, of that I was sure. Yeah. Right. Maybe I should put another ad in the paper. I thought about that for a while and then I ordered dinner from across the street.

After Zsa Zsa and I ate – she had one slice of pizza and I had two – I lit a cigarette and went into the back room and checked my email. I'd gotten one reply from the kennels I'd queried earlier in the day. Labradoodle Farm told me that they'd sold dogs in my area to families in Dewitt and Manlius.

I was printing out the emails when the shop bell went off. Zsa Zsa started barking and dashed out front. I followed. A girl was standing by the counter. She had on an oversized parka, boots with high heels, and hair that had been shellacked into place. Her eyes were rimmed with black eyeliner and she was wearing a dark purple lipstick, which gave her brown complexion an offish, ashy undertone.

She didn't look as if she had a lot of extra spending cash, but I've learned that appearances can be deceiving in that regard. Besides, as I keep telling Manuel, today she could buy a can of fish food for two bucks, tomorrow she could come back in and purchase a fish tank.

'She doesn't bite,' I told the girl, referring to Zsa Zsa, who was now dancing around the girl's feet. 'She just wants you to pet her.'

The girl gave me a faint smile and bent over and gave Zsa Zsa a tentative pat on her head, at which point Zsa Zsa turned around, went under the counter, and curled up on her bed.

'You're Robin Light?' the girl asked.

I told her that I was.

'I'm Cecelia. Freddy's sister.'

All I could think of as I stood there looking at her was that her mother probably wasn't really pleased with her daughter's appearance. But maybe I was projecting.

'I'm sorry about what happened to your brother,' I told her.

'Me too.' She looked towards the ceiling for a moment as she fought to get herself under control. 'What they said in the papers about him . . . my mom's real upset about it.'

'I can understand why,' I replied. 'You think what they said was true?'

'Maybe . . . I don't know.' Cecelia began twisting the bottom hem of the parka with her left hand. 'My mother would kill me if she knew I was here.'

I didn't say anything. In the background I could hear the squeak of the wheels as the hamsters ran around on them.

'But Freddy was into some bad shit.'

'So you're saying that the papers are right. That his death was gang related?'

'Yes. No.' Cecelia's grip tightened on the material. 'My mom always thought everything Freddy did was perfect. He was her little baby. Her angel.' She paused again.

'Unlike you and your brother,' I prompted.

Cecelia nodded. 'Maybe because my dad wasn't around when Freddy was raised. We weren't very nice to him.'

I clarified. 'We're talking about Freddy here, right?' I asked.

She nodded again. 'But he was always sneaking around and doing stuff – only he never got caught. He was good like that. And when he did get caught he blamed us.'

I reached for my cigarettes and lit one. 'Is that what you're here to tell me?'

Cecelia didn't say anything. I watched as she wandered over to look at the hamsters. After a moment I came up behind her.

'They look like rats,' she said without turning around.

'Rats have tails.' I put in some food so Cecelia could see how the hamsters stored the seeds in their cheeks. 'Pretty neat, huh?' I said as they scurried around.

Cecelia shrugged. 'They still look like rats to me.' And she started drifting over to the reptiles. 'Freddy hated snakes,' she said as she gazed at a ball python. 'He couldn't even watch a show with them.'

'But he liked his dog,' I said.

'Yeah.' Cecelia grimaced. 'One day I brought home this puppy that someone was giving away and mom made me take it back. But Freddy, he brought one home and it was wonderful. Freddy's shit didn't stink if you know what I mean.'

'I think I do. So you know where he got it from?'

'No.'

'You guys didn't talk?'

'I told you we weren't tight.'

'How about Freddy and his brother?'

'They got along a little bit better.'

'Would he talk to me?'

Cecelia shrugged. 'You'll have to ask him.'

'Where can I find him?'

She touched the top of her hair lightly. 'He moves around a lot.'

'So. He's a travelin' man?'

Cecelia smiled. 'Yeah. That's exactly what he is.' Then her eyes misted over. 'Freddy, he was my baby brother.'

She shook her head, turned, and walked out the door. I followed her twenty minutes later. I wound my scarf around my neck to keep the snow from going down my jacket front. Even though it was nighttime the sky was whitish-gray.

For a moment I debated shoveling the walkway to the parking lot again, but I was just too tired to bother. I'd do it in the morning. Zsa Zsa ran around in circles sniffing at whatever lay under the snow while I trudged towards the Taurus. A moment later she followed. When I opened the door on the passenger side, Zsa Zsa started growling. Ordinarily that might have gotten my attention, but she's been barking at nothing, or at least nothing that I could see, for the last two weeks. So I told her to knock it off. She didn't listen.

'What is the matter with you?' I asked her. Zsa Zsa kept going. It's not good when even your dog won't listen to you. 'Jeez,' I warned her. 'If you don't stop this I'm going to put you on doggy downers.'

I was reaching inside the car to get my brush so I could clean the snow off the windows when a guy's voice came from the back seat.

'Don't let her bite me.'

I jumped back. 'What the hell?' I cried.

'It's Jose Flores,' the voice said.

Thirteen

I peeked in the back of my Taurus. There was Jose crouched down between the seats, looking for all the world like an escapee in a bad prison movie.

'What are you doing in my car?' I demanded.

'Waiting for you.'

'That's fairly self-evident. I'm asking why.'

'I'll tell you when you get in.'

But I wasn't sure I wanted to get mixed up in whatever it was Jose was involved in. After all, you gotta figure that unless it was serious he wouldn't be crouching in my car in ten degree weather. Plus whatever happened to asking permission?

'No. Get out of my car or I *will* have my dog bite you.'

Like Zsa Zsa would ever do something like that, although I have to admit she sounded pretty ferocious at that moment.

'All I'm asking you to do is listen to me.'

'Why didn't you come in the store if you wanted to speak to me? In fact, why don't we go in there now? At least it's warm.'

'Because I don't want anyone to see me.'

'As in who? There's no one out here.'

'Please get in,' Jose begged.

Something in his voice made me relent. 'All right.' I calmed Zsa Zsa down and introduced Jose to her. She immediately went into full-tilt welcoming mode. She was licking Jose's ear as I turned on the heat.

'You should lock your car doors,' Jose told me as Zsa Zsa sniffed at his hair. 'I could be anyone.'

'I can't lock my doors,' I told him. 'The locks are broken.'

'I know someone who can fix them cheap.'

'I may take you up on that at some point. Now you want to tell me what this is about?'

'How about you drive?' Jose said.

'Someone after you?'

Jose didn't say anything.

'A rival association?'

He still wasn't talking.

'The cops? Look,' I told him when he didn't answer. 'Either you start talking to me or you get out of this car right now.'

'Manuel said you'd help me.'

'Sometimes Manuel presumes too much.' The heater was beginning to work. Thank God, since the tips of my fingers were burning from the cold.

'Why you got to use words like that?' Jose complained as he pushed Zsa Zsa away.

'You mean like presumed? Because it fits and if you'd stayed in school you'd know what that meant.'

'I wanted to stay in school,' Jose replied as Zsa Zsa settled down next to him. 'They kicked me out.' He started scratching behind her ears. She sighed and tilted her head towards him. My little girl was in doggie heaven.

'To answer your question,' I continued. 'What I meant was that Manuel expects too much. Understand now?'

'Yeah.'

I turned around so I could see Jose's face. 'So. One last time. What's going on?'

Jose didn't say anything, he just pointed. I turned back. I could see a patrol car coming towards us. From the way it was moving I could tell the cop inside was looking for someone.

'Is he by chance searching for you?' I asked Jose.

'Please,' Jose replied. His voice was muffled because he'd ducked down again.

Even though I knew I'd probably regret it, I told Jose to use the coat on the back seat to cover himself up as I began to pull away from the curb. By now the patrol car was level with me. I expected him to signal for me to stop, but he kept going. I took a deep breath, released my grip on the steering wheel, and finished pulling out into the street.

'You can come out now,' I told Jose as the patrol car rounded the corner. I watched his head popping back up in my rearview mirror. 'Talk,' I told him. 'Or I'll go find that patrol car.'

'You know what I was saying to you when you was at my place?' he said as I cruised down South Geddes and took a turn onto Fayette.

'You said a lot of things to me,' I answered.

Jose coughed. 'I'm talking about the stuff I said to you about the police going to lay Freddy's thing on me and my guys.'

'You mean his death?'

'Yeah.'

'What about it?'

'Well they're gonna scoop me up.'

I stopped for a red light. 'And you know this for a fact.'

'Yeah.'

'May I ask how you know?'

'I got friends.'

The light turned green and I went. 'And I should care why?'

Flores let out a yelp. ''Cause I didn't do it.'

'So what?'

'I thought you were a nice lady.'

'Not when I'm cold and tired and hungry. And, anyway, I don't know you didn't do it.'

'Ask Manuel. He was with me when Freddy got it.'

I braked for a couple of kids who'd decided to cross in the middle of the street. You'd think they'd figure out that it was hard to see them in this kind of weather.

'Doing what?' I asked.

'Moving stuff. Call him if you don't believe me.'

'I will.' And I reached over and got my cell out of my backpack. I had trouble hearing Manuel due to the music in the background.

'I thought you were sick,' I said.

'I am. I'm home in bed,' he assured me.

'Well I have your friend in the back seat of my car.'

'Who?' Manuel sounded alarmed.

'Jose. He says you told him I'd help him out.'

'That *pendejo*. Honest to God, Robin. That's not what I meant.'

'Let's save that for another time. What I want to know is whether you were with him when Freddy was killed.'

'Ah . . . yes.'

'He said I was, right?' Flores asked me from the back seat.

'Right.' And I said goodbye to Manuel. 'So what is it exactly that you want me to do for you?' I asked Flores.

I stopped again to let a couple more people go by. Even through the veil of snow I could see the top of the Niagara Mohawk building with its green and red lights. To my mind it's one of the best buildings in Syracuse.

'I need you to spot me the money for a bus ticket down to the city.'

I should have guessed. The city is where everyone from Syracuse goes when the cops are after them. Then they come back up when things have quieted down.

'Ask your friends Tony and John.'

'They're not my friends.'

I tapped my fingers on the steering wheel as I waited for another light to change. The timing on the traffic lights in downtown Syracuse sucks.

'So you gonna help me or what?' Flores asked.

'That depends,' I replied.

'On what?'

'Tell me what Manuel was helping you with and I'll give you the money for your ticket.'

'And if I don't?'

'Simple. I won't.'

'How about you give me the money first and then I tell you?'

I snorted. 'Despite what you obviously think, I'm really not an idiot.'

'That's not fair. I didn't have anything to do with the Freddy thing,' Jose cried. 'You know I didn't.'

'Life is unfair,' I pointed out. 'Anyway,' I continued, 'maybe you didn't have anything to do with the Freddy thing, as you so nicely put it, but I'm willing to bet you've done lots of other stuff.'

'But not this kind of stuff.'

'Too bad.'

'That's cold.'

'Yes, it is,' I agreed. 'Now I'll give you what you want if you give me what I want. So what's it going to be?'

'Manuel's going to kill me,' Jose muttered.

'Then ask him for the money,' I told Jose. 'Or ask your family.'

'Okay. Okay.' Jose threw up his hands. 'Manuel and I were unloading guns.'

'Where'd you get them?'

'That's not part of the deal.'

'I want to know anyway.'

'I got this guy from the National Guard that sells them to me. Satisfied?'

'Yes.'

'Give me the money.'

'I have to go get it.'

'You don't have it?' Jose yelped.

'No. But I will.'

'You lied to me,' Jose cried.

I ignored his whining and made a U-turn and headed towards Shamus's.

'A word of advice,' I told him as I drove over there.

'What?' Jose asked.

'You might want to think about taking your ear plugs and your piercings out. They make you visible.'

Fourteen

The usual crowd was sitting at Shamus's. Given the weather that surprised me. Normally people don't come out in a blizzard, but we'd had so much snow that everyone was going a little stir crazy.

I walked by Bill and Shelley, who were arguing with someone I didn't know about something I probably didn't want to hear about, and went by Carmen, who was staring into her beer. I nodded to Ulysses, who didn't respond, because he was having an animated conversation with himself, went around to the side, and beckoned to Ian. He slid off his stool and came towards me.

'And what brings you out on this lovely night?'

I explained the situation.

Ian laughed. 'And you want me to give you some money for this?'

'Yes, I do.'

'Why?'

'As a favor.'

'I don't do favors.'

I just stood there and looked at him. Finally he relented, went over to the register, and opened it.

'Here,' he said when he came back. 'Fifty bucks. Just like you asked.' He counted it out. 'Which I'm taking out of your salary.'

'But . . .'

He held his hand out. 'You want it or not.'

'I want it.'

'You'd better pay this back,' I told Flores when I returned to my car.

'I will. Is anyone coming?'

I looked around. 'No one.'

'You sure.'

'Wait.' I held up my hand. 'I see the Canadian Mounties.'

'Ha. Ha.' Flores opened the door and started down the street. He turned when he got to Shonnard. I didn't know how he was getting to the bus station and I didn't want to know. That way if I were asked I could honestly proclaim ignorance.

I got out of the car, whistled for Zsa Zsa, and went back into the bar. It had been a long day and I needed a drink.

I needed one even more when a cop came into the bar fifteen minutes later and started asking everyone if they'd seen Jose Flores. To make matters even worse he began with me.

'Have you see Jose Flores?' he asked me, notebook at the ready.

I told him I'd seen Flores yesterday. Which I had. So I didn't lie, I just didn't tell the cop the truth. There is a difference – fine though it may be – between the omission and the commission of an act. I was gearing myself up for another question from the cop – something along the lines of 'Well, what about today? Have you seen him today?' – but he just nodded and moved down to Ulysses. Watching the cop's bored expression I got the impression that his performance was strictly pro forma and that he'd rather be home watching TV.

'Why you want to know?' Carmen demanded of him when he got to her.

The policeman muttered something about Flores being

wanted for questioning in the commission of a felony and tried to move on, but Carmen plucked at his sleeve.

'She's the one you should arrest.' And she pointed at Shelley. 'Always saying bad things about me.'

'I'll do that ma'am,' the cop said as he freed himself from Carmen's grasp.

He looked young enough to be Carmen's grandson. And just as uneasy. He didn't have much better luck with Shelley and Bill. Bill started telling the cop that this Flores person was hiding up on top of the Upstate Medical Building at the same time that Shelley was telling him to take Carmen in for lewd and obscene behavior.

'She just wants my Bill,' she said and she leaned over and patted Bill on the arm.

Well, if the cop wasn't sorry before, he was sorry now that he'd come in here, I thought as I watched him try and disentangle himself from Shelley's clutches and move on down the line. From what I could see he wasn't having any better luck getting information from anyone else.

Ian leaned forward when the cop got down to the other end of the bar and whispered to me, 'Aiding and abetting, Robin. Not bad. Not bad at all.'

I lifted my beer and toasted him. 'I try.'

A moment later the cop's radio kicked into life and he left.

'By the way,' Ian asked me, 'how's the Freddy thing going?'

'Not too well. I get the feeling Freddy was a good kid till something happened.'

'Like birth?' Ian deadpanned. 'I didn't know you believed in original sin.'

'What I meant was he seemed to have had a radical turnabout a year ago.'

'Yeah,' Ian said. 'He got into crack.'

'But my question is why?'

'Because it's in his environment. Anything else?'

'Yeah. He got shot with a forty-five caliber bullet.' Sometimes it's nice to have a journalist as your best friend.

'Interesting.' Ian went over to the soak sink, ran a few glasses over the brush, put them on the apron to dry, then moved back to me. 'If I were you, maybe I'd start thinking about who uses a forty-five.'

I knew what he was getting at. A forty-five is a more conservative weapon. Hood rats these days usually used 0.9mms. That's because a 0.9mm has more firing power and they didn't care if it goes through two rooms and hits some kid who's sleeping in his bed. On the other hand, maybe the fashion now is for forty-fives or twenty-twos with silencers. These kids change the style of their weapons the way Park Avenue ladies change their handbags.

Ian was about to say something else when the door opened and John Philips and Tony Shepard came strolling in. I expected Ian to throw them out, but he didn't.

Instead he moved towards them. 'You're lookin' good,' he said to Tony, ignoring Philips. 'You were real skinny the last time I saw you. Now you're looking healthy.'

'He's a tub of lard,' John said.

Tony ignored his friend's comment and grinned. 'Hey,' he patted his gut with both hands. 'When you got something big like I do, you gotta have a shelf to protect it.'

I was trying not to laugh when he turned to me. 'I didn't know you knew this guy.' And he jerked his head in Ian's direction.

'She works here two days a week,' Ian answered before I could.

'Buy you a beer?' Tony asked me.

I pointed to my glass. 'Thanks, but I already have one.'

'She was just finishing up and going home,' Ian said.

I looked at him. He pointed to the television set. The weatherman was telling everyone how bad the driving conditions were outside, but somehow I didn't think the weather was why he wanted me to leave.

'Nice to know you care.'

'I care about all my customers,' Ian blandly replied as Tony asked him for two beers and a couple of dollars' worth of quarters.

It looked as if Tony and John were settling in for a while. I watched them move over to the pool table. While they were busy setting up I turned my back on them so they couldn't hear what I was saying – not that that would have been easy to do, since Tom Petty was now playing on the jukebox.

'Didn't you throw the Philips kid out?' I asked Ian

He leaned his elbows on the bar apron. 'No. I told him he couldn't deal in here. That's different.'

I looked at Ian. He seemed uneasy.

'What's going I?' I asked.

'Probably nothing,' he replied.

'Are these guys part of the group you were having problems with?'

'Could be. They're third or fourth cousins to those people. Or something like that.'

There'd been trouble at the bar a couple of weeks ago. Four kids had come in – three Mohawks and one Onondaga. They'd had a couple of beers then one of the kids in the group had started shoving one of the other customers around.

Ian had stopped him as he'd been putting on his black leather gloves – talk about telegraphing your move – and told him he couldn't do that kind of thing in Shamus's. And he'd explained why fighting in his bar was a bad thing that could only lead to the cops being called. But the kid hadn't listened, so Ian had thrown him into a snow bank, accidentally managing to bang the kid's head into the doorframe on the way out. Two days later the spotlights over the bar had been smashed. A week after that some other kids had come in and started a fight. Ian had thrown them out, too. Hopefully that was the end. But with stuff like this you never knew. I took another sip of my beer.

'You finished with that beer?' Ian asked, indicating my drink.

'Don't hurry me or anything.'

Ian just looked at me. I stuck out my tongue. He didn't laugh.

'Fine,' I said.

'Can you take the late shift day after tomorrow?'

'Absolutely.' I drank up and put on my jacket. Then I went into the back and got Zsa Zsa. She looked at me and wagged her tail. She was ready to go home.

'Hey,' Philips called out to me as I stood up. 'You seen Jose Flores around?'

'No,' I told him. 'No. I haven't. Why?'

Philips shrugged. 'Just wanted to ask him something.'

Maybe, I thought. Or maybe he wanted to give the cops the info in return for a favor or two.

'I thought he was your man,' Philips observed.

'News to me,' I replied.

I was turning to go out the door when Bill brushed by me on his way to the bathroom. I don't know whether he brushed against John or not, but John pushed him against the wall really hard.

'Hey,' Bill cried.

'Then watch where you walk,' John told him.

In probably less than two seconds Ian had ducked underneath the bar apron, come out onto the floor, and grabbed John by the back of his neck with his right hand. John tried to free himself. But he couldn't. He began wincing in pain as Ian drove his fingers deeper into his neck.

Tony came up from behind. He had his pool cue in his hand.

'Watch it,' I yelled to Ian.

I didn't have to. He was already turning. Somehow he managed to ram John's head into the bar at the same time that he turned and grabbed the pool cue out of Tony's hand. Then he clamped his hand on Tony's shoulder and pressed down.

'I've told you about this kind of thing before,' he said to both of them as he herded the bruised and bleeding pair towards the door.

Shelly gave John a nice little kick as he went by. Carmen gave him another one.

'I'm going to call the cops,' Philips yelled, which was pretty funny when you think about it.

'You do that,' Ian said, 'and I'll press charges.' And he threw them out into the street. 'Everything's fine,' he told everyone. 'They took off.'

I pointed towards the pool table. 'What about their jackets?'

'What about them?' Ian said.

'Well, what are you going to do with them?'

'Sell them on eBay.'

'I hope they're not going to be coming in here when I'm working.'

'Don't worry,' Ian said. 'They won't.'

'How do you know?'

'Because I'm going to straighten this out. Any more questions?'

'As a matter of fact, yes.'

Ian sighed. 'Okay. What?' he asked in a grudging tone.

'Bea Sanchez.'

'What about her?'

'Why do you really want me to do this?'

'I told you. She's a customer.'

'Excuse me, but you'll have to do better.'

'She's my neighbor.'

'Tell me,' I demanded. 'Or I'm going to quit.'

'No. You're not.'

'Oh yes I am.'

'What about poor Jose?'

'Don't try the guilt thing with me. I was raised by a Jewish grandmother.'

Ian thought that over while he rolled a cigarette. I watched him take a piece of rolling paper out, put the tobacco in the center, tamp it done with the edge of his finger, then roll it up, give the ends a little twist, and light it.

'Okay,' Ian said after he'd taken a hit. 'Her husband owes me money. If she builds a lawsuit against the city and wins maybe I can get some of it back.'

'At least that makes sense.'

'Good,' Ian said. 'I was worried.'

'Then I get some of it too.'

'No,' Ian said as he escorted me out. 'You get to put the fish tank in the bar.' He waited till I got in my car to make sure that John and Tony weren't lurking around anywhere.

I'd been going to talk to Manuel, but that could wait. Right now I just wanted to get to my house, take a hot bath, and crawl into bed.

Fifteen

'So what are you going to do?' Calli asked me.

She had to raise her voice to be heard over Bertie, who'd started screeching when Calli had walked in the door.

I went over and scratched the cockatiel's neck. I knew from experience that if I didn't he could keep this up for a long time. After a minute or so he twisted his head so I could get the other side. Then he settled back down on his perch and began pulling on a rope with a bell that I'd hung from a hook on the ceiling earlier that day. Tomorrow I'd put up another toy. I tried to rotate them throughout the week otherwise Bertie got bored. Cockatiels are like people in that way. They crave novelty.

'Why did he do that?' Calli asked when I came back to the counter.

'Screech like that? He wanted some attention.'

'Don't we all,' Calli said.

She'd come by Noah's Ark after she'd gotten off work. Originally I was supposed to have met her at Barnes & Noble at five but that was before Manuel's mother had called in with a family emergency. Her sister was sick and Manuel and Bethany had to watch his nieces and nephews for the day.

'He's a good boy,' Manuel's mother told me, and I agreed, not having the heart to tell her about her son's latest escapade.

The net result was that I was stuck in the shop for the day, so Calli, bless her soul, had come over here bearing gifts. In this case, a large breve for me and a latte for her, two pieces of cheesecake, and a mammoth chocolate chip cookie.

'So what are you going to do?' she repeated as I broke off a piece of the cookie and put it in my mouth.

Scotch is good but at a pinch chocolate isn't bad either.

'What am I going to do about Manuel?' I asked, even though I knew Calli wasn't referring to him.

'Were you calling me about Manuel at two o'clock . . .

'One-forty-five,' I corrected.

'Okay. One forty-five in the morning.'

'No.'

I'd taken one of Calli's sleeping pills and gone up to bed after I'd gotten home last night, but it hadn't helped and I was still tossing and turning when George had come in at one in the morning. I'd put on my bathrobe and come down the stairs.

Before I'd even opened my mouth George had snapped, 'I know what you're thinking and you're wrong.'

'You don't know what I'm thinking,' I'd told him.

'Okay, I don't,' George had said as he headed for the kitchen.

'Let's talk,' I'd replied as I followed him.

George hadn't even looked at me as he gotten himself a drink of water. 'I told you before, now is not a good time.'

'I know what you said but we're both up. We're both here.'

'I have an early meeting tomorrow.'

'So?'

He'd whipped around and snarled, 'You always have to get in my face, don't you?'

I wanted to scream back at him. But I didn't. I can never seem to say anything when my feelings are really hurt. Instead I'd gone into the living room and turned on the TV and George had gone upstairs to bed. I'd poured myself a hefty shot of Scotch and downed it, after which I'd remembered I'd taken the Ambien. Not a smart thing to do. So I'd panicked and called Calli.

'No, it's not the smartest thing to do,' Calli had agreed. 'But you'll be fine. It's hard to OD on Ambien.'

'That's comforting.'

'I think so. Now go to sleep.' And she'd hung up.

And she'd been right. I'd just woken up muzzy headed with a numb feeling in my leg because I'd slept on it the wrong way. I sighed. Calli hadn't wanted me to get back together with George and she really hadn't wanted George to move

97

into my house, but she was kind enough not to remind of that fact more than once a day.

I took a sip of my coffee, ran a finger along the side of the cup where the foam was, and licked it off.

'I'm thinking of finding out if he's going to see Natalie or not.'

'I see,' said Calli. She leaned an elbow on the counter and broke off a piece of her cookie. Zsa Zsa barked and Calli looked at me.

'You can give her some,' I told her

'I thought chocolate was bad for dogs. I thought it could kill them.'

'Unsweetened is. Anyway, if she can drink beer, she can eat chocolate.'

'I suppose,' Calli said and she held out a piece.

Zsa Zsa grabbed it out of her hand and tore into the back.

'Lucky I still have my finger,' Calli told me.

'You should have told her "take nice."'

'Oh. So her almost biting me is my fault?'

'Don't you start in on me too,' I told her.

'I was kidding,' Calli said.

'Sorry.' I took another sip of my coffee. Nothing like cream to make something taste good. 'So what do you think about my doing that?' I asked her.

'Finding out about George and Natalie?' she asked.

I nodded.

'This is your big news?'

'I thought you'd be happy.'

'I am. It's just that you picked the wrong time to do this. You know, Mercury is retrograde right now,' Calli told me as she broke off another piece of cookie and ate it.

'What the hell does that have to do with anything?'

'Because Mercury is the planet of communication. When it goes retrograde things get fouled up.'

'George and I don't have any communication so it doesn't matter.'

Calli wiped the corners of her mouth with the paper napkin she'd brought, took one of the forks, and began eating the cheesecake. 'I'm sorry,' she said, 'I didn't have time to eat lunch today.'

'That I understand. I don't understand what Mercury has to do with me and finding out about George and Natalie.'

'And the baby,' Calli added.

'This has nothing to do with the baby so let's leave her out of it.'

I wouldn't admit this to anyone, but I hate hearing about Natalie's and George's baby. I hate thinking about the baby. Immature, but there it is.

'Fine.' Calli rubbed her shoulders and hugged herself. 'I don't know what it is but I can't seem to get warm these days. I'm just telling you about Mercury,' she continued, 'because things don't proceed smoothly during this period.'

'They never go smoothly for me anyway.'

'Yes. But they're going to get worse.'

'Thanks for the helpful information.' I watched a UPS truck drive by. Was it going to stop for me? I was expecting an order. No. It kept going. Drats. I picked up the thread of what I'd been saying. 'Maybe I should just check myself into the psych unit. Or dig a big hole for myself somewhere in the desert.'

Calli leaned over and gave me a hug. 'I'm sorry things are such a mess.'

I hugged her back. 'Me too. And you were right. I never should have let George move in with me.'

'Probably Venus was—'

I held up my hand. 'No more.' I'd gone through Calli's feng shui period and her brush with EST. Enough was enough. 'You know what really worries me?' I continued.

'What?' Calli asked.

'Maybe what George says is right. Maybe I really am the paranoid jealous bitch he says I am. Maybe I am nuts. Maybe he isn't doing anything with Natalie.'

Calli snorted. 'Get real. Of course he is,' she assured me. 'In case you need me to remind you, he's cheated on you before.'

'I know. I know.'

'Then what's the problem? Why not kick him out?'

'The problem is me,' I admitted.

Calli rolled her eyes. 'Finally she speaks words of truth.'

I started biting my cuticles. 'I just feel I need to get him dead to rights so he can't wiggle out of it. I need to do it for my own mental health. Does that sound crazy?'

'It sounds a little obsessive, but then who am I to talk?' Calli ate another piece of her cake and pushed the plate towards me. 'You'd better get started otherwise I'm going to eat yours too.'

I picked up my fork and had a piece. The taste of pumpkin lingered in my mouth.

'I just need to know once and for all.'

'You already know.'

'There's knowing and then there's *knowing*.'

'You want a picture?'

'No. I just want to catch him coming out of her house. Or with her. I want to catch him in his lie.'

'And then you'll make him leave.'

'I will.'

'You swear?'

I put up my hand. 'I swear.'

Calli pointed her fork at me. 'I'm going to hold you to that.'

'You know what I'm going to miss,' I told her.

'What?'

'The sex. George is really good in bed.'

'Was,' Calli reminded me. 'Was good in bed. You're not having any now, so what's the difference? Anyway, you'll find someone better. Someone you can trust. Someone who doesn't cheat on you. What a concept.'

'Hopefully,' I said.

'Definitely,' Calli replied.

So far in the faithfulness department I'd been zero for two. Both George and my late husband had stepped out on me. Obviously I wasn't doing well with men.

'Maybe I'll become a lesbian,' I mused.

Calli lifted an eyebrow. 'They have problems too, you know.'

'Yeah, but they'll be different problems.'

'No, they'll be the same,' Calli retorted. 'People are people no matter what their sexual orientation is.'

'Is there something you're not telling me?'

'Ha. Ha. Being a reporter and all, I'm a trained observer of people.'

'That's right. I forgot.'

Calli and I ate in silence for a moment. When the cake was gone I looked at Calli and said, 'Promise me that when we're old, if we're not married we'll live together.'

'Deal,' Calli said.

Somehow that made me feel better. I took another sip of my coffee.

'So are you going to hire someone to nail George?' Calli asked.

'No. I can't afford to. I'm going to do it myself.' I gave Calli my best smile. 'I was hoping I could borrow your car. Please,' I said to her when she didn't say anything. Maybe it was because she had a Beamer. 'I figure the next time he tells me he's going out, I'll follow him and see where he goes.'

'Why can't you use your car?' Calli asked.

'Because he might spot it.'

'Not if you keep in back of him.'

'If he were someone else I'd agree, but he still has cops' eyes.'

Calli wrinkled her nose. 'Cops' eyes?'

'He notices everything.'

'I see.' Calli picked up a cookie crumb that was lying on the bag and ate it.

'You're just looking for an excuse to drive the Beamer,' she said.

'Well, there's that too,' I admitted. Who wouldn't? The Beamer had heated seats, while my Taurus had a heater that blew out puffs of slightly warm air when it was in a good mood. 'I mean,' I continued when Calli remained silent, 'it's hard to sit someplace when your fingers are freezing.'

'And my car has a CD player.'

Unlike mine.

'And since we both agree that getting George out of my life would be a good thing and since you're my friend I thought you'd want to facilitate the process. And I'm not even going to mention the fact that I found your dog for you and untangled you from your last bad relationship. I charge most people thousands for that kind of service. All I'm asking from you is the loan of your car.'

Calli ate another crumb. She seemed unmoved by my little speech. 'That car is my baby.'

'I respect that.'

'You don't respect anything.'

'I respect my friends.'

Calli pursed her lips while she thought. 'I should have bought two cookies,' she observed. Another moment went by and she said, 'You can't smoke in the car.'

'No problem.'

'And no wild chases.'

'None.'

'And you'll drive my car in a responsible manner.'

'Don't I always drive in a responsible manner?'

She gave me a who-are-you-kidding look. 'No, you don't.'

'I absolutely will when I'm in the Beamer.'

'Okay. When do you want to do this?'

'I don't know. Sometime this week, maybe?'

Calli nodded. I hugged her again. Calli always came through when I needed her. She yawned. 'As for the stuff about Freddy's uncle that you asked me to find out,' she said, 'because obviously I have nothing better to do with my time than be your personal research assistant . . .'

'Hey, I'm paying you.'

'With what? A slice of pizza.'

'I've offered to buy you at least three. So did you get anything?'

'I couldn't get too much more then what was in the papers.' Calli dug her notebook out of her pocket and riffled through the pages until she found the one she was looking for. 'Okay. Here we go.' She looked up at me to make sure I was paying attention.

I was. She began reading her notes.

'The cops are definitely treating this guy's death as accidental. Evidently Juan Sanchez got into an altercation with someone at the Lennox. At which point he went outside, slipped on the sidewalk, and hit his head. The police have two witnesses that will testify to that fact.'

She stopped to take a sip of coffee before continuing.

'The blow caused bleeding into the brain. The consensus of opinion is that if this man had sought medical treatment immediately they might have been able to do something for him. Unfortunately he didn't, so he collapsed and froze to death.'

I thought of the picture of him lying in the driveway that I'd seen. He'd seemed so forlorn lying there.

'Did you find out where he lived?'

Calli ran her finger down her notes. 'His last known address was on Detrich Street.'

That was over on the near west side, not too far away from where he'd been found. So much for my theory about Juan's death and Freddy's death being connected, because if they were I couldn't see how.

'So that's that.'

'Yup.' Calli turned the page. 'Ah. Here's something else. He was working for Industrial Enterprises in a janitorial capacity.'

'Hum.' I ate the last piece of cheesecake. Then I licked the fork. I would have licked the plate if that weren't considered unseemly. 'Anything else?'

'He's a convicted felon.'

My ears perked up. 'For what?'

'Drugs.'

'Selling?'

'Yup. A little weed. A little coke. The usual thing in this part of town. So how are you doing with the Freddy thing, anyway?' Calli asked. 'Anything in it for me?'

Zsa Zsa came out of the back room and I put the plate down for her to lick. The advantages of being a dog.

'If there's a story in this other than the normal sorry-state-of west side, I don't see it. I've talked to three . . .' I stopped to consider for a moment – 'No. Make that five. No. Make that seven people, and I haven't learned very much. I mean I've learned that Freddy was a stellar elementary school student. That he played chess. That he had an expensive laptop, an IPod, and a fancy dog. That he was, as they liked to say in the old days, the apple of his mother's eye. That his sister really didn't like him too much.' I bit my cuticle. 'The whole thing is so nebulous. Was Freddy Sanchez killed for gang-related reasons or wasn't he? I don't think he was.

'And now, according to Ian, it turns out that the mother wants me to look into this because she's thinking about initiating a suit against the city.'

'Grieving mother fights for son's good name,' Calli said. 'I like it.'

'Good for you.'

'So why are you involved in this?'

I mentioned the fish-tank angle.

Calli didn't look as if she believe me.

'It's true,' I insisted.

'This is me you're talking to, remember?

'I just . . . I don't know . . . I just get the feeling there's something else going on, but I can't put my finger on it.'

'Fair enough. So what are you going to do now?' Calli asked me.

I downed the last of my breve, crumpled the cup up, and threw it in the trash basket under the counter. 'What I usually do.'

'You mean cause trouble?'

'Ha. Ha. I was thinking more along the lines of poking around and seeing what turns up. I'll talk to Freddy's friends. His neighbors. Chat up his brother. Maybe find some of the people he played chess with.'

Calli flicked a piece of lint off the neck of her rust-colored angora crewneck. 'Like I said, cause trouble.'

I was just about to reply when Manuel walked in the door.

'Well, well,' I said as Zsa Zsa ran towards him. 'If it isn't our own miscreant.'

Sixteen

'Robin, don't be like that,' Manuel said as he stamped the snow off his boots. Then he bent down and scratched Zsa Zsa's rump. She was wagging her tail so hard her body was moving from side to side.

'Like what?' I asked.

'Pissy.'

'I'm not being pissy.'

'Yes you are. Jose is my cousin. I was just helping him out.'

I turned to Calli. 'Have you noticed how everyone is everyone's cousin around here? Just like in Chinatown.'

'I can't help it if I have a large family,' Manuel replied. Then he said, 'Can I speak to you in your office for a moment?'

Calli shrugged. 'Go ahead,' she said.

When I got there Manuel handed me an envelope.

'What's this?' I asked him.

'Open it,' he said.

I did. Inside was a twenty-dollar bill. I took it out.

'And this is for?' I asked.

'It's a retainer.'

'For what? From who?'

'It's for Jose.'

'He gave you this money?' I was confused.

'No. I'm giving it to you.'

'Why?'

''Cause I want to make sure that if he gets himself arrested he'll have someone on his side.'

I put the twenty-dollar bill on my desk. 'How forward thinking of you, Manuel, but the answer is no. And even if I were to say yes, I don't work for twenty dollars.'

Manuel drew himself up. 'I'm planning on giving you more, but I just want to remind you that you've worked for less.'

'Not these days.'

'Come on, Robin,' Manuel whined. 'You're looking into the Freddy Sanchez thing and you're not getting any money for that.'

'I'm not investigating, I'm making inquiries. There's a difference. And as for the money thing – I'm looking into Freddy Sanchez's death because it might net me a business opportunity.'

'I can get you a computer if you want,' Manuel said.

'No, no computer. I've already told you that.'

'But you know you want one.'

'That's not the issue. Anyway,' I continued, 'why should you be worried about Jose when he has such a good alibi?'

Manuel gave me 'the glare'. It didn't work well with me but I'm sure it was effective with his buddies.

'That's cold, Robin. Just cold.'

Because, of course, Manuel couldn't testify on Jose's part. If Manuel did that it would mean admitting he had committed a felony.

'Feeling a little guilty are we?' I asked him.

'You saying that just because I want to help someone out?' Manuel asked.

He tried doing outrage next. That didn't work either. I left the office and went out front. Manuel was right behind me. Calli was petting Zsa Zsa with one hand and paging through today's edition of the local paper with the other. She looked up.

'You don't want to know,' I told her.

'Come on, Robin,' Manuel wheedled. 'Please.'

'No,' I told him. 'I'm not doing it. You've lied to me up and down the line and I'm tired of it.'

'That's not fair,' Manuel protested.

'It's true.'

'Don't take out George on me,' Manuel cried.

'Now that is totally uncalled for,' I snapped.

Calli had put down the paper and was now following

Manuel's and my conversation with rapt interest. 'Children, children,' she remonstrated.

Manuel and I shut up.

So what's this about?' she asked.

'Tell her, Manuel,' I ordered.

'I can't,' he mumbled.

'Yes, do tell me,' Calli said. 'Mother Calli wants to know.'

'You told me,' I pointed out to Manuel.

'That's different,' Manuel said.

'I assume we're talking about some illegal activity here,' Calli said.

Instead of replying Manuel began studying the ceiling fan.

'You'd do better to confide in me if that's the case,' Calli told him. 'Really. You would. If you tell me something and the cops want to know what it is I can always claim journalistic immunity. If you tell her,' Calli indicated me with a nod of her head, 'and she doesn't answer the cops' questions, they can charge her with obstruction of justice. Plus I have better contacts.'

'Is that true?' Manuel asked me.

I nodded.

'So,' Calli said. 'What is it you want Robin to do?'

Manuel looked at me.

'Go on,' I told him.

Manuel swallowed. He yanked up his pants. I watched him trying to decide. After a few moments he began to speak. Calli sat still and listened. When Manuel was through she turned to me and said, 'Robin, you know you're going to do this, so stop giving Manuel a hard time.'

Manuel smirked.

'I'm not going to do it,' I said to Calli. 'How can you say that I am?'

'Because you are,' Calli told me.

'That's certainly a good answer,' I observed. 'I bet you write all the articles in the paper like that.' I framed an imaginary article with my hand. 'I can see it now. So and so is doing such and such. Why? Because I just know they are.'

'May I continue?' Calli asked.

I bowed. 'By all means. I wait on your words with breathless anticipation.'

Calli bowed back. 'Funny thing. Everyone does.'

'Must be why you're working for the *New York Times*.'

She shot me a hurt look and I apologized. I'd hit her sore spot. Sometimes I really need to think first and speak second.

'Okay,' Calli continued after a moment. 'You'll do it for two reasons,' she said.

I raised an eyebrow. 'Only two?'

Calli ignored my sarcasm and continued. When Calli wants to say something it's impossible to sidetrack her.

'One.' She held out a finger. 'Because you're curious, and things around Freddy Sanchez's death aren't adding up for you.'

'I'm not that curious.'

'It's your leading characteristic.'

Or fault, depending on whom you spoke to.

'And two?' I asked.

'Guilt.'

'What guilt?'

'You still feel responsible for Freddy Sanchez's death.' Calli smiled. 'Which of course corresponds with the guilt Manuel feels about Jose. No wonder you two get along.'

'Cute,' Manuel said.

'You think you know me pretty well, don't you?' I demanded of Calli.

'Yeah I do. You'll just keep on turning the problem over in your mind. You're not going to be able to let it go.'

The irritating thing is that Calli was right. She knew it. I knew it. Manuel knew it.

I turned to Manuel. 'Okay. Go get the twenty bucks.'

'So how deeply involved in the Freddy Sanchez thing are you?' Calli asked him when he came back.

'I already told you, I'm not,' Manuel protested as he handed me the money. 'I just don't want Jose picked up for something he didn't do.'

'Out of the kindness of your heart,' I observed.

'Yeah. Out of the kindness of my heart,' Manuel repeated. 'What's the matter? You don't think I got any finer emotions?'

'Finer emotions? What have you been reading?'

Manuel looked away. 'Some book that Bethany has,' he muttered.

'Reading is good,' I told him. 'And as to your finer emotions, I'm sure you have them. Somewhere. I'm just not sure you act on them.'

Manuel bit his lip.

'Manuel, it seems to me,' Calli interjected, 'that the simplest thing to do would be to get you immunity from prosecution. That way you could furnish Jose with an alibi.'

'I can't do that,' Manuel objected.

'Why not?' Calli asked.

Manuel shifted his weight from one leg to another. 'Because the DA ain't gonna do that for nuthin'. He's gonna want something from me.'

'And you don't want to give it to him?' Calli asked.

'I gotta live here,' Manuel told her. 'I don't wanna be watchin' my back twenty-four-seven.'

'I suppose you're right,' Calli allowed.

'You know it.'

I tapped my fingers on the counter. Bertie began screeching again.

'Go give him something,' I told Manuel.

Manuel headed off at the same time Calli took her jacket off the counter and put it on. She looked out the window. 'I can hardly wait till it starts getting light out again. I hate this dark by five o'clock business.'

'Me too,' I agreed.

'Call me,' she said.

'I will.'

'And don't do what you did last night,' she cautioned as she left.

'I thought you said it was okay,' I replied. But she didn't hear me.

'What did you do last night?' Manuel asked.

'Nothing.'

There were some things that Manuel didn't need to know.

Seventeen

I was just about to tell Manuel that I thought we should rearrange the pet food shelves when Calli came walking back inside. Zsa Zsa ran to greet her in a manner that suggested she hadn't seen her for eons.

'I've been thinking,' Calli said.

I waited.

'I don't have any appointments right now. I'll stay here and keep an eye on Manuel while you see if you can find out what George is up to.'

'You're following George?' Manuel said.

'I'm verifying information,' I told him.

'You're seeing if he's with Natalie.'

'That's a crude way of putting it – but yes.'

'It's about time you kicked his ass,' Manuel said.

'Out of the mouths of babes,' Calli remarked as I reached for my cell.

George didn't pick up the phone at home. I tried his office next. Sometimes he stopped there after class to check his phone messages. No luck. I tried his cell and got his voice-mail. I hung up without leaving a message. I looked at Calli.

'He really could be anywhere,' I told her.

'See what you can find out.' And she handed me the keys to the Beamer. 'If you find him call me, if not I'll see you back here in an hour.'

I spent the next hour cruising around. The first place I went was Eastwood, which was where Natalie's apartment was located. Ten years ago Eastwood was a thriving area, but now half the storefronts on the main drag were empty and graffiti was beginning to creep in and make a home on the walls of the buildings.

The houses on the street that Natalie lived on were changing from owner-occupied to rental properties and it showed in the trash that dotted the streets. Six twenty-six Collingwood was marked out by a large half-dead pine tree, partially screening the front of the small bungalow from the street. A line of dead ivy clung to the telephone wires that ran from the house to the utility pole on the sidewalk.

George had told me that the bungalow contained two bedrooms, which made it just large enough for Natalie and her kid. I wondered if he'd go there when I asked him to leave my place since he was a man that always liked his privacy. It would be interesting to see what happened.

The house was lit up, but there were no cars parked in the driveway, a fact that led me to make the stunning deduction that no one was home. Then I remembered that George had told me that he'd had to follow Natalie over to the dealership to get the power steering hose on her Skylark replaced. So maybe it was still at the shop.

From where I'd parked I could see through the living-room window. A young girl was sitting on the sofa watching TV. The babysitter, I guessed. In which case Natalie was out. Possibly with George. But the girl could also be Natalie's cousin. In which case Natalie could be in. Impossible to know unless I rang the doorbell.

I turned that course of action over in my mind while I reached in my backpack for a stick of gum. The whole object of this enterprise was to surprise George. Even if Natalie weren't there the babysitter would tell her I'd come by. It wouldn't matter if I didn't use my real name, because once the babysitter described me Natalie would know who I was and she would tell George. Ergo, I reluctantly concluded that knocking on the door was out. That being the case I headed over to Pat's, a bar on Burnett Avenue that George liked to hang out in.

When George and I first began seeing each other we used to go there. We'd have a couple of beers and shoot some pool, but we hadn't done that for a long time. Of course, I thought as I checked the lot and the street adjacent to the bar for

George's car, he and I really didn't go out together anywhere anymore.

I didn't see George's new Subaru but I went into Pat's just to make sure. They'd smartened the place up since I'd been in last. The owner had put up new wallpaper and wainscoting. Pictures of Syracuse in the old days were hanging on the walls. The crowd had gone upscale too. There were fewer blue-collar guys and more professional types.

Over in the dining room, a handful of people were scarfing down Pat's famous hamburger and sweet potato fries. I briefly thought about getting an order to go, but I didn't want to get grease over the leather seats of Calli's Beamer. Never say I'm not considerate.

'Can I get you anything?' the bartender asked me.

I shook my head and went outside. I nosed the car back onto Burnett, made a left, and then made another left at Teall. I stopped at the gas station to get a cup of coffee and then headed towards the university. There were a couple of bars on the hill that George frequented from time to time. As I went up and down Crouse and M Streets, I caught glimpses of knots of college kids as they hurried down the streets hugging their jackets to their chests. I remembered when I'd studied for my finals. Once, I'd learned four hundred pages in twenty-four hours. Of course, I'd forgotten everything as soon as I'd taken the final.

After I'd spent ten minutes driving around and not finding George's Subaru, I headed over to Westcott Street and drove around there for a while. The area is mixed residential, student, and Section Eight – read welfare – housing. For a while the neighborhood looked as if it was going downhill, but it's stabilized. Now it's got three good restaurants, a diner, a couple of bars, a movie theater that shows foreign and independent films, and a store that sells art stuff.

Basically it's the closest thing Syracuse has to Greenwich Village. A lot of the houses on the side streets had Christmas lights on the shrubbery outside their doors or lit candles in their windows. Large silver stars were mounted on the street poles along the main drag. They'd gone up right after

Thanksgiving and would stay up till after New Year's.

I could see the flickers of color from the TV screens as I negotiated my way through the neighborhood streets. Between the snow and the cars parked on either side of the road, it was like driving down a series of one-lane country paths.

So far I was striking out, but I figured what the hell, as long as I was out I might as well try one more place. I felt happier then I had any right to. Maybe it was because I was driving around in a nice car, or maybe it was because I was finally doing something about George.

I turned up the Dixie Chicks another notch and headed to the last place on my list, Armory Square. If the Westcott Street area is Syracuse's Greenwich Village, then Armory Square is Syracuse's answer to SoHo, except without the shopping. Once the place had been a jumble of warehouses and unoccupied buildings, but it had been yuppified with a vengeance. Now it was mostly populated with bars, restaurants, and nightclubs.

Even though it was the middle of the week there were no parking spaces on the streets. White lights were wrapped around the trees. The candles on the restaurant tables reflected in the windows. Office-party people toasted each other. Couples held hands as they scurried to their cars.

For a second I felt like a child pressing her nose against the window, but then I shook the feeling off and started looking for George's car. If it was down there I wasn't seeing it. For all I knew he and Natalie could be at the mall catching a picture or doing some last-minute Christmas shopping. Or they could be doing separate things – although for some reason I didn't think so.

Finally I turned around and headed back to Noah's Ark. It had been a little under an hour and I needed to get the Beamer back to Calli. Even though I'd never spend that much money on a car I could see why Calli had. Riding in it made me feel invincible. I wondered if that's how the rich felt as I made a right onto Fayette Street.

'She's a sweet ride, isn't she,' Calli said as I walked through the door of Noah's Ark.

'I like my car better,' I told her as I bent down to pet Zsa Zsa. 'I like to be one with the struggling masses.'

Calli laughed. 'Sure you do. Everyone does. So I'm assuming you didn't have any luck.'

I straightened up and took my jacket off. 'No George. No Natalie.'

Calli searched my face. 'But you're not giving up?'

'No. I'm not.'

Zsa Zsa barked. I went around the counter, got a liver treat, and fed it to her.

'Even if you can't nail him, you're going to ask him to leave, right?' Calli said.

'Right,' I replied.

She brushed back a strand of hair that had fallen over her eye. 'You'd better.'

'I just said I was,' I told her.

'You've said that before,' Calli reminded me. 'Several times, in fact.'

'I know. But this time I mean it.'

'I really hope so.'

'I will.'

I don't know why or how or when but somewhere inside me a switch had clicked off. I wanted to catch George with Natalie for the sheer pleasure of watching him squirm, but if I couldn't he was out anyway. Maybe, I thought as Calli got her jacket on, I'd just move his stuff out onto the street.

Eighteen

Manuel and Bethany were bickering when I left the store the next day to motor out to Dewitt and Manlius to talk to the Labradoodle owners. I'd gotten their phone numbers from the kennel and called and asked to come visit. Both owners had agreed that I could come and see their dogs.

It took me ten minutes to clean the snow off my car before I got underway. The traffic on East Gennie was tortoise-like. When I finally got to Maplewood Drive I took a hard left and started looking for Applegate Lane. The problem was seeing. There are no streetlights on the road and the darkness of the night and the blowing snow it made it hard to read the street signs, let alone stay on my side of the road. In fact, I had to double back because I missed the sign the first time around. I made a U-turn, which was maybe not the smartest move, but I couldn't see anyplace to turn around. I must have hit a greasy patch, because I skidded out and almost slid into a mound of snow on the shoulder. The tires spun as I put the car in reverse. Great. Here I was in the middle of the road and no one could see me until it was too late for them to stop.

Finally I got some traction and made my turn. I definitely had to find the money to buy some tires, because the treads on mine were almost bald. Basically, I shouldn't have been out on the road with them in weather like that. But then I shouldn't have been out on the road with my car in any weather. Unfortunately, unless I won the New York State jackpot I wasn't getting a new car any time in the foreseeable future, and if I waited until road conditions were more suitable I'd never leave my house. But this was the only time the Labradoodle owners that I'd got in contact with could talk to me. Plus I had to work tonight at Shamus's and Manuel was going to be gone tomorrow – to help a friend move he said. So this was really it.

I considered Manuel for a moment as I peered over the icy smear my wipers were leaving on the windshield. The thing with Bethany aside, he seemed stressed out these days. But then ever since that Russian thing we'd been involved in he'd had periods when he wasn't quite himself. It occurred to me that maybe he was suffering from Post Traumatic Stress syndrome. Given what he'd been through, it wouldn't have surprised me to learn that he was, I decided as I finally turned onto Applegate Lane.

The house I was looking for was built on a cul de sac. I parked my car in the circular driveway, got out, and rang the bell. Deep inside the house I could hear the sound of a dog barking. Must be the Labradoodle. The noise got closer. I could hear scratching on the door.

Someone said, 'Down, Abby. Sit.'

The door swung open and I stepped inside. The house smelled of pine and cinnamon. The moment my feet touched the tile floor Abby barreled towards me, jumped up, and started scratching at my pants. Her tongue lolled out of the side of her mouth.

'I can't get her not to do that,' the woman said, laughing.

'She's just a puppy,' I said as I scratched Abby behind her ears.

'She's almost a year old.'

That would put Abby at more or less the same age as Freddy Sanchez's dog.

'You're Constance O'Meara?' I asked.

The woman in front of me nodded. Backlit by the hall chandelier, her skin looked as if it were as poreless as bone china. She had one of those perfect bodies, thin, but not too thin. The jeans and the turquoise cashmere sweater she was wearing made sure you knew that.

As I moved my hands down and scratched Abby's sides, I noted that she didn't look like Freddy Sanchez's dog at all. She looked like a poodle with slightly longer legs and shorter ears. That was the thing with Labradoodles. Since they weren't an established breed you could and did get different conformations in the same litters.

'Thank you for seeing me,' I told Constance O'Meara.

She beamed. I could see her teeth were white and even. Everything about her was expensive. 'Well, I just think that Abbey is so special I want to do everything I can to encourage other people to own one.'

As if on cue, Abby licked my hand, put her two feet back on the floor, and ran off.

'She's going to bring you a toy,' Constance said. 'I know I should train her better, but she's so cute I have trouble doing that.'

'I can understand.' And I could. Training dogs has never been my forte. When they're puppies they're so cute I let them get away with everything and when they're older it's too late.

I slipped my boots off and Constance took my coat and hung it in the hall closest. She pointed to the large silver vase filled with pine boughs standing on the table by the wall.

'I love decorating the house this time of year, don't you?' Constance said.

I nodded. It was easier then telling Constance O'Meara that I was Jewish. The last time I'd done that I'd gotten into a discussion with someone who kept on asserting that Christmas was a secular holiday.

A moment later Abby came back with a bright blue rubber squeeze toy – I recognized the brand; we sell it in the store – and dropped it in my hand. I thanked her and tossed it and she went running after it. Then I followed Constance into the kitchen.

'I hope you don't mind,' she said as I trailed behind her, 'but I'm in the middle of decorating Christmas cookies for my son's school party.'

The kitchen looked like Constance did. Perfect. The colors – yellow and white – were warm and inviting. There was a fireplace with a fire going in it towards the far end of the room, flanked by two comfortable-looking sofas. One had a blanket on it, which I presumed was for the dog. There were toys strewn all over the floor.

'Excuse the mess,' Constance said. 'But you know what kids are like. Then of course Abby gets Jonathan's toys and chews them up and then he gets upset.' She sighed. 'Hot chocolate?' she asked, changing the subject.

I told her that would be nice if it wasn't too much trouble.

'No trouble at all,' she said as she walked over to the kitchen cabinet on the left. The cabinets were oak with glass doors and white pulls. Everything in them was perfectly arranged – just like my cabinets were. Right.

Abby came back in and sat on my feet. I bent down and scratched underneath her chin.

'So you like her?' I asked.

'She's wonderful,' Constance gushed. 'Aren't you?' she cooed to Abby, who wagged her tail but kept her eyes fixed on me. 'We wanted a dog that was good with children, one that didn't shed, and something that I could manage on my own since my husband is gone a lot these days.'

Then Constance straightened up and made us both hot cocoa the old-fashioned way. First she heated up some milk and then she measured out sugar and cocoa into two cups and put a pinch of cinnamon in. 'From our time in Mexico,' she explained. Then she slowly poured the milk into the cups, stirring as she went. When she was done she handed me a cup.

I took a sip. 'It's delicious,' I told her.

And it was. She smiled. 'I try to use foods in their most unprocessed state. It's so much healthier, don't you agree?'

'Oh absolutely.' Well, it was healthier. I just didn't do it.

I took another sip of my hot chocolate and got back to the matter at hand. 'You're perfectly satisfied with Abby, then?' I asked.

'Absolutely.' Constance had taken little containers filled with silver sprinkles and balls out of one of the cabinets and placed them on the worktable in the middle of the kitchen. 'I wouldn't trade her for anything.'

Next she went over to the fridge and took out two cookie

sheets. When she put them down on the table I could see they were filled with gingerbread men.

'A family tradition,' Constance said. 'Later this week Jonathan and I are going to make our gingerbread house.'

I felt as if I was in the middle of a Disney movie. Normally I'd want to puke, only Constance seemed so nice that I couldn't bring myself to feel that way.

'So,' I continued, 'you feel Abby was worth the money you paid.'

Constance was getting bowls of icing out of the fridge. 'Every penny,' she replied as she set the bowls down on the worktable.

'May I ask how much?'

'Three thousand,' Constance said as she gently removed Abby's paws from the worktable. 'You have to get down,' she told her. 'I'll get you a bone.' A few seconds later she was back with a rawhide chew. The moment Abby got it she ran off.

'I know it sounds like a hideous amount,' Constance continued. 'But it really isn't when you think that this dog is going to be with you for ten to fifteen years.'

I took another sip of my hot cocoa. I could do this myself, I thought. It really wasn't that hard. 'Is there anyone else you know that has one of these dogs?' I asked.

'Well there's Mike Barron out in Manlius,' Constance answered. 'Abby's actually the reason he got one.'

I nodded my head again – I was doing a lot of nodding in here – and took another sip of my hot cocoa. He was my next destination. I was going to ask if there was anyone else when I heard the front door open.

'That's Jonathan,' Constance explained. She glanced at the clock on the kitchen wall. 'He's early,' she said to me as he came in with Abby trailing behind him.

'They canceled the ski race,' Jonathan said.

I figured him for somewhere between nine and ten.

'Jonathan placed first in his last meet, didn't you, sweetie?' Constance said to him.

'Mom,' he wailed.

119

'And he just got straight As on his report card,' Constance informed me as he grabbed a bag of Doritos and scampered off. 'Hey, don't eat all of those,' Constance yelled after him. 'We're having dinner soon.'

'He's adorable,' I said to Constance.

'I know.' She grinned. 'He's just like his dad. I'm so lucky.'

'You're busy,' I said. And I thanked her for seeing me and handed her my cup. She put it in the sink, got my jacket, and walked me to the door.

'Drive safe,' she said as she ushered me out into the night.

If possible it was snowing even harder now then it had been when I'd gone inside the house. I brushed the snow off my car again, got in, and called Mike Barron to see if he still wanted me to come out. He did. I told him I'd be there as soon as I could.

Next I called Manuel and asked how everything at the store was. It was fine, that is if you didn't count the fact that Zsa Zsa had eaten half a box of doggie treats and that they hadn't had any customers since I'd left.

'Check on the birds and then go home,' I told Manuel.

'I'll take Zsa Zsa home with me and Bethany,' Manuel said.

I told him that would be great and hung up. Then I put my car in gear and took off. It took me the better part of an hour to get out to Manlius.

Manlius is another affluent Syracuse suburb full of historic housing. The place I was looking for was in the town proper. It turned out to be a hundred-year-old farmhouse that had been meticulously restored.

'We wanted to be true to the period,' Mike Barron told me as he showed me through the place.

I kept wondering where the Labradoodle was as he gave me the obligatory guided tour. I saw a dog food bowl in the kitchen, and a leash hanging over the stair railing, but no dog.

'That's why we kept the rooms the way they were,' Mike Barron continued. 'Most people don't realize that farmhouses were a series of small, low-ceiling rooms. They were built that way to conserve heat.'

I pointed to the wide-plank floors. 'They're very nice.'

'Aren't they though. We had to go to Pennsylvania to get them.' Mike pointed at a hook rug lying in the center of the floor. 'Mother made that the old-fashioned way. In fact, she's made all the rugs in the house.'

'Very admirable,' I said.

'Well, she's doing well with them online. I wish you could meet her. Unfortunately she and Jacques won't be back until tomorrow.'

'Jacques?' I said.

'Our Labradoodle.'

Ah. Mystery solved. 'He's not here?'

'No. He's with my mother. Is that important?'

'Well, I did want to see him.'

Mike clapped his hands over his mouth. 'I am so sorry,' he said. 'I should have realized. I thought you just wanted to chat and see pictures of him. I'll have her call you as soon as she gets in. Would you like to look at the pictures anyway?'

When I told him I would, he bounded out of his seat. A moment later he was back with a handful of photos. The tail was slightly different. So were the ears. The legs were longer. It could be True's littermate. Or not. I couldn't decide.

'Do you know where Jacques's other littermates went?' I asked him.

'If I recall one went to the O'Mearas, two went to someone in Westchester, and as for the others I'm not sure.'

Which left me with the same question: Where had True come from?

It's true Freddy could have stolen him, but I didn't see him coming out here or cruising around Dewitt. The local cops would have picked him up in two seconds. It's what they're paid to do. According to Bea, someone had given the dog to Freddy. But who? And why? It occurred to me that maybe it was time to go back and take another look at Freddy Sanchez's room. Then I'd see what Freddy's brother had to say – if I could find him. Perhaps I could get some information there.

Mike and I chatted for a little while longer and then I left. I was anxious about getting home, but the ride back was better than I'd expected. The plows had been out and most people were inside so I had the road to myself.

As I drove over to Shamus's I put Guns N' Roses on my tape deck and thought about how Barron's suburban world and Freddy's urban world could intersect. The only answer I could come up with was some kind of charitable rescue – the benighted child type of deal. Or maybe Freddy had met someone when he was in rehab – if he was in rehab. Rehab was always a great leveler.

'Hey,' I asked Ian when I came through the door. Amazingly there were people in the place. Three of the old regulars, a kid with a knit cap pulled down around his ears, and a couple of skanky looking characters shooting pool. 'Do you know if Freddy Sanchez was ever in rehab?'

'Not to my knowledge,' Ian said. He pointed to his watch. 'Your shift started half an hour ago.'

'The driving was horrible.'

'Then you should allow time for it. And Jose Flores was in looking for you.'

'I thought he was in New York,' I said.

'Apparently not,' Ian said.

Nineteen

B y the time I got home from Shamus's I was so exhausted my bones were aching. This getting four to five hours shut eye a night was killing me. You'd think that I'd have fallen asleep instantly, but I knew from experience that I wouldn't be able to. I was too wound up. Or maybe it was that George was upstairs and I didn't want to have to deal with him. I don't know. But it didn't really matter, because I did what I always do. I threw my jacket on the hall table and kicked off my boots. Then I went into the kitchen, got myself a glass, and poured myself a shot of Black Label.

I used to drink the aged-twenty-years-in-a-barrel stuff, but that was when my finances were in better shape. Actually, I shouldn't even be spending my money on Black Label. I should go down a notch, but everyone needs one luxury in their life. Besides, the cheap stuff tastes like paint thinner.

The Scotch burned slightly as it slid down by throat, but it was a good burn, like fire cleansing away the day's events. I could feel the tension I'd accumulated in my shoulders and the back of my neck begin to slide away.

I petted my cat, James, for a while, my fingers running through his thick black fur. I think he enjoyed Zsa Zsa's absence. Then after I made sure he had food and water I took the bottle of Scotch and my glass with me into the living room, sat down on the sofa, and turned on the television to the home shopping network. That or the weather channel helps me unwind.

I poured myself another shot and drank it down while I watched a lady on television talk about how good the vacuum cleaner she was selling was. She almost made me want to call up myself. I knew I should go upstairs and go to bed but instead I poured myself another shot and went and got my cigarettes out of my backpack. I lit one and inhaled, then watched the smoke coming out of my mouth drift up to the ceiling. I definitely had to do something about the drafts coming through the windows, I thought, as I reached over and pulled the blanket that had been lying on the far end of the sofa over me.

I took another couple of puffs and stubbed it out in the ashtray on the coffee table. Then I poured myself another shot of booze. It occurred to me as I downed it that I hadn't eaten anything since breakfast and that I was going to feel terrible when I woke up the next day. But then I decided I didn't care. I'd deal with tomorrow when it came. And that was the last thing I remembered thinking until James woke me up the next morning by sitting on my face.

I pushed him off and stumbled into the bathroom. God, I thought, gazing at myself in the mirror, I looked terrible and felt even worse. I took a couple of aspirin and went into the kitchen. I fed the cat and made myself some coffee. I was sitting at the kitchen table drinking it when I heard George come downstairs.

He was immaculate. As always. He had on dark brown corduroy pants, a lighter brown button down shirt, a light blue and brown patterned tie, and a tan jacket. His female students loved him. They thought he was really hot. A kind of black Harrison Ford. He looked at me but didn't say anything. I watched as he went over to the kitchen drain board, got a cup off it, checked to make sure it was clean, then poured himself a cup of coffee.

'Look at you,' he said.

'Yes.' My head hurt too much to listen to his spiel.

'I'm worried about you,' he said to me.

'That's nice to know.'

'This thing with Freddy Sanchez isn't good for you. I could kill Ian for getting you involved in this.'

'He had nothing to do with it.'

George evened out his cuffs. 'I think you should call your old therapist and make an appointment to see him. Your need to help every stray, be it animal or human, that comes along is symptomatic of a general underlying issue. It's a sickness, Robin. One that's interfering with your life. With our life.'

I didn't say anything. I wasn't rising to the bait. I just took another sip of coffee.

'Or,' he said, 'if you don't want to go back to him I could ask around and see if I can get you another name.'

I put my cup down on the table. 'I want you out of here.'

George looked at his watch. I might as well have been talking about the weather. 'I have to be on campus in twenty minutes for a meeting,' he said. 'We'll discuss this tonight when I get back.'

'No more discussions,' I told him. 'I'm sick of discussions. You're an asshole, pure and simple.'

'Robin, I keep on telling you you're assuming things about Natalie that aren't true.'

'So I'm paranoid on top of everything else.'

George put his coffee down and walked over to me. 'That's not what I meant.' He stroked my hair. Then he lifted my chin and kissed me. Normally, I would have kissed him back. This time I didn't.

'You'll see,' George murmured. He put his hand under my shirt and rubbed my nipples. 'It'll be fine.'

'No. It won't.'

I pushed his hand away from me. I caught an expression of uncertainty on George's face. I knew what he was thinking. This had always worked before. What was going on?

'I know things haven't been the best between us, but I've been stressed between my teaching load and applying for jobs. You can understand that, can't you?'

I thought about what I'd said to Calli the other day about missing sleeping with George. That was gone. Amazingly I felt . . . nothing. Something had happened to me. I didn't know what, but it had. I'd gone to sleep feeling one thing and woken up feeling another.

George straightened up.

'We'll talk,' he said. 'I'll see if I can get out of my evening meeting early.'

'It won't make any difference,' I told him. As far as I was concerned he could talk all he wanted. It didn't matter. I didn't even care about catching him dead to rights with Natalie anymore. Calli had been correct about that. That had just been an excuse to postpone doing what had to be done.

He gripped my arm hard enough to hurt and bent over me. I could feel his breath on my ear. 'I want you to come with me when I move to Old Miss,' he told me.

Evidently he'd gotten a teaching job. It would have been nice if he'd informed me of said fact.

He must have read my mind, because he said, 'I just heard yesterday afternoon.'

I winced because his fingers were digging into my skin. 'Congratulations. Now can you let go of me,' I told him while I tried to twist out of his grasp.

He opened his hand. 'Sorry,' he murmured as he straightened up. 'I didn't mean to do that.'

I rubbed my arm while I digested this new piece of news. George was going to be gone in a few months anyway. I could ride it out and wait. The thing was I didn't want to.

After several seconds George said, 'So we'll talk tonight.' It was a statement not a question. 'I mean it,' he said into the face of my silence.

'I know you do.'

That seemed to satisfy him and he turned and walked out the door. I could hear him opening the hall entrance closet door, hear the wire hangars jangle as he took his coat off one of them, hear the front door close, hear the growl of his car as he started it. A couple of moments later I heard him backing out of the driveway.

James jumped up on the table and mewed. I rubbed the tips of his ears. Then I rubbed my thumb under his chin until he'd had enough and clawed at me. It was a small scratch but it still hurt.

'Nice,' I said as I sucked the tip of my finger.

I guess I always have to have one sonofabitch in my life. I suppose it's better in the scheme of things that it be a cat. James swished his tail once or twice, then spread his considerable bulk across the place mats and closed his eyes. I petted him again and got another scratch for my trouble.

I finished my coffee and went upstairs, stripped down, and got into the shower. As the water poured over me I started to think about the color I wanted to paint my bedroom when George left. Something nice. Something pretty. Pretty was good. I hadn't done pretty for a long time. I'd decided on something Mediterranean as I got out of shower. Maybe a robin's egg blue. Or an aqua.

I put on jeans and my black cashmere turtleneck. Then just for the hell of it I dug into my jewelry case and got out my turquoise studs and put those on. After that I went into the bathroom, blow-dried my hair, and applied some lipstick and blush and a little bit of mascara. Not bad, I thought as I studied my reflection in the mirror. Not bad at all. I could still pull it together when I wanted to.

I went downstairs. George was in the hallway. I stopped in

surprise. He must have come in when I was in the shower or running the hairdryer. Otherwise I would have heard him. He looked up when he saw me.

'What are you doing here?' I asked.

'I forgot my papers.'

The phone rang. I didn't go get it. After four rings my message kicked in. Then I heard a voice. I caught the words 'detective' and 'get in contact with' before the caller rang off.

'I'm going to be so pissed if someone's broken into the store again,' I said as I started for the kitchen so I could call the guy back.

'It's not about the store,' George said.

I wheeled around. 'How do you know?' I asked him.

George started buttoning up his leather jacket. 'Jose Flores was around here looking for you last night.'

'And you didn't tell me?'

'No, I didn't.' George's car keys jingled as he picked them up off the hall table. 'I don't want you any more involved with him than you already are.'

'What gives you the right to make that decision for me?' I demanded.

George gave me one of his how-stupid-can-you-be looks. 'For God's sake, he's wanted on suspicion of homicide.'

I began to suspect where this conversation was going. 'What else did you do besides not tell me?'

'I called the police and reported him. But he left before they came.'

I don't know what infuriated me more. The fact that George had done it or the fact that he was proud of it.

'You sonofabitch. Who the hell do you think you are?' I was so angry I could hardly get the words out of my mouth.

'No. I was right. Haven't you read the morning paper?'

'What's that got to do with anything?'

George gave me a superior smile. 'They found another kid – Tony Shepard – dead in an abandoned building on Shonnard Street. They're looking for Jose Flores for that, too. Read the

127

article if you don't believe me. It's on the second page of the metro section.'

'Tony Shepard?' I repeated.

'You know him, too?'

I felt numb all over.

'That's great, Robin, just great.' George looked at his watch. 'When you have a chance you might want to get in touch with Detective Paul James. That's the guy on the answering machine. I gave him your work number too.'

I told him to go screw himself. It was a really weak come-back but I was too upset to think of a snappy one.

He leaned forward. 'Hey,' he said. 'I'm sorry you don't like what I did. But I did it for your own good.'

'My own good?' I could hardly believe what I was hearing.

'Yes. Your own good. I made a judgment call and when you calm down you'll see I did the right thing. One of us has to act like an adult.'

As I looked at George, I wondered how the hell I'd ever liked this man. What had I ever seen in him?

'Don't come back here except to move out your stuff,' I told him. Then I turned and went back upstairs. Now I understood what people meant when they talked about not wanting to look in someone's face. As soon as I heard the front door slam I went back downstairs and checked out the paper. Yup. There was the story, just where George said it would be. I read it slowly.

It really didn't say much other than that Jose Flores, head of the notorious Ash Street Gang – Ash Street? Couldn't they have come up with another name? And notorious? Please. Al Capone was notorious. These kids were punks – was wanted for questioning in the deaths of Freddy Sanchez and Tony Shepard. Evidently a Ni Mo guy who had been checking out a reported gas leak in the vicinity had found Shepard early in the morning.

He'd been shot just like Freddy had been. When I got to the end of the article I reread it just to make sure there was nothing I'd missed the first time around. I reached for the phone and dialed Calli. I tried her house phone, figuring she wouldn't have left for work yet.

Twenty

When Calli picked up I told her about the latest killing. 'Not even a good morning?' she said. 'Not even a how did you sleep last night?'

'Fine. Good morning. How did you sleep last night? Now can you find out what happened for me?'

'Robin, come on. It's too early for this.'

'Well, it's too late for Tony Shepard.' I could hear the sound of water running. 'Where are you?' I asked her.

'In the bathroom putting on my mascara.'

Then I heard an 'Oh damn.'

'I just poked myself in the eye,' Calli explained.

I didn't say anything.

She sighed into the receiver. 'And I'm doing this for you why?' she asked.

'A bottle of wine.'

'I'm not drinking. I'm on the South Beach Diet.'

'You're always on a diet.'

'But this time I'm serious.'

'Okay. Then dinner in a nice place.'

'That's not good enough. I want to know what's going on.'

'I already told you.'

'Sorry. You wouldn't be calling me this early in the morning for something like this. You'd be upset, but not that upset. So, let me think.' I pictured Calli putting her index finger to her cheek. 'Hmmm. Can we say the word George?'

Even though I hadn't been going to, I broke down and told Calli what George had done.

There was a brief pause and then Calli said, 'Have you considered the possibility that for once George is right?'

'George is a sanctimonious prick.'

'Well, we know that.'

'At the very least he should have called me and told me what he had done. Anyway, I thought you hated him.'

'I do,' Calli replied. 'The man can't keep his fly zipped up. But what if Jose did do what the police said he did?'

'That doesn't change the principle involved.'

'This isn't about you and George.'

I switched the receiver to the other ear and drained the rest of an open can of Diet Coke that was in the sink. 'I know that.'

'I'm not sure you do. Tell me,' Calli said, 'do you think that this kid Jose did kill two people?'

'Obviously not.'

'Why?'

'My gut.'

'George is right,' Calli said. 'You need help.'

'No. I don't. My instincts are usually correct and you know it. Besides, Jose's been trying to see me for the last two days. I need to hear what he has to say.'

'Maybe that's not such a good idea.'

'I'm going to be safe. He's asked me for help. Why would he hurt me?'

'I wasn't thinking about that. I was thinking that maybe the police are watching you, hoping you'll lead them to him.'

'Maybe, but probably not.'

'You could get in trouble for this,' Calli pointed out.

'I'm not doing anything,' I protested.

'Yes you are,' Calli said. 'You're aiding and abetting and you know it.'

James jumped back up on the kitchen table. I gave him a very circumspect pat. He hissed and I stopped.

'Fine. I'm aiding and abetting. Are you going to help me or not?' I asked Calli.

She sighed again. 'I'll see what I can find out for you. I gotta finish getting my make-up on. Later.' And she hung up.

By now it was 8:30 in the morning and I still felt awful. My head was hurting, my heart was pounding, and I had a bad taste in my mouth that I couldn't seem to get rid of. It took me ten minutes to get the Taurus to turn over.

I decided to stop at Dunkin' Donuts to get my morning chocolate fix. I pulled in, parked, and tried to open the door. It was frozen shut. Again. I took a deep breath. Finally I managed to roll the side window down and depress the door handle. I went inside and picked up three chocolate peanut donuts, two glazed strawberry ones, and a large coffee with cream and sugar. Then I headed to the store.

After I parked the Taurus I shoveled the sidewalk and cleared a space from the curb to the pavement. Then I opened up and turned on the lights and greeted Bertie and Ernie, after which I played with the two ferrets for about half an hour. Then I let them run around while I hung a new hammock in their cage and did the rest of the small mammals. When I was through, I scooped them up, got them situated, and called Ian, even though I knew it was too early to do that.

'What time is it?' he mumbled.

'Nine thirty. I'm sorry to wake you up.'

'Crap.' There was a pause. Then Ian said, 'Just a minute.' I heard the sound of footsteps and water running. The water got turned off. A door slammed. He was back.

'What's the matter?'

I told him about Jose Flores and about what George had done.

'Nice guy you're living with,' Ian said.

'I'm not going to be living with him anymore.'

Ian went into a coughing spasm

'You okay?' I asked him when it was over.

'I'm fine. Just getting rid of a few brain cells. I got plenty to spare.'

'That's good. I was worried for a moment.'

'Your boyfriend. He used to be a cop, right?'

'Yeah. You think Jose knows what George did?'

'I don't have a clue.'

'Because he's been trying to get in touch with me.'

'Okay,' Ian said.

131

I waited for Ian to say something else. When he didn't I went on. 'So if he doesn't know,' I told him, 'it would probably be better if he didn't come to the store.'

'Stuff happens,' Ian said.

'I'd rather it didn't,' I told him.

'Good for you,' Ian said. 'I gotta get back to sleep. I have to open. Later.' And he hung up the phone.

Maybe Ian knew where Jose Flores was and maybe he didn't. But I had a feeling that he did, or that he knew people who did, and that he'd pass the word along. At least that's what I was hoping.

Poor Tony Shepard. He'd impressed me as an okay kid. Oh well. As Ian said, 'Stuff happens.' And it had been happening around here a lot lately. I finished the coffee I'd gotten from Dunkin' Donuts and went in the back of the store to my office and brewed myself some more of the stuff. I poured some in a cup, added a ton of cream and sugar, and took a chocolate peanut donut out of the box, ate it, and got to work.

Manuel came in a little bit later, with Zsa Zsa. He nodded a hello and went in back to put his coat away. A moment later, Mrs. Lee came in. She bought fish for her grandson's forty-gallon tank. She lingered trying to make a decision and in the end went with a swordtail and two gouramis, instead of an angelfish.

'Make sure you get them home as fast as possible,' I told her as I wrapped the plastic bag containing the fish in a triple sheet of newspaper to insulate them from the cold before I put them in a paper bag. Tropical fish are extremely sensitive to cold temperatures – no big surprise there. Newspaper is an excellent insulating material – that's why street people stuff their jackets with it – but with the temperature hovering at zero, there was only so much protection it could provide.

Mrs. Lee raised her hand to indicate she'd heard me, tucked the bag of fish under her black quilted jacket and headed out of the store. A moment later Manuel came out of the back. He was eating one of the donuts.

'I wish Bethany would get off my back,' he complained. 'Now she wants me to stop drinking. She gets pissed when I go out with my buddies and have a beer,' Manuel fumed. 'Why does she have to always be messing in my business?'

'I think that's called commitment,' I told him.

'Well, it sucks,' he said.

'You could say that,' I replied thinking of George.

I took a close look at Manuel. He didn't look well. His eyes were red rimmed and he had that tic thing going underneath his left eye that he always gets when something is going on.

'You heard about Tony Shepard, right?'

Manuel nodded. He began peeling his fingernails. 'Yeah.'

'And that the police are looking for Jose Flores.'

Manuel ran his hand over the top of his head. Recently he'd got it cut really short, almost buzzed, but he was letting his sideburns grow. The effect was weird

'Because if you know where Jose is hanging out,' I continued before he had time to answer, 'it would be nice if he knew that George blew him in to the cops when he was over at my house last night.'

Manuel put his hand down. His jaw muscles started working. 'That motherfucker,' he said.

I assumed he was talking about George. 'I would have chosen a different word but I agree with the sentiment,' I told Manuel. 'You know what's going on?'

'No.' He started to move off. 'I gotta take care of the parakeets.'

Since Manuel hated cleaning the birdcages I thought it was safe to assume he knew more then he was saying. 'You want to tell me what's happening?' I asked him.

'Nothing.'

'You're flat out lying.'

Manuel yanked his pants up. 'Why ya dissin' me?' he whined.

Manuel always trotted out the hood talk when he didn't want to answer something. Usually I got a kick out of it, but I didn't today.

'You can cut the Ebonics,' I told him. 'It's not working.'

I was about to say more, something along the lines of once in a while it would be refreshing to get a straight answer from him. But before I could the shop door opened again and a man came in.

From the look of him I knew he wasn't a customer. He was a cop. Even though he was out of uniform, he still had that cop stance, those wary eyes. I took another sip of my coffee and watched him knock the snow off his shoes. If I were betting, I'd bet he was the detective George had told me I'd be hearing from.

As the guy came nearer I could see that his skin color wasn't so good. He had that grayish color people get when they have circulation problems. His gray hair was clipped short and he had a mole over his left eyebrow that looked as if it should probably be removed. His coat was gray too. He had quite the color scheme going on.

'Robin Light?' he said when he got up to the counter.

I gave him my best customer smile. 'How can I help you?'

He badged me and told me his name. Detective Paul James. I always like it when I'm correct. It happens so infrequently.

'I'm looking for Jose Flores,' he said.

I took another sip of my coffee. 'I haven't seen him.' I gestured towards my cup. 'Can I get you some?'

Always be polite. That's my motto. He shook his head. Not even a 'no thanks'. Ann Landers would not have approved.

'We got a call that said he showed up at your house last night.' His voice was nasal. Maybe he had a cold.

'Really.'

Suddenly Manuel was at my elbow. 'Robin,' he said.

I turned towards him. He had his jacket on.

'Where are you going?' I asked him.

'To make that delivery you were talking about.' And he left.

'We deliver pet food,' I explained to Detective Paul James. 'Our elder customers can't manage the big bags. I feel that it's nice to give back to the community, don't you?'

He nodded. I could tell he wasn't interested in giving back or serving the community.

'So have you talked with him?' he asked.

'Jose Flores? No. I wasn't home when he came by.'

'You could have met him somewhere else.'

'I suppose I could have. But I didn't.'

'Are you sure?' Detective Paul James's voice took on an edge.

'Yes, I'm sure. Why would I lie to you?' I asked.

'Because you helped him out the first time. You gave him fifty bucks to get out of town. Maybe he wants you to help him out again.'

Screw George. Evidently he'd felt it necessary to relay all the details of my activities to the detective. How nice of him. Why had I told this man anything? I decided that when Manuel returned, before I did anything else I was going to change the locks on my doors at home. If George thought he was spending another night in my place he was sadly mistaken. Let him stay with Natalie and the baby. Or out in the street. I really didn't care.

'Well?' The detective prompted.

'You're wrong,' I replied. 'I didn't give the kid the money so he could, as you put it, get out of town. I paid him the money I owed him. I had no idea he was in trouble.'

'What did you owe him the money for?'

'Helping out at the store.'

The detective moved forward. From the look on his face I could tell that he thought he had me now. 'You have a record for that?' he demanded.

'No. It was off the books.' I flashed him a smile. 'I guess ya got me.' I put out my wrists. 'Here. Snap the cuffs on.'

Detective Paul James didn't crack a smile. The corners of his mouth didn't even turn up. But then I didn't really expect that they would. I think I'm funny, but most people don't.

'Did you know Tony Shepard?' he asked, continuing down his list of questions.

'I've spoken to him a few times. Why?'

'He was Jose Flores's second lieutenant.'

'Okay.'

'And now he's dead.'

From what I'd seen calling Tony Shepard a second lieutenant

of anything was a massive overstatement. That kid probably couldn't have organized a shopping trip to Sam's Club. But, since I was fairly certain that my views on the subject wouldn't be welcome, for once I kept my mouth shut. I watched as the detective took a business card out of his wallet and laid it on the counter.

'What do you have to say about that?' the detective demanded.

'That I'm sorry.'

'That's it?'

'That the area needs better law enforcement?'

The detective's eyes narrowed. 'Jose shows up you call me,' he said. 'He calls you, you call me. You see him on the street, you call me.'

'Oh, I definitely will,' I lied.

Detective Paul James tapped the card with a stubby, nicotine-stained finger. 'Because aiding and abetting is a felony. You could do jail time for that.'

I thought about what Calli had said as I nodded.

'This is no joke. I'm serious,' he said.

'I know you are.' I could tell from the look he gave me that he didn't believe what I was saying. 'I have a question for you?' I told him.

'What?'

'Is it hard going around with two first names instead of a first and a last one? I mean do you ever get confused and sign your name James Paul instead of Paul James?'

He wagged his finger in my face. 'Don't be playing games.'

'I'm not. I'm curious. I mean it must have been hard in elementary school.'

The color in Paul James's face rose.

'You know,' I told him, 'stress isn't good for your system.'

'You'd better watch yourself,' he warned. Then he turned around and left.

Funny, but lots of people have said that to me over the years.

I finished my coffee and got back to work.

Twenty-One

M anuel came back in the store a little over an hour later. 'So. Was your errand successful?' I asked him as he went by me on his way to the back room.

He nodded as I put out my hand to stop him. I could feel the cold lingering on his jacket.

'What, Robin?' His tone was impatient.

'Let me ask you this.'

Manuel shifted his weight from one leg to the other while he waited to hear what I had to say.

'Is everything all squared away?'

'Yeah. Everything's fine.'

We looked at each other for a minute.

Finally I said, 'What the hell have you gotten yourself into?'

Manuel shrugged and studied the floor.

'Yes, it needs mopping,' I said.

Finally he looked up at me and said, 'You know, I'm trying to do the best that I can.'

'No you're not.'

'I am. That other stuff.'

'What stuff?'

'School shit and all. The stuff you keep telling me I should be doin'. It doesn't work for me.'

'That's because you're not trying. Listen, Manuel . . .'

He held up his hand to stop me. 'I appreciate what you're doin',' he said. 'But you gotta understand my point of view. You gotta give me a little credit for knowing what I'm doing.'

'I do—'

'No, you think you do, but you don't. You're always all over me. My world ain't your world.'

I reached under the counter and got my cigarettes out of my backpack. I took one and offered the pack to Manuel. He took one too. I lit mine and passed Manuel my matches. He lit his cigarette and put the matches on the counter next to the register. I watched the smoke drift away from us.

'Maybe you're right,' I told him. 'I just don't like seeing you involved in this kind of stuff. It always ends badly.'

'Hey. Shit happens. You deal with it and go on.'

There it was. Those phrases again.

'If you can,' I said.

Manuel shrugged.

'That's a stupid philosophy,' I said.

'Not in my world,' Manuel replied.

'Our worlds are the same.'

'No. They're not.'

'You're right. They're not. But they are.'

'You are wacked,' Manuel told me. 'Totally wacked.'

'You may have a point.' I tapped my ash into the Coke can I was using as an ashtray. Then I moved the can over so it was between Manuel and myself.

Manuel took another hit off his cigarette. 'I didn't think things would get so screwed up,' he allowed, but I noticed he looked away as he said it.

'That's not true. You thought something was going to happen. Otherwise you wouldn't have given me that retainer for Jose Flores.'

A flicker of concern passed over his face. 'You're still going to do that, right?'

'Yeah. With all the money you've given me how can I say no?'

Manuel smiled for the first time since I'd seen him today.

'Maybe things will die down,' he said.

'You wish. Two homicides? I don't think so.'

Manuel flicked his ash in the Coke can.

'You can take your knife back if you want to,' I told him. I was through being his keeper.

'Thanks,' he replied. 'But I already have.'

'Nice, Manuel. Stealing from my drawer. Very nice.'

He didn't say anything.

'At least you could act remorseful.'

He laughed. I had more questions for him, but I figured they could wait for a little while.

From eleven to two we had a total of two more customers come into the store. They bought a total of fifty-seven dollars and thirty-two cents' worth of merchandise: a small dog bed, one giant rawhide bone, and a dog sweater for a beagle. This was not good. The Christmas crowd was passing the store by. I'd talked to some other storeowners that I knew and they were having the same problem – it looked as if people weren't buying or they weren't buying yet – but that didn't help me.

Finally I broke down and did what I probably should have done three weeks ago: put an ad in the local paper. I know the motto that you have to spend money to make money, but it's hard to do when you don't have much in the bank. Sometimes you have to do it anyway, though. I composed the ad and phoned it into the *Post Standard*. Hopefully it would bring some more people in. I couldn't just sit here and watch the business go down the tubes. At least this way I was doing something.

After I got off the phone, I finished off the donuts and the pot of coffee I'd brewed up earlier. While I was doing that I went through my bills and tried to figure whom I had to pay and whom I could put off and whom I could negotiate with. The bill on the top of the heap was my utility bill. They were going to shut me off if I didn't come up with $1,439.50 by tomorrow, and that wasn't happening. I took a deep breath and called up the power company. It took talking to three people about paying my Noah's Ark bill, but I finally worked out a deal. To celebrate I lit a cigarette and reflected upon what I was going to do with the rest of my day.

I decided that now would be as good a time as any to run back to the house and change the locks on my doors. Might as well get that over and done with. When I was through with that I'd call Bea Sanchez and see if she would let me take another look at Freddy's room. I wanted to make sure I hadn't missed anything when I was up there the first time. Then, if the weather wasn't too bad, I thought I'd motor out to Carousel Mall and talk to some of the people in the chess club and see if they could shed some light on Freddy.

I had three doors on my house. I'd called locksmiths. Their quotes had ranged from two hundred and twenty to three hundred two dollars and fifty cents, which was way more then I wanted to spend. I mean how hard could doing it be? You went to the hardware store, bought some new locks, popped out the old ones, and put in the new ones. End of subject. I even had a screwdriver at home.

'You sure you want to do this?' Manuel said when I explained my plan.

'You don't think I can?' I asked while I zipped up my jacket. 'Because I certainly don't want to give the locksmith my money.'

Manuel took a spray bottle of cleanser from underneath the counter and started wiping it down. 'I was thinking more about George,' he said. 'Maybe you should tell him what you're doing first. He's gonna be pissed when he finds out.'

'Good,' I said as I told Zsa Zsa to stay. 'Let him be.'

Manuel put the spray bottle down and tugged on his ear. 'Maybe that's not such a good idea.'

'Just because George is two hundred and thirty pounds and I'm one hundred and forty?'

Manuel nodded. 'And the fact that he's an ex-cop.'

'I'll be fine,' I told him.

Manuel looked doubtful.

'Honest,' I said.

'Well, call me if you need me.'

I picked up my cell and waved it in his direction. 'Same goes for you.'

'You're going to see about Jose Flores, right?' Manuel asked as I wound my scarf around my neck.

'That's next on my to do list,' I told him, even though I wasn't sure how much I could do. 'Of course,' I continued, 'it would help if you'd tell me where you were the night that Tony got shot.'

Manuel folded the cloth he'd been using to wipe the counter down into half and then he folded that in half as well. 'Why do you want to know?'

'Why do you think?' I said impatiently. 'Come on, Manuel,' I went on when he didn't answer. 'Give me a break. I want to help you, but, not to belabor the obvious, I can't unless you tell me what's going on.'

'What if I shot him?'

'Tony? Did you?'

'No.'

'Then why are you saying that?'

He bent down and rubbed Zsa Zsa's ears. 'I don't know. I guess . . . I wonder . . . Would you turn me in if I did?'

I thought my answer over for a moment. Then I said, 'This is a terrible thing to confess, but no. I don't think I would.'

'I wouldn't turn you in if you shot someone either,' Manuel said.

'That's a relief.' I paused briefly then said, 'And this is something you've been giving a lot of thought to?'

Manuel shrugged and pulled up his pants. I studied him for a minute.

Then I said, 'You're thinking about George, aren't you?'

'No,' Manuel said, but I knew him well enough to know he was lying.

'It's not going to come down to that,' I promised him. 'I swear.'

'My friend's mother—'

'This is different,' I told Manuel. Latisha had been shot by her live-in when she'd tried to throw him out of the house. 'Honest.'

'I guess,' Manuel allowed.

'So now that we've got that out of the way are you going to tell me what you were doing the night Tony was shot or aren't you?'

Manuel gave Zsa Zsa another scratch. 'Jose and I were moving some stuff,' he mumbled. Because he was talking to the floor it was hard to make out what he was saying, but I managed.

141

'Like what?'

'More computers. Jose got a good deal. He had to take them off this guy's hands.'

I just bet he did. Manuel stowed the bottle of spray cleaner and the rag under the counter.

'Oh. Where did they come from?'

'Jose's got this supplier in Canada.'

'I see.' And I did. People have been using the North Country route to smuggle things into this country since Prohibition. Why should they stop now? The border was, despite the efforts of the Border Patrol, still porous. With thousands of miles of water and woodlands, it was impossible to patrol all of it.

For a while now people have been growing weed on the Canadian side of the border then muling it back into the U.S. by a variety of devices. Or they smuggle in guns. Or undocumented workers. Or cigarettes. Or anything that makes money. The process is the same, but the product varies.

'Was Bethany with you?' I asked him.

Manuel gave me one of his are-you-out-of-your-mind looks. 'She's not down with any of the stuff.'

That was good at least. 'So where is all this money you're supposed to be earning?'

Manuel shrugged. 'Things got fucked up.'

'Ah.'

'What do you mean, ah?'

'Just that.'

'You're not going to ask any more questions?'

'No, Manuel. I don't think I am, because I really don't want to know.'

He gave me a quizzical look. 'You're not usually like that.'

He's right. I wasn't. Usually I wanted to know everything. Maybe I was wising up in my old age. I bit off a hangnail. 'Well, if the cops come by and I have to answer any questions about you I don't want to have to lie. This way I can just tell them I don't know anything.'

Manuel nodded. 'The cops aren't going to come by.'

'Good.'

'Call me if you have problems with George.'

'I will,' I lied. Like I would really do that and make things even worse.

'Seriously,' Manuel said.

'Seriously,' I agreed.

Fifteen minutes after I'd put my jacket on I left the store.

Twenty-Two

The man behind the counter at the local hardware store had said that changing the cylinders on the locks would be, and I'm quoting here, 'a piece of cake.' 'Just follow the instructions and you can't go wrong,' he'd said.

Ha. This of course presupposed two things: that I could comprehend the instructions and that I had the right tools for the job. And I'm not even going to mention the joy of doing this with fingers so numb with cold they couldn't feel anything. The only consolation I had was that at least it wasn't minus twenty like it had been the week before, because at minus twenty metal shatters. Of course, I didn't have the right tools. Or if I did I couldn't locate them. First I couldn't find my screwdriver so I used a butter knife. That was a total failure. I had to go down in my basement and start looking in a serious way.

I finally found a screwdriver in back of the dryer, but it was way too small. Finally, after looking through all the shelving, I went down the street and knocked on my neighbor's door and asked if I could borrow her husband's electric drill. Once I had the DeWald in my hand the job was a lot easier. It wasn't a snap, but at least it was doable, and even though I was standing out in the cold getting the old cylinders out and putting the new ones in, just thinking about the expression on George's face when I told him what I'd done was enough to make it worth it.

The question I was considering was did I pack up his things and put them in the garage or let him do it himself? After some thought and a quick smoke break I opted for the latter, because, frankly, I had too much to do.

Then I thought: I could always throw his stuff out into the snow. That was pretty mean. But it would be really satisfying. I was fantasizing about that when I felt a tap on my shoulder. I spun around. Jose Flores was standing in back of me.

'What are you doing here?' I hissed at him. Jeez. Just the person I didn't want to see at the moment.

'I need to talk to you,' he said.

I dragged him inside. Luckily the neighbors on either side of me and the ones across the street were at work and didn't get home until a little after six o'clock, although on reflection I was probably being overly paranoid. The odds of anyone recognizing Jose were minuscule. With his black watch cap pulled down over his ears and the hood of his parka pulled up he looked like every other hood rat in the city. On the other hand, George could have been home and that wouldn't have been pretty.

'You shouldn't come here. Or the store. The cops are searching for you,' I told him.

'I know,' Jose said.

He was shivering. I told him to sit on the radiator in the dining room to warm up while I made him some hot cocoa. It was instant, not nearly as good as the stuff Constance O'Meara had used, but it was good enough.

'My mom used to make that for me.'

'Where is she now?'

He didn't say anything and I didn't want to press it. When I came back he was rubbing his hands together. I realized he hadn't worn gloves.

'You could get frostbite,' I said as I handed him a mug full of hot cocoa. I put both hands around my mug. I could feel my fingers start to loosen with the heat.

'I know.' Jose grasped the mug in both hands like I was doing and held it for a moment before taking a sip. 'The radiator is nice,' he said. 'We used to have a house that had them.'

I sat down beside him on it. The metal on the radiator was hot enough to feel through my jeans. But given the temperature outside I wasn't complaining.

Jose took another sip of his cocoa.

'You shouldn't be here,' I told him. 'The guy who lives with me is the one who blew you in.'

'I know,' Jose said.

'Manuel told you?'

'No. Someone else.'

'Who?'

Jose shook his head. 'You don't know them.' He took another sip of his cocoa. 'Doesn't matter anyway.'

It might, but I wasn't about to get into a debate with him about it. We had more important things to discuss.

'How come you didn't go down to the city?' I asked him. 'You said you were.'

Jose stood up for a moment. I guess the heat was getting to him. 'Something came up,' he said.

'That thing with Manuel?' When Jose didn't answer I said, 'Manuel tipped me off.'

Jose whipped his head around. 'What did he say?'

I held out my hands. 'That you were moving computers.'

I could see Jose's shoulders relax. 'Yeah. That's right. We were.'

I wondered what they'd really been doing, as Jose took another sip of his hot cocoa. Probably moving weed, I was guessing. As I watched Jose I decided he looked as if he were being sandpapered to a thin edge.

'So what do you want?' I asked.

'I thought maybe you had some more money you could give me.'

Naturally. I have so much to spare. I drained the last of my hot cocoa and put the mug down on the windowsill.

'Don't you have family?'

'Please, Robin.'

'Why me?' I swear I must have the word sucker stamped

on my forehead. 'What did you do with the last money I gave you?'

Jose studied the dining room. 'You don't have any Christmas decorations up,' he observed.

'That's right. I don't.'

'How come?'

'Because I'm Jewish. Now how about answering the question.'

'I gave the money to someone I owed.'

'I thought you were going to get out of town.'

'I was. But then I met up with someone . . .'

'And . . .' I prompted.

'I owed him fifty bucks.'

'So you gave it to him, just like that?' I snapped my fingers.

'Not quite like that.' He involuntarily touched the side of his jaw. I noticed that the skin there was discolored.

'Nice bruise,' I commented. I wondered who he owed. His dealer maybe? The guy he'd gotten the computers from? The butcher, the baker, the candlestick maker? 'You get that from anyone I know?'

Jose shook his head as he sat back down on the radiator again. He rubbed his hands over his thighs.

I didn't believe him, but I didn't push it. 'So where have you been sleeping?' I asked him instead.

'Abandoned houses, mostly.'

Of which there were a plentiful neighborhood supply. 'You look it.'

And he did. He needed a shave, his jacket had small white patches of something on it, and he smelled as if he could use a bath. I studied the sky outside. The gray in the sky was turning from steel to slate. We were going to have another storm.

'You know Tony,' Jose said.

'The kid that was killed?' I replied even though I knew it was a rhetorical question.

'Yeah.'

'You gave me his name to go talk to, remember?'

Jose didn't say anything. He pushed the drape away from

the window and studied the view outside. There wasn't much to see on my block. Just two-story houses and snow-banked curbs. Nothing was moving outside. Everything was in gray and white, except for the Christmas decorations. They brought the only note of color into the scene.

'Is there something you want to tell me?' I asked Jose.

He kept his eyes fixed on the scene outside. 'No.'

I lightly touched his shoulder. 'Are you sure?'

He nodded but I could tell he wasn't sure at all. Another minute went by and he turned to me. 'I didn't kill Tony,' he blurted.

'That's a relief.'

He gave me a quick look.

'I'm kidding,' I told him, even though I hadn't been.

'I found him though.'

I didn't reply.

Jose looked down at the floor. 'He wasn't dead yet.'

I waited. Jose began rubbing his thighs again. As if he could rub the scene away. 'He was groaning. That's how come I saw him. I heard this noise and I went to see what was up. He was layin' behind this car. And then he started twitchin' and shit. People dyin'. It ain't like in the movies.'

'No, it's not,' I agreed.

The movies make death neat and clean, but in the real world death smells bad.

Jose fell silent again. I watched a few snowflakes swirl around the lamppost. A school bus went down the street. I could hear the fridge in my kitchen clunk as it started another cycle.

'So after he died, what did you do?' I asked, after a couple of minutes had elapsed.

'Who says I did anything?' he demanded.

'I do.'

Jose studied the tree in my neighbor's yard.

'Well?' I said.

'What kind of tree is that?' Jose asked.

'Pine. You moved him, didn't you?' I was guessing, but what else could he have done?

Jose touched his jaw again.

'But he's a big guy.' Now I was thinking aloud. 'And you couldn't manage it by yourself, right?'

Jose remained silent, but his eyes were looking everywhere but my face.

'So you called one of your friends,' I continued.

Suddenly I flashed onto Manuel. It would certainly explain his conduct better than his Canada story. I thought about Manuel's comment about how things had gotten fucked up. Yeah, I guess you could say that.

'It was Manuel you called, wasn't it?'

Jose looked away.

'If you want me to help you, you'd better start talking to me. Otherwise you can leave now.'

Jose glared at me. I shrugged. 'Your choice,' I told him.

'Yeah,' he finally allowed after a few seconds had gone by. 'It was Manuel.'

I bit at my cuticle. Wonderful. The kid was just getting in deeper and deeper. 'What else is he involved in?' Not that aiding in the disposal of a body wasn't enough.

'Nothing else,' Jose said.

I decided to take him at his word, maybe because it was easier that way.

'So why did you move Tony?' I asked Jose.

He snorted. 'What do you mean why? Think I had a choice? He was lying in the driveway of the place I was staying at.'

'Which was?'

'This house they're gonna pull down on Shonnard. The one with the second floor that's tilting like that wacked out tower I seen on TV.'

Jose meant the Leaning Tower of Pisa. I knew the house Jose was talking about. The edge of the roof was gone and water was pouring into the structure. My guess was that the building was going to collapse if someone didn't take it down soon.

'I mean what the hell was I supposed to do?' Jose demanded. 'Leave him there and call the cops? They're all over my ass as it is.'

'So you put him in another abandoned building?' I said, remembering the newspaper article I'd read. Like I said there were enough of them in the area.

'It was the only thing I could think of to do. And anyway,' Jose's tone softened, 'it didn't seem right leaving him out there like that all uncovered and everything.' Jose wiped his nose with the back of his hand. 'What difference does it make anyhow? Dead is dead.'

He was about to say something else but he stopped when James leaped up between us. James focused his gaze on the cardinal that was sitting on a branch of the shadberry tree. I watched his tail twitch. Then he made the chirruping noise he always makes whenever he sees something he wants to kill.

'Not today, buddy,' I told him.

James gave me a look of contempt.

'I didn't know you had a cat,' Jose said, leaning towards James.

'He's not very friendly,' I warned.

Amazingly James let Jose pet him. Usually he claws strangers.

'Cats and me, we usually get along fine,' Jose said.

'So I see.' Out of the corner of my eye I saw a flash of red. The cardinal was gone. 'Where's your dog? What did you do with her?'

'Frieda? My old girlfriend has her.' Jose sighed. 'I was really lookin' forward to gettin' that baby iguana, too.'

'Maybe when this is over you will,' I replied.

'Yeah. Maybe.'

Jose and I sat in silence for a while. Then Jose broke the silence. 'Are chameleons hard to keep?' he asked me.

'They require a warm climate,' I told him.

Jose nodded. 'I was thinkin' of going back to school and becoming a zoo keeper or something like that.'

'Maybe you could volunteer there,' I suggested.

'They let people do things like that?' Jose asked.

'Yeah. They do.'

'Even someone like me?'

'Even someone like you.'

'That would be cool,' Jose said as he gazed out the window again.

I felt bad about dragging Jose back to his present reality. I did it anyway. 'Do you think Tony was coming to see you?' I asked.

He shrugged. 'I suppose.'

'Was anyone else staying in the building besides you?'

Jose shrugged again. 'People come and go all the time. It's a crack house.'

'Did Freddy ever stay there?'

'Probably. I just said it was a crack house, didn't I? You don't think I should have moved him, do you?' Jose asked me.

'It doesn't matter what I think, the only thing that matters is what the cops think.' I looked at Jose. At least he wasn't shivering any longer. 'Do you have any idea what Tony wanted to talk to you about?'

Jose thought about that for a moment, then said, 'I owed him some money. Maybe he wanted to see about gettin' it before I left town. All I know,' he added as he stroked James's back, 'is that someone is trying to set me up.'

'Why would they do that?'

He shrugged again. 'Maybe they want me off the street.'

'Why?'

'So they can do more business.'

It was a possible motive. It just didn't seem very likely to me is all. It was way too complicated. I mean why not do a drive-by and get it over with if that was the aim of the enterprise? Anyway, whatever Jose was doing it was strictly small-time.

'Who are they?'

Jose looked outside. James looked with him. Then he jumped off the windowsill and wandered away.

'Do you know?' I asked.

He obviously had someone in mind. The question was whether he was going to tell me or not.

Jose's lips tightened across his teeth. He began tapping his fingers against his thigh. 'So can you give me some cash?'

'I take it you're not going to answer my question.'

He bit down on his lip. 'It could be anyone,' he said after a couple of seconds had gone by.

'Give me a name.'

'I don't know. The Dreaming Saints.'

'You'll have to do better than that. The Dreaming Saints operate on the north side of town.'

Jose rubbed his hands on his thighs again. 'Could be the guys living across the street from Freddy. They're expanding.'

'Okay.' At least that made a little more sense. 'Do they call themselves anything?'

Jose shook his head.

'Do they have names?

'Gallo and the Dog.'

'Real names.'

Jose hesitated for a second. Then he said, 'Ernesto and Fernando. So are you going to give me the money or not?'

'Yeah,' I said, thinking of Detective Paul James's words. 'I am, but I think it would be better if you'd let me call the DA's office and try and arrange something. Or let me call up one of my lawyer friends and see what your options are.' Not that they'd be happy with the request.

'I ain't doin' that,' Jose said.

If I remembered rightly Calli had made the same offer to Manuel. He hadn't taken it up either. I got up off the radiator and started out of the room.

'Where are you goin'?' Jose cried.

'To call the cops.'

'Funny,' he said. 'Very funny.'

'I'm going upstairs. I'll be right back.' When I returned I was carrying a pair of George's gloves, one of his cashmere scarves, and one of his sweaters. 'Here,' I said, giving them to Jose.

Karma at work. I knew that George's stuff was going to be too large for Jose, but Jose didn't seem to mind when he put it on.

'Thanks,' he said as he wound the scarf around his neck.

At least he wouldn't get hypothermia now. It seemed like

the least George could do to make up for what he'd done – not that he would agree. I was wondering if George would even miss the stuff I'd taken as I drove Jose to the ATM machine over by Key Bank and withdrew another fifty bucks.

'Here,' I held the bills out to him. 'This is it. I don't have any more.'

Jose bobbed his head to indicate he understood what I was saying as he stuffed the money in his jacket pocket. I was about to ask him if there was anyone I should talk to when my cell rang. It was George. He was at the house. And he was really pissed.

'Wait,' I cried to Jose as he stepped out of the car.

'Who are you talking to?' George demanded. 'Is it that kid?'

I ignored him and called to Jose again. But he just waved at me and kept going. I could see a Centro bus coming down the road. He started running for it. A moment later he was gone. I turned my attention back to the phone.

'What is going on?' George bellowed. 'Why can't I get into the house?'

I told him.

'You wouldn't dare.'

'Hey. I already have. I don't want you there anymore. Go live with Natalie and the baby. You'll be happier with them anyway.' I took a deep breath and let it out. 'As for your stuff, anytime you want to make arrangements to come and get it, I'll be happy to let you in.'

He called me a name. Instead of answering, I turned my cell off. I didn't want to hear it.

I went to Sam's Club next, did a few more errands, then drove on over to Bea Sanchez's house. The kids in the Jeep Cherokee were parked across the street again. Just like the last time I was there. I got out of my vehicle, stuck my hands in my jacket pockets to keep them warm, and walked over. In light of my conversation with Jose, it seemed time to talk to them about their neighbor Freddy Sanchez. And other things as well. If we got that far.

Twenty-Three

'Are you Ernesto or Fernando?' I asked the kid in the driver's seat after he'd rolled his window down just enough so that he could talk to me. He was smooth shaven, but now that I was closer, even in the dim, afternoon light I could see the acne pits on his cheeks. I figured him for seventeen although he could just as easily have been in his late twenties.

'Ernesto. Why?'

'Well, Ernesto, I was wondering if you could answer a couple of questions for me about Freddy.'

Ernesto's face worked itself into a scowl. 'What do you want to know about him for?' he demanded.

Actually, he put the question a little less politely. I had to raise my voice to be heard over the CD he was playing as I explained about Freddy's mom to him. I'd decided to keep Jose out of the equation for the time being.

I watched Ernesto and Fernando look at each other. Fernando's cell phone rang. He took it and turned away to talk. Obviously he didn't want me to hear what he was saying, but then given the volume of the music coming out of the car I couldn't have heard it even if he hadn't turned his head away.

'I don't know what I can tell you, man,' Ernesto said to me. He reached out and flicked the air freshener hanging from the rearview mirror. It swung back and forth. He watched it for a moment then leaned back in the driver's seat.

'So Freddy didn't hang with you?' I asked him.

The cold was seeping through my boots. I moved my feet forward a little so I could keep them out of the snow bank behind me.

'Freddy didn't hang with no one,' Ernesto told me.

I could understand why he was called El Gallo. There as something cocky about him. A car sped down Onondaga. Ernesto followed it with his eyes, checking it out. Fernando didn't bother. A couple of seconds later I heard brakes squealing, then the screech of metal on metal. A couple of seconds after that I heard the sound of people yelling at each other.

'Guess they should have been going slower,' I said to Ernesto.

He shrugged. Mr. Cool.

'Was the reason Freddy didn't hang with anyone that he was a crack head?' I said.

Ernesto's eyes flickered as he checked the rearview mirror before bringing his gaze back to me.

'You know where he got his stuff from?' I asked.

Fernando stopped talking on his cell and turned towards me. 'No man,' he answered, although how he could hear what I was saying through the music was a mystery to me. 'We don't do that kind of shit. That's bad news. What you sayin' something like that for?'

'I wasn't saying he got it from you.'

'We just gotta clarify that. You know what I'm sayin'.'

I found myself studying him to see if I could figure out where he got his nickname from. I couldn't.

'You can get that on any corner.' Then his cell went off again and Fernando turned around to answer it. 'Yo,' he said before he turned away.

'Your friend is popular,' I said to Ernesto.

'People like him,' Ernesto said to me. His tone was carefully noncommittal.

I just bet they liked him. Or rather they liked what he had for them.

'Maybe you could tell me how Freddy got his money?'

'What money? Freddy didn't have no money.'

'He had an expensive laptop. An expensive dog. Where did they come from?'

'How the fuck should I know?' Ernesto said to me as he

checked his rearview mirror again. He was beginning to look nervous.

'Expecting someone?' I asked him.

'A couple of friends. Why?'

I took a cigarette out of my backpack and lit it. Then I offered one to him. He shook his head.

'I was just thinking,' I continued, 'that your friends would probably like it better if I wasn't here when they came around.'

'You can be wherever you want,' the kid said. 'I don't care. And neither will they. Why should they?' But I could see from the expression on his face he agreed with my assessment of the situation.

I took a drag of my cigarette. 'On the other hand,' I told him, 'I can go sit in my car and read the paper and wait for Freddy's sister to come around.'

'She don't come home till two in the morning. She works over at one of those food places on Erie Boulevard.'

'Exactly,' I said to him.

'That's crap,' Ernesto said.

'Yes, it is.' I agreed. 'So what's it going to be?'

Ernesto's eyes narrowed. I could see the muscles in his jaw working. I stayed where I was, although it did occur to me that getting into a pissing contest with this kid wasn't the smart way to go, especially since I realized I had another alternative.

'Or I could call Ian,' I told Ernesto, banking on the fact that Ian's name would carry weight with this kid, Ian being a neighbor and all. 'He was the one that pulled me into this thing in the first place.'

'Good for him.'

But the expression on Ernesto's face had softened. I realized I could have used Ian's name to begin with and saved myself the last five minutes of conversation.

'Yeah. He did,' I reiterated. 'Otherwise I wouldn't be here now.' Which was the truth. I pointed to his friend's phone. 'Call Ian up if you don't believe me.' As I said that I wondered if George was trying to call me. I almost pulled my cell out of my backpack to check but I decided not to. It was better to focus on the matter at hand.

The kid thought it over for a moment. Then he nodded. 'Fine,' he said.

I repeated my question in case he didn't remember. 'So how did Freddy get his money?'

'He did a little of this, a little of that.'

We were advancing, but not by much.

'Like what? I mean I'm not asking you to name names here, but could you be a little bit more specific?'

The kid wiped an invisible speck of something off the steering column with the tip of one of his fingers. 'What difference does it make?' he asked me.

'It could. If I can find out what was going on maybe I could help some people out,' I said, keeping it vague.

Ernesto thought about that for a moment, then he said, 'Like I told you, Freddy did a little of this and a little of that. You know.'

'The same kind of stuff that Tony did?'

'Yeah. They were both in business.'

A police car sped by. Probably going to the scene of the accident down the hill.

'What kind of business?' I asked.

'Private business.'

'What kind of private business?'

'None of yours.'

'Cute,' I told Ernesto.

He looked pleased with himself.

'Ian already told me,' I said to him.

Ernesto smirked. 'Hey, man. Then you already know. So why you askin' me?'

As I suppressed an urge to punch Ernesto out, I realized that Ian probably *did* know and that I should have asked him first.

'All right,' I said to Ernesto. 'I'll get out of here if you tell me where Freddy got the laptop from? Did he steal it? I mean it's not like it matters anymore.'

I knocked the ash off my cigarette while the kid worked his shoulders into the back of his chair. I could tell from the expression on his face he was considering whether to answer me or not. He asked for a cigarette and I gave him one. I handed him my lighter. He lit up and took a puff.

'I guess it don't matter,' he told me after he'd handed my lighter back to me. He waited for another moment. Then he began. 'Freddy told me some wacked out story about some guy giving it to him. He was always telling me stories.' Ernesto reached up with his free hand and scratched under his hat.

'Such as?'

'Stupid stuff,' the kid said. 'Like he was going to Syracuse University next year to study some sort of biology shit. Like he was gettin' this record contract for this big label. Like he was gonna be a recording star. You know, stuff like that. We was trash, but he was gonna be famous.' Ernesto snorted. He took another drag from his cigarette. 'Yeah. Right.' He jabbed his finger down towards the floor. 'So who's up here and who's in some box in the ground? That's what I'd like to know.'

I wiggled my toes to keep the circulation going. 'Do you think there's any chance this guy that Freddy was talking about was real?'

He raised an eyebrow. 'Hey, come on. Like you said, Freddy was a crack head.'

As if that said it all. Well, maybe it did. These were Freddy's pipe dreams. I flicked my cigarette into the snow bank and watched it extinguish itself. Even though I wasn't quite done with it I figured that any puff not taken was a good thing.

'Give me a break here,' the kid continued. 'He didn't even have his GED.'

'Okay then. Answer me this. Did Freddy come home at night?'

'How the hell should I know?' Ernesto replied.

'Well, your house is right across the street from his.'

'Ya think I got nuthin' better to do with my life then keep track of Freddy?'

Before I could answer Fernando nudged Ernesto. 'We gotta go,' he said.

'I thought we were waitin'.'

'Plan's changed.'

Ernesto nodded and put up his window. I was out of the picture. I stepped away from the car just as the kid slammed the clutch into reverse and the car tore out of the driveway. I could feel a rush of air as the Jeep Cherokee whooshed by me. Of course by this point my feet were so numb I probably wouldn't have felt it if he had run over them.

As I watched the Cherokee making its way down West Onondaga it occurred to me that if these kids were coming out of the Harvard Business School, they'd be CEOs by the time they were in their thirties. They understood business.

They worked hard. They kept in contact with their customers. And most importantly, they understood that getting your product to the point of sale in a speedy manner is key.

As I walked across the street to Bea Sanchez's house, I tried Ian's number, but all I got was his voicemail. I clicked off without leaving a message. I'd try back later.

Twenty-Four

B ea Sanchez opened the door before I had a chance to ring the bell. Her mouth had formed itself into a downward bow. I guessed she'd been watching me out the window, a supposition her next comment bore out. 'What you talking to those kids for?' she demanded as I took my boots off and placed them by the closet door. 'I seen you out.'

Like I'd been trying to hide.

'I wanted to hear what they had to say.'

'I told you they were trash.'

'I still wanted to hear what they had to say.'

Bea closed her eyes for a second and bit her lip. Then her eyes opened. 'They should be arrested,' she said.

I nodded in the direction I'd just come from. 'Then why don't you call them in?' I asked her.

'Because they'll be back on the street again. What's the point?' She shook her head. 'Anyway, the Lord Jesus says you have to show kindness to everyone, even garbage like that.'

'That's very compassionate of you,' I told her.

The expression on her face told me she'd missed the sarcasm, which was probably a good thing.

'I don't see why you want to see Freddy's room again,' she asked me, changing topic.

As I moved by the living room I noticed there were a few more presents under the tree, but otherwise the house looked exactly the way it had when I'd first visited it. It made me want to move something – a vase, a chair – to see what would happen.

'What do you hope to find there?' Bea Sanchez wanted to know.

'I'm not sure,' I told her as Freddy's dog, True, danced around my feet.

'Then why are you here?'

I pushed back a strand of hair that had fallen over my eye. 'I just think I should check to make sure I haven't missed anything.' That sounded better than telling her I was taking another look to see if anything in his room connected him with Tony Shepard, the other kid who had been killed. I didn't think it would, but I just wanted to make sure.

'Like what?'

'I wish I could tell you.'

Bea worked her mouth down a little more. I was impressed. I didn't think that was possible. I thought she was going to order me out of her house. Instead, she tugged at the jacket of the charcoal-gray suit she was wearing. She was definitely dressed for success *à la* the style suggestions from the women's magazines.

'Well, hurry up.' She tapped her watch face with a

French-manicured fingernail. 'I have a meeting to go to.' Then she turned and stomped in the direction of the kitchen. Evidently I was going to go up to Freddy's room by myself. Which was fine with me.

'By the way,' I called after her. 'You wouldn't happen to know where I could get in touch with your other son, would you?'

She made a dismissive noise and said, 'That one.' And kept walking into the kitchen.

I took that as a no. Great family relationships everyone had here. I tried one more time. 'Freddy have any friends I can talk to?'

This time Bea turned to face me. 'He didn't have friends. He had vultures circling around him.'

'Even vultures are called something.'

'Not in my world.' There was a certain note of satisfaction in her pronouncement.

'He must have mentioned their names.'

'I never listened.'

Wow. All I could think of was how hard Freddy must have had it growing up. By now we were at the sink. It had several mugs sitting in it. They were white with the letters EI in a logo printed on them in black copperplate letters. I'd been planning on putting the name of my shop on some mugs and giving them away for free with every purchase over thirty dollars. That way when people drank their morning coffee they'd think of me. Unfortunately the mugs I'd liked had turned out to be too expensive. I'd settled for pens instead, but looking at the mugs in Bea Sanchez's sink I wished I'd gone with my original concept.

'Anything else?' Bea Sanchez asked as she snapped on a pair of yellow latex gloves.

I shook my head.

'Good,' she said and turned on the water faucets full blast.

I lingered for a moment then started out of the kitchen. True followed me. When I got to the doorway I turned and looked. Bea Sanchez was bent over the sink with her feet planted on the linoleum and her hands in soapy water.

'So what do you think?' I asked True when we got to Freddy's room. 'Where would you look if you were me?'

True wagged his tail, ran inside, and jumped on Freddy's bed. I paused for an instant and surveyed the place. From what I could see nothing had changed from the last time I'd been here. Everything was neat and orderly. Spic and span were the words that popped into my mind. Not the description one usually applied to the room of a teenage boy. Once again I thought that either Bea had cleaned up her son's room or her son had been OCD. Before I started I decided I should go downstairs and asked her again. She'd turned the water down so she heard me approaching.

'Yes?' she said, looking up from the dishes she was washing. I asked my question.

'I told you already,' she said, her voice dripping annoyance. 'That's the way he kept his room. He was always a very neat child. Not like my other two. That's how I knew he was going to do well. He takes after me.'

'Unlike your other two,' I couldn't resist saying.

Bea glared at me.

'Sorry,' I said.

This time I got to work immediately. I started with Freddy's desk. Now I not only opened the drawers, I went through all the contents. I don't know what I was hoping for. Maybe a secret compartment? Something taped to the bottom of one of the drawers? A cigar box with Freddy's most cherished possessions, one of which would furnish me with a clue to Freddy's killer? But there was nothing there except Freddy's school supplies, all neatly lined up, waiting to be used. I wondered when was the last time he'd been to school.

I sighed and closed the drawers and transferred my attention to Freddy's nightstands. There were two of them, one on either side of the bed. One of the drawers contained two packs of Kleenex, a flashlight, and a pack of gum, while the other held three pennies. I started biting my cuticles. Then I started moving the zipper on my jacket up and down.

There was no sign of the kid I'd seen in the bar that night, the one that had been trying to sell me a headboard, the one

161

who had stolen the collars out of the store, the one the kid across the street was talking about. Everything in this room spoke of a different identity. Of a 'good' kid. Maybe one that was too good.

It must have been hard. His father was in jail. The brother and sister were a disappointment to the mother. So here was Freddy. Who had to be perfect. Who had to do everything just right. Only he hadn't. Or had tried to and couldn't.

So where did this other kid live? Where did Freddy's alter ego, Jimmy Slade, reside? Where did he hang out? A series of crack houses would be my guess. Given the way he'd looked he sure wouldn't have been at the mall. Security would have kicked him out in a flash.

I sat down on Freddy's bed. True licked my hand as I thought about smoking another cigarette. Then I discarded the idea. Sometimes with drugs – weed or heroin – if you're at all circumspect, no one knows what you're doing because you maintain the same appearance. At least for a while, in most cases a long while.

But that's not true of crack. People go down fast with that. Crack heads are skinny and twitchy and startle easily. Freddy looked like what he was. Surely his mother had to have seen that. Seen him losing weight before her eyes. Seen him wiping his nose. Seen him growing more and more fragile every day. Surely she knew something was going terribly wrong. That something was going on. That he was no longer her good little boy.

My best guess was that she couldn't bear to face that so she pretended it wasn't happening. Pretended that her kid was still going to school. Still doing all the right things. I got up and went over to the bookcase. I picked up each model on the shelf above Freddy's bed, studied it, and then put it back down. They were all perfect. Unlike the ones I'd done when I was a kid. Freddy has been a careful worker. There were no lines of hardened cement leaking out of the sides of his models.

I went through Freddy's dresser next. It was all tee-shirts, underwear, and knit shirts. I could have been looking through the possessions of a traveler in a hotel room.

The real Freddy Sanchez wasn't here and I suspected that he never had been. At least not for a long time. I opened the door to his closet. His pants were hanging in precise rows. He had seven pairs of jeans and eight sports tops. A pair of gray slacks and a tweedy jacket hung a little ways away. His going-to-church clothes, I was willing to bet.

He had three pairs of shoes; two of them were sneakers and one pair was high-quality black leather. They looked like something a forty-year-old man would wear. Something his mother had bought for him.

The clothes I'd seen him in that night in the bar had been strictly ghetto-rat garb. Plus they'd been dirty. They'd looked as if he'd slept in them for days. What had Bea Sanchez thought of her son going out into the world like that? Odds were she hadn't seen him. Odds were he'd been sleeping somewhere else. I ran my hand over the top shelf. I came away with dust on the tips of my fingers.

I went through the pockets of his pants and jackets. All I found were gum wrappers, some loose change, a few game tokens from an arcade, a wadded up Kleenex, and a matchbook from a place called the Spindle. I palmed it. At least it was something. Then I went back downstairs with True trailing behind me. Bea was in the entrance hall.

'Good,' she said when she saw me on the steps. 'I was going to come and get you. I was just getting ready to leave.'

She picked her purse up off the table in the hall. I bent over to put my boots on. When I straightened up Bea was standing there holding my jacket for me.

'Did you find anything?' she asked as I took my jacket from her hands. The leather was cold from being in the closet.

'Just this.' And I showed her the matchbook. 'I found it in the pocket of a pair of Freddy's jeans.'

I thought I saw a flicker of something on her face. Was it recognition? Anger? Fear? I wasn't sure.

'Freddy didn't smoke,' Bea stated. Then before I could stop her she plucked the matchbook out of my hand, walked out to the kitchen, and deposited it in the trashcan sitting by the door. She held it as if it were a dead mouse. 'It must have been somebody else's,' she explained. 'No need to waste your time.'

'Then why did he have it?' I asked.

Bea glanced at her watch again. 'I'm sure he confiscated it from someone. That's the kind of person he was.'

For a moment I thought about going into the kitchen and getting the matchbook out of the trash, but then I decided against it. Bea Sanchez needed all the help maintaining her illusions that she could get.

'You know Tony Shepard got shot,' I told her as we walked out the door.

She turned and locked it. 'Doesn't surprise me in the least.'

The wind had picked up since I'd been inside. The skin on my face started to sting. As I pulled my collar up, I thought about Bea's throwing the matchbook away and how a psychologist would have a field day with that gesture.

As I stepped off the porch, I noticed that the kids in the Jeep Cherokee were back. They were sitting across the street in the exact same spot they had been before they'd taken off. I wondered if they ever got out of their car. I caught Bea Sanchez's disapproving glare as I headed in their direction. Too bad. This time she didn't say anything to me.

I tapped on the driver's side window about the same time Bea Sanchez took off. Ernesto lowered the window a little.

'You still here?' he said.

'Guess so. Have you heard of a place called the Spindle?'

'Why?'

'Just curious. I heard good things about it. I thought I might want to check it out.'

Ernesto sniggered. 'You're a little old to be going to someplace like that, aren't you?'

'Am I?'

'Yeah,' his partner threw in. 'Plus it's all the way out in Liverpool. What do you want to go out there for?'

'Liverpool?' I said. 'You sure?'

'Of course I'm sure,' Ernesto said as his cell phone rang. He looked at me and I moved away. I heard him say 'Wassup?' as I headed for my vehicle.

I turned my cell back on when I got into my Taurus. I checked my voicemail. George had left eleven messages. They got progressively nastier as they went on.

I tapped the phone against my teeth. I should call him back. I knew that. It would be the prudent thing to do. But I wasn't going to. At least not yet. First of all it was going to be unpleasant. But that wasn't the real reason I wasn't returning his calls. The real reason was that I wanted to give him back a little of his own.

Twenty-Five

On the way back to the store I decided on a whim to stop at the place where, according to Jose, Freddy had been crashing. I was hoping there was someone there I could talk to about him. As it turned out, there wasn't and I could have saved myself the trip, but that's the way it goes with things like this. You never know what's going to happen until you try.

The house Jose was talking about had gone past the point where it could be saved. Slats of wood had sprung free from its sides, exposing its bones, drywall, and two by fours. The middle two steps to the porch were missing, but the snow was packed down enough to offset that, and I could see where people had come and gone.

I followed the path of footprints to the door, pushed it open, and yelled hello. When no one answered I went inside. It was dark and I couldn't see much. The living room smelled of smoke and when I squinted I could see char marks on the floor from where someone must have tried to build a fire.

I walked into what had once been the kitchen. Someone had ripped out the sink and the piping – probably to sell. The far corner of the room looked like a midden heap. A sleeping bag was thrown in another corner. Someone had papered the windows over with newspaper. I didn't try and go upstairs to the second floor. There were gaps in the steps. Instead I walked a little further down the hall into what must have been a sitting room at one time but now had plaster piled up against one wall from where the ceiling had fallen down. I stepped inside. The floor creaked at my weight. I stopped and looked around.

There was a mattress over by the corner. Part of the mattress was a dark color. So was the floor around it. Probably blood. Something bad had happened here. I took a couple more steps inside. There was nothing to see except the support beams from the second-story ceiling staring back at me. I turned and left.

On my way out a kid who could have been Freddy stumbled by me and mumbled something. I asked him if he knew Freddy Sanchez but he moved off without answering me. I'm not sure he'd even heard me. He hadn't bothered to close the front door. It was wide open and snow was blowing into the hallway. I left, closing it behind me. On my way to the store I stopped off at Domino's and got a large plain pizza and a two liter bottle of Coke for Manuel, Bethany, and me.

When I walked into Noah's Ark I could tell from the tight expressions on Manuel's and Bethany's faces that they'd been arguing again. It seemed as if that's all they did these days.

'George called,' Manuel announced as I laid the pizza down on the counter. 'He sounded really pissed.'

'That's because he is.'

I knelt down to greet Zsa Zsa. She licked my chin and the bottom of my cheek. I petted her for a few moments then stood up.

'You should call him,' Bethany said.

'I will,' I told her. 'After I eat.'

I went in the back and hung my jacket up. When I came out front again Manuel and Bethany were already working on the pizza.

'Have either one of you heard of the Spindle?' I asked them.

Bethany shook her head, while Manuel volunteered that he had. 'It used to be called the Wasps' Nest,' he said.

'Nice name,' I commented as I broke off a small piece of pizza and fed it to Zsa Zsa.

'A kid got stabbed there,' Manuel said.

Now I remembered. About six months ago some seventeen-year-old kid had gotten into a fight with another seventeen-year-old kid and put him in the hospital with two stab wounds and a broken jaw.

At that point the authorities had moved in and closed the place down. Evidently there had been numerous violations over the six months before the stabbing. The place had reopened a month later with a new name.

The owner, some businessman whose name I didn't remember, had expressed shock and dismay. None of this had happened on his watch. He'd just put up the money. Didn't have a clue what was going on. He was appalled. Simply appalled. Blah. Blah. Blah. Hey, I may be naïve but it seems to me that if you've named your place the Wasps' Nest you should be expecting trouble.

I took another bite of my pizza then got up and gave two small pieces to Bertie and Ernie. Who would have thought that parrots like pizza? But then who would have thought that dogs like beer?

'Anything else about it?' I asked Manuel.

'It's a sketchy place.'

Guess things hadn't changed much since its last incarnation.

'Sketchy as in how?'

'You can get weed, E, vitamin K. Whatever.'

I wondered if that's why Ernesto had sniggered when I'd told him I was thinking of going there.

'Could Freddy have been getting his crack there?'

Manuel gave me a withering look. 'Why go all the way out there when you can get it on the street corner here?' He was about to say something else when the store phone rang. He picked it up.

'It's George,' he mouthed while he covered the receiver

with his hand. 'You want to take it or should I tell him you're not here?'

I motioned for him to give me the phone. Now seemed as good a time as any to get this over with.

'You know how many times I've called?' George began by saying.

'Sorry. I was busy. I had my cell turned off,' I explained. 'Just like you do,' I wanted to add, but didn't. I'd had my moment, now it was time to be civil. 'So when do you want to come by and pick your stuff up?' I asked him.

'I don't want to pick my stuff up. I want to talk.'

'I have nothing to say to you.'

'Give me one hour.'

'No.'

'Please. One hour for all the time we've been together.'

I could feel myself weakening, but then I remembered what George had done.

'This is over,' I told him. 'We're through. I'm going to be busy, so we need to arrange a time for you to get your stuff.'

'Robin . . .'

I heard a baby crying in the background.

'You're at Natalie's, aren't you?' I asked him.

George hesitated for a few seconds then replied, 'I had to get diapers and Neosporin for the baby.'

As if that made everything okay. I couldn't believe him.

'At least have the decency to call me from someplace else.'

'See. This is what I'm talking about. My getting stuff for the baby has nothing to do with us.'

'It has everything to do with us.'

I heard a noise. George walking. A door closing. I didn't hear the baby crying anymore.

'Better? Are you happy now?' he asked.

'Not really.'

There was a slight pause. Then George said, 'You're still doing that crap for Ian, aren't you?'

'What does that have to do with what we're talking about?'

'Because if you weren't that kid wouldn't have come to the house and we wouldn't be having this discussion.'

168

'You mean Jose?'

'Is there another one?'

'This would have happened anyway. He was just the precipitating factor.'

'So you say.'

'Make your point, George.'

I took the squirt bottle of Top Job that I kept under the counter and cleaned the smudge marks off the area around the register. Manuel never does it. I don't know if he doesn't see them or he sees them and doesn't care. Either way the marks drive me nuts. When I was through I reached for my backpack and groped around inside for my cigarettes. I really needed one in the worst possible way.

'What I want to know is what the fuck else you're doing with Ian?' If a person could growl George was doing a good impersonation here.

I lit my cigarette and took a puff. Then I said, 'I'm screwing him on top of the bar with everyone watching, if you must know. The video should be in the stores next month. If you're interested I'll let you know when and you can go buy it.'

So much for being civil.

Bethany lifted an eyebrow.

'Hey,' I continued. 'Don't you dare put your shit on me. I'm not the one who's stepping out. You are.'

'You know what your problem is?' George asked.

I moved the empty can of Coke closer to me and knocked my ash into it.

'Don't bother to tell me. Our business is over with.'

'Your problem,' he continued, despite what I'd just said, 'is that you're never satisfied.'

Which was a pretty funny comment when you thought that I wasn't the one with two people in my life; I wasn't the one that was always screwing around with someone else. I took another drag and picked a piece of tobacco off my tongue. Smoking really is a disgusting habit.

'Hey,' I told George. 'Let's leave my problems out of this, if you don't mind. Do you want to arrange a time to pick up your stuff or don't you?'

'I already told you I'm not picking it up.'

'Then I'm throwing it out.'

'Don't even think about,' George warned.

'Your decision.'

I clicked off. Okay. If that's the way he wanted it I'd just pack up George's stuff and move it out to the curb for the garbage men to collect.

'That didn't go too well, did it?' Bethany observed.

'You could say that.' I reached for another slice of pizza. I usually lose my appetite when I'm stressed, but this time I was ravenous.

Twenty-Six

Manuel picked a piece of cheese off the inside of the pizza box and ate it. I'd just played him George's messages to me.

'You should have someone with you when George comes over,' Manuel said.

'I'll think about it.'

'I'm serious.'

'I know you are, but if you don't mind I don't want to talk about this now,' I told him. I just couldn't deal. 'So what happened here when I was gone?'

Evidently, not much. We'd sold a leash for four dollars and eighty-five cents, a large bag of dog food for twelve dollars and fifty-nine cents, a cat toy for a little under two bucks, and a used fish tank with hood, air pump, gravel, plants, and a rock for a little over a hundred.

'The guy's going to come back for the fish over the weekend,' Manuel informed me.

Well that was good at least. What wasn't good was that my

reptile supplier had called and left me a message. I wasn't getting the bio-engineered snakes after all. He'd had a massive die-off and he didn't have the stock to send me. What he said was possible. More likely he'd gotten a better offer from someone else. Damn. I'd had people asking about them, too. One of them had been as good as sold. Oh well.

I beckoned to Bethany and asked her to take care of the gerbils and make sure they had enough food and water. 'Please,' I said to her to forestall her protests. For a moment I thought she was going to say no, but she headed off in the direction of the small-mammal section. When she was gone I told Manuel I'd like to talk to him in my office for a second.

'About what?' he asked.

'I'll tell you when we're inside.'

Zsa Zsa ran ahead of us. She was settling herself on her doggie bed when Manuel and I came in.

'I was just going to remop the floor,' Manuel said.

'Good. I'm glad you're not too tired to do that.'

Manuel gave me one of his she's-taken-leave-of-her-senses looks. 'Why would I be too tired?' Manuel asked.

'After what you did.'

'I didn't do anything.'

'That's good to hear. I was afraid you might have pulled a muscle or something moving Tony. I mean he's not exactly light.'

'I—'

'Jose told me,' I said before Manuel could say anything else. 'So don't bother trying to deny it.'

'Robin—' Manuel began, but I cut him off again.

'I don't want to hear it,' I told him. 'What you did was a felony.'

Manuel shrugged and pulled up his pants. 'I know what it is.'

'See.' I started pacing. I couldn't help myself. 'You want to know what's wrong with the activities you're currently involved in? This is what's wrong with doing what you're doing.'

'This was a one-shot deal.'

171

'Maybe. Maybe not. But bad attracts bad.'

Manuel shook his finger at me. 'I'm not living my life in a bubble.'

'I'm not asking you to do that. But you could have walked away.'

'Would you?' Manuel demanded. 'No you wouldn't have. You would have done the same thing for me if I'd asked you to. You know you would.'

I didn't argue with him, because I couldn't. He was right. I would have done what he had if he'd asked me to.

'Fine,' I agreed. 'But most of my friends don't call me up and ask me to help them move a body. They ask me to water their plants when they're away.'

Manuel yanked up his pants again. 'I guess this is it, hunh?'

'What do you mean?'

'I guess you're going to fire me?'

'No. I'm not going to fire you.' And I went over and gave him a hug. I could feel his body stiffen in surprise. 'I'm just really worried. I don't want anything to happen to you.'

Manuel nodded and turned around, but not before I saw his eyes misting up. Before I could say anything else he made his way out of my office. I thought about his reaction as I logged on to my computer.

I was checking my email when Bethany materialized at my elbow.

'What did you say to him?' she asked.

'Manuel?'

She nodded.

'Why?'

'Because he's acting all weird. I asked him if he wanted a soda and he snapped my head off. I just don't get him,' she said.

I swiveled around in my chair and faced her. For a few seconds I debated telling her about what was going on with Manuel, then decided against it. It was really his decision.

'Weird is not a descriptive phrase,' I felt obligated to point out.

Bethany absentmindedly pinched the roll of puppy fat on

172

her midsection while she thought. Finally she said, 'He's always thinking about something else. It's like he's not there. You know what I mean?'

I did.

'And he jumps down my throat for every little thing.'

'Maybe he's got other things on his mind,' I suggested.

Bethany frowned.

I clarified. 'Business things.'

I emphasized the word business slightly. Okay. I wasn't going to tell her, but I could throw her a hint. Her next comment showed that she didn't get it.

She twisted a lock of her hair around her finger. 'I don't think he likes me anymore.'

It was a classic female interpretation of a situation. Everything is always personal.

'He was talking about getting his own apartment with you,' I pointed out to her. 'That should say something.'

'I don't know.' Bethany studied her shoes for a second. Then she looked back up. 'I think maybe he's seeing someone else.'

'Why are you saying that?'

Bethany shrugged. 'What else could it be?'

'Lots of stuff. Do you have any proof?'

She hesitated for a moment and then said, 'Guys suck.' After which she turned and walked out the door.

Amen to that, I thought, as I turned back to my computer. It's amazing but no matter how old you are some things never change. I scanned my email. There was nothing in it but spam. I logged off. Then I called Calli and updated her on the George story.

'Well, be careful,' she said.

'Of George?'

'He's got a big ego. And you've just hurt it pretty badly.'

'Excuse me. What about my ego?'

'You're a woman. You're expected to eat it.'

'So what are you telling me?'

'Just that it might be wise to have someone with you when George comes over. Someone big.'

'That's what Manuel said.'

'For once I agree with him. Gotta go.' And she hung up. I called her back and asked her to see what she could find out about a place called the Spindle.

'Why?'

'Just do it.'

'I repeat my question.'

'Because you love me and I'm your friend and I need some help.'

'That's not a good reason.'

'That's very cold, Calli. How about because you still owe me?'

'I can get behind that.'

This time I was the person who hung up. It's nice to be first in something.

I swiveled my chair around and put my feet up on my desk and considered what Calli and Manuel had said. If they both were saying the same thing, maybe they were right. Maybe someone should be there when George came by – if he came by.

The only one guy that I knew that was bigger then George and could handle him was Ian. However, since George disliked him, having him there would make the situation worse, not better. I took my feet off the desk and stood up. I guess I'd figure that out when the time came.

I lit a cigarette and started thinking about the matchbook I'd found in Freddy Sanchez's pants. The more I thought about his mother's reaction, her throwing it away, the more I realized it had been an impulsive act. As if she'd wanted to rid herself of something that brought back bad memories.

She felt about the matchbook the way I felt about George's things. I wanted them out of my house, the faster the better. Why? Because something bad had happened to her son there and she didn't want any reminder of it around her.

I went back to my desk and dug my phonebook out from underneath a pile of old newspapers and looked up the Spindle. There was no ad, but there was a number. I picked up the phone again and called Ian. I could hear the sound of people talking when he answered.

'Hey,' he said. 'I got a visit from this detective.'

'The one that's looking for Jose?'

'He has two first names?'

'That's him.'

'I told him the kid's probably long gone by now,' Ian said.

'That's what I said too.'

'I don't think he believed me.'

'He didn't believe me either.'

'They're probably watching your house right now.'

I laughed. 'And your bar.'

'Especially my bar. So what's up?' Ian asked.

'Not too much. Have you ever heard of a place called the Spindle?'

It's out in Liverpool,' Ian said. 'That's the place where the kid got stabbed. Used to be called the Wasps' Nest, right?'

'Correct.' Zsa Zsa pawed at my leg. I fed her a dog biscuit from the box that I keep on top of my computer.

'Was a big Bud Light place. Why do you want to know?'

I told him about the matchbook and Bea's reaction to it.

'Interesting,' Ian said. I could hear people shouting in the background.

'Interesting as in how?' I asked.

'It's out of Freddy's area.'

The volume of noise flooding into Ian's phone increased. I had to strain to hear what he was saying. 'I thought I'd check it out,' I told him.

I snugged the phone against my ear with my shoulder so I could lift the top off the monitor's cage that was presently residing next to the side wall of my office and put some cat food in. Monitors are funny. Feed them canned food and they're really friendly. Feed them live food and they turn mean.

'Well, be careful going out there,' Ian said as I repositioned the phone. 'We're supposed to get another storm sweeping through.'

'That's sweet of you to worry.'

He chuckled. 'I'm not worried. I just don't want you to get stuck out there and miss your shift. I don't want to make this a fifteen-hour day.'

'Lovely.'

'What were you expecting? I already told you I'm not a nice guy.'

'So you keep saying.'

'Well, believe it. They don't say Ian is Satan spelled backwards for nothing.'

'That makes no sense.'

'It does if you think about it.'

'I'm not going to,' I said and hung up.

For some reason I realized I was smiling. Then I realized I hadn't asked Ian about Tony. And then I realized something else. I'd have to do that in person. This wasn't the kind of thing you talked about on the phone, especially with someone like Ian.

Twenty-Seven

I could have waited to talk to Ian until I went to work at the bar, but I didn't. I wanted to talk to him now. Maybe that was because I thought that if I kept moving I wouldn't have to think about George. Or my business. Or the taxes that were coming due and that I had no idea how I was going to pay. So I left Manuel and Bethany in charge of Noah's Ark and took off with Zsa Zsa for Shamus's. If the two of them needed me they could always call me on my cell and I'd be back at the store.

I made an illegal U-turn on South Geddes and parked in front of the Mobil Station. Then I skirted the snow bank by the curb, which was five feet high if it was a foot, and made my way through the partially shoveled sidewalk.

The lone neon beer sign that Ian had managed to pry from the distributors winked in the gloom. Somehow having one seemed worse then having none at all. Maybe because it called attention to its condition. It's funny, but if you run a bar in one of the better areas of the city the distributors are willing to give you everything. If you run a bar down in the hood you get nothing. It's the usual rich get richer while the poor get nothing story.

As I opened the outside door I noticed the icicle above it was growing to impressive proportions. Someone would definitely feel it if it came down and clocked them on the head. I opened the second door and went inside. Zsa Zsa ran in front of me. For a second all conversation stopped as people dumped their cigarettes in empty beer cans or shielded them from view with cupped hands. Then they saw it was just me and it was back to business as usual. Not that hiding the cigarettes would have helped if I had been the health inspector. You could smell the smoke; you could see it hanging in the air. I scanned the crowd. The usuals were here. Probably had been for the past five hours or so. By the time they left to toddle off to bed the younger crowd would have started drifting in. Between the two groups I liked the old-timers better. Maybe they told you the same story over and over again to the point where you could recite it with them, but at least you didn't have to worry about them stabbing anyone.

Carmen, swathed in an oversized men's tweed coat that smelled of mold, was sitting in 'her' seat in the middle of the bar, hunched over her can of PBR. Stuttering Sam was sitting at the far end of the bar, down towards the window, also holding a can of PBR, and having an animated conversation with himself.

A couple of seats down from him three truckers that come in once in a while for a quick one or two were arguing sports. The last of the crew, Bill and Shelley, were sitting in their usual spots, directly across from the TV set. Bill was wearing a gray shirt; I think that's all he had in his closet, while Shelley had on a pink jumpsuit. They were also drinking PBR. Shamus's goes through fifteen to twenty cases of the stuff a week. It's what most of the clientele drink.

Bill raised his can when he saw me. 'Hey,' he mumbled as I went by. 'You solved the murders yet, because we got another one here.'

'I'm working on them,' I told him.

I took another step. Shelley plucked at my jacket sleeve. The smell of old beer, tobacco, and cheap lily of the valley perfume drifted off of her.

'Are you working on my stuff?' she asked me.

'What stuff?' Bill demanded, turning to her.

'My stuff,' Shelley said. She nodded in my direction. 'She knows. Tell him,' she ordered.

'Later,' I said at the same time that Bill said to Shelley, 'You ain't got private stuff.'

Shelley lifted her chin up. 'I most certainly do,' she informed him.

Bill stuck his face in hers. 'This is about the house again, isn't it?' he said. 'Goddamnit!' He pounded the bar with his fist. 'How many times do I have to tell you nothing is going on? She's crazy,' he said to me. 'She can't remember anything. Even her sister won't take care of her any more, let alone her son.'

Shelley arched her back at the same time she pushed the bottom of her pageboy up with the palm of her hand. It was a flirtatious gesture, one I'm sure she'd been using since she was fifteen. She was smiling. She had Bill's attention at last. I left them to it and walked over to where Ian was seated.

He was perched on a bar stool near the end of the bar smoking one of his hand-rolled cigarettes. They looked like joints. He smoked those, too, but not in here. Today he was wearing jeans and a faded plaid flannel shirt over a green long-sleeved tee-shirt that had Shamus's written on it in small letters on the left-hand side. Come to think of it, I'd never seen him in anything else.

'I like the icicle,' I said.

'Yeah.' He nodded. 'Nice, isn't it? I keep talking to the landlord, but he's too cheap to fix the roof so I'm not paying rent until he does.'

'Seems fair,' I said.

If you looked closely you could see that the second story of the building was leaning slightly. Actually, the building Shamus's is in should be closed for multiple code violations, the most important one being the hole in the furnace venting system. Fortunately the broken window in the basement lets the carbon monoxide out, so no one has died yet.

But the roof isn't going to get fixed and neither is the furnace, because the owner of the building is a friend of the guy who inspects it. On the other hand, Ian isn't paying rent, so I guess things even out. I'm only hoping the building doesn't fall down around my ears when I'm in it.

'So what are you doing here?' Ian asked. 'Your shift doesn't start for another,' he consulted his watch, 'three hours.'

'I couldn't stay away. Neither could Zsa Zsa.'

'I told you about her.'

'She needed a change of scene.'

Ian got up and flicked the ash off the cigarette he was smoking into the Coke can he was using as an ashtray. Then he put the cigarette back in his mouth, where it hung. I wondered how he managed to do that. It was a trick I'd never been able to master. I've tried a couple of times and managed to get burn marks over my clothes.

'I'll put her in the back.'

Ian nodded.

'Can I leave her here until my shift starts?'

'I suppose so,' Ian said.

'I have a question for you,' I told Ian after I'd gotten Zsa Zsa situated.

Ian waited.

'It's about Tony.'

'I know a lot of people with that name. Even some girls.'

'This is the Tony that got himself shot. The one the detective was asking you about.' Like he didn't know.

'What about him?'

'What did he do?'

Ian pushed his hair back behind his ears. It was long and black with a few gray streaks near his temples. Then he readjusted his glasses.

'Let's see.' He pretended to think. 'Tony hung out, he played pool—'

'As in a job.'

'He didn't have a job.'

179

'You're being purposely dense.'

Ian smiled. The dimple on his cheek showed. 'I am dense. It's a well-known fact. Didn't anyone tell you that?'

'Like they told me that you were Satan?'

'Exactly.'

Ian is one of those extremely smart people who take real pleasure in having people think he isn't that bright. He reminds me of one of those country lawyers in the movies that tries a case in a New York City courtroom and kicks the Harvard lawyer's ass.

'Okay. Let me rephrase that. How did Tony make his money?'

Ian's eyes narrowed slightly. 'Who said he had any?'

'Oh, come on. He was wearing a gold necklace, and don't tell me that was a present from his girlfriend.'

'I wasn't going to. Why do you want to know?'

'Because I want to know if Tony was involved with Freddy.'

'Everyone is involved with everyone. Haven't you heard of the six degrees of separation?'

'Cute,' I said.

Ian's cell went off. 'Hold on,' he said to me as he got it. He walked a little ways away.

'Business,' he explained when he came back.

I moved in closer and turned my back away from the crowd so they couldn't hear what I was saying. 'Jose and Manuel moved Tony's body.'

'And you know this how?'

'Jose told me. And Manuel confirmed it.'

Ian made a circular motion with his hands. 'And they did this because . . .'

'Because Jose found Tony in the driveway of the house he was staying in. Jose moved the body because he didn't want the police there.'

'If it had been me, I would have just left,' Ian said. 'But what do I know?' He looked around the bar to make sure no one wanted anything before bringing his gaze back to me. 'By the way, thanks for sharing,' he said. 'I always enjoy being an accessory after the fact.'

180

'No problem. Happy to oblige.'

I took off my jacket and without thinking about it threw it over his.

Ian looked at my jacket, then looked back at me. 'You know on the west side you could get killed for doing something like that.'

I smiled even though he wasn't. 'This is the west side.'

'Exactly. Are you going to move it?'

I folded my arms across my chest. 'Maybe. Are you going to tell me what I want to know? I mean we're not talking state secrets here.'

'You know you can be extremely annoying.'

'So I'm told.'

Ian thought for a moment. Then he said, 'Tony carried a weapon. Satisfied?'

'Big deal. Everyone here carries a weapon.'

'He did it in a professional capacity.'

'I see.'

'I thought you might.'

So Tony had been an enforcer. When people are moving drugs they typically handle large volumes of cash. That means they need protection, and since they can't go to the cops for that they come up with alternate strategies – like Tony. But I was having trouble picturing Tony in that role. I kept seeing him at his house taking care of his brothers and sisters. He had a real baby face. But then hadn't there been someone in the thirties called Baby Face Nelson?

'You're sure?' I asked.

Ian rolled his cigarette around in his mouth. 'No. I'm making it up. He was parking his car around the corner last month because he'd shot at the wrong person and they were looking for him.'

'Maybe they found him. Maybe that's who shot Tony.'

'Trust me. It isn't.'

'How do you know?'

'Because I do and no I'm not telling you how I do, so don't even bother asking me. Now if you don't mind.' Ian pointed to my jacket.

'You're serious, aren't you?'

'Yes, I am.'

'Fine.'

I put my jacket back on. It was cold in here anyway.

'You want anything?' Ian asked.

I settled on a hot cocoa. It seemed more in tune with the weather than a beer. Ian placed the mug in front of me and moved off to get Stuttering Sam another PBR. I finished my cocoa and left. Tonight was the night the chess club met at Carousel Mall. I wanted to talk to someone there if I could.

Twenty-Eight

The driving had gotten worse since I'd gone into Shamus's. The roads were extremely slick. When the Elantra in front of me did a 180, I decided to take Route Eleven over to Carousel instead of 690 and 81. Even though it took longer going through the city, it was worth it. At least that way I wouldn't have some idiot rear-ending me because he was going too fast and couldn't stop in time.

I spent the drive over listening to the Dixie Chicks and thinking about what Jose and Manuel had told me. Freddy's laptop, the dog, his crack use all said one thing to me. Which was that, contrary to what his mother wanted to believe, her son was involved in some sort of drug-related activity, which in my book meant gang-related activity. People like Freddy weren't into the heavy end of things, like Tony had been. They were too unreliable for that. They were fringe players. Sometimes they made small deliveries, sometimes they ran errands.

What I needed was confirmation. I drummed my fingers on the wheel of the car. I had no doubt that there were a lot of people out there who knew what Freddy was doing, but none of them wanted to talk to me about it. I'd already spoken with Freddy's mother, sister, neighbors, and kindergarten teacher. The only person close to Freddy that I hadn't spoken to was his brother. It was his turn up at bat.

I dug my cell out of my bag and called Ian.

'Do you know where Freddy's brother is?' I asked him.

'And hello to you too.'

'Hello. Well, do you?'

'I can find out,' Ian said.

'Thanks. Gotta go, there's a cop up ahead.'

And I clicked off and dropped my cell on the seat. The last thing I needed right now was a hundred-dollar ticket and a couple of points on my license. And then I saw why the cop was there.

He was directing traffic. There was a long line to get into the mall. For a moment I thought about turning around and doing this next week – I hate crowds – but next week would be even worse because it would be closer to Christmas. Oh well. As someone said, 'The time is now.' And it was.

Three-quarters of an hour later I'd finally made it to the mall food court. The place was bedlam. It had taken me fifteen minutes to get into the mall parking lot and another half an hour to find a space. Ten-foot piles of snow that had been left by the snowplows towered over everything, obstructing lanes and turning them into dead ends. Cars were wedged in wherever they could fit.

Watching the hordes of shoppers I remembered why I never came to the mall during this season of the year. Of course, to be accurate I didn't go to it any time of the year unless absolutely necessary. Calli enjoys shopping. She thinks it's fun. I don't and I never have, much to my mother's chagrin.

As I looked around at the throngs of people I had a moment of jealousy as I thought of all the business that passed through here and how little came through the area around my shop. After the original Noah's Ark had burned down I'd considered relocating to the mall, but I couldn't afford it. The rents were sky high. So were the utilities because lessees were charged for heating the common area as well. And because I'd have to stay open more hours I would have had to have hired more staff. When I'd costed it all out I'd decided that it wasn't worth the money. Now I wondered if I'd made the right decision. At least if I were here there'd be people walking by the shop, people with money to spend. Unlike where I am now, where everyone was either broke, on the verge of being broke, or living from social service check to social service check.

Oh well. I studied the food court. The palm trees decorating the place were wrapped in strings of white lights. Christmas carols competed with the music from the carousel. People talking and laughing and children screaming added to the din. People rushed by me their arms laden with bulging shopping bags. Occasionally, one of the sparrows that lived in the trees swooped down, picked up a crumb from the floor, and flew back up to its perch. I took a deep breath and tried to locate the chess players among the mass of people eating at the tables in the food court.

After several minutes of wandering around, I finally spotted them. They were seated next to the escalators to the third floor. I went over and stood beside a man in his thirties and a boy who was probably fifteen. I guess they were used to having people watching them, because no one looked up.

'Yes?' the thirty-year-old said as he moved one of his pawns.

For some reason I noticed that he and his partner were playing with classic Staunton design pieces. I remember reading that it made it easier to follow the game.

The man's face was thin, making the pouches under his eyes look even bigger. You expected them to belong to someone who was twenty years older. He had a scar that ran across the left side of his mouth. Whoever had sewn it up had done a bad job, because that side of his mouth had a permanent pucker.

The boy didn't look up. He had his elbows on the table. His hands were supporting his head. He was studying the board intently while he drummed his fingers on the table. Finally, he moved his bishop.

The man grunted. 'Interesting,' he commented. He went back to studying the board. I noticed he was rocking back and forth in his chair.

'I need some information,' I told him.

He glanced back up at me reluctantly.

'About someone who might have played here.' And I gestured to the dozen people with their heads down over their boards. 'His name was Freddy Sanchez.'

The man shook his head. 'Doesn't ring a bell. Do you know him, Ivan?' he asked his opponent.

'Nope.' Ivan kept his eyes on the board.

'Are you sure?' I asked him.

Ivan frowned in annoyance. Obviously he wanted me gone as soon as possible. 'He mostly watched. He wasn't very good.'

'Anything else?'

Ivan pointed to a man sitting three tables down. 'No. But Carl might know something.' I got the feeling he was telling me that so he could fob me off on someone else.

I went over to talk to Carl. Whereas Ivan and his opponent were just beginning their game, Carl and his opponent were finishing theirs.

'Freddy Sanchez,' he repeated when I asked about him. His eyes were focused on the game and he tore his gaze away reluctantly, but he kept one of his fingers on his knight. 'I played him a couple of times.'

'And?'

'His offensive game was very underdeveloped.' He tipped the knight back and forth.

His opponent, a man I judged to be in his sixties, who had a ring of white hair and freckled scalp, said, 'He liked the game though.'

'I told him he had to learn to read chess,' Carl said. 'He had to study.'

I took off my jacket. It was warm in here. 'But he had that game. Electronic chess.'

Carl's opponent made a dismissive noise. 'It's good for practice, not for learning.'

Carl spun his knight around with his finger. 'I don't know,' he said.

I realized he was talking to himself about the move he was going to make.

'So what else about Freddy?' I asked.

Carl kept his eyes on the board this time. 'Nothing.'

I waited.

Carl finally must have realized that some further explanation was called for, because he said, 'People come and watch all the time. Sometimes they come for a couple of weeks, sometimes they come for a month. It's not unusual.'

'But Freddy played,' I persisted.

Carl finally looked up. 'He came for about two months. Then he stopped.'

'Do you know why?' I didn't know where I was going with this. I was fishing around.

'He got that electronic gizmo. I guess he decided it was better then we were.' Carl shook his head. 'Machines.'

'Do you know who gave it to him?'

Carl shook his head. 'Some man. He told me the man said he was a genius. That he was sending him to school. Nonsense. I tell you the kid could have been a low-ranked player – if he'd studied. But he wanted it all to happen fast. That's the problem with people these days. They want instant everything.' He turned his attention back to the board and moved his bishop. 'Checkmate,' he announced.

His opponent tsked. 'I must be getting old,' he said. 'I should have seen that coming.'

They turned the board around and started setting up pieces for another game. I watched them for a few minutes then went over and asked the other players about Freddy. They pretty much said the same thing Carl had. I left my business cards with everyone and told them to contact me if they remembered anything, which I didn't think would happen, and went on to the Spindle.

Twenty-Nine

I've always hated Liverpool. Maybe it's because I always get lost out there. Maybe I'd like it better if I knew my way around, but that isn't likely to happen soon. Since I don't have any friends out there, I don't go out that way. But I'm in the minority. The area north of Liverpool, in Clay, is one of the fastest growing areas in the county. Superstores and strip malls have sprung up all over Route 57. Capitalism at its best. Suddenly the Lake Road has become congested with people trying to get home. Usually people drive fast on it. Today was no exception, and I felt as if I was playing bumper cars.

Visibility was poor. I could barely see Onondaga Lake. The water that I could see was gray, the same color as the sky. Old rusted-out towers were faintly visible in the distance. In the summer people biked and walked along the paths that went around the lake, but no one was out now. For some reason a picture of mutated fish swimming just below the surface, fish the color of skin with three red eyes and ten fins, flashed through my mind. I shook my head to clear it. The lake has been an object of controversy for as long as I've been in Syracuse. Someone once told me it was one of the most polluted lakes for its size in the world. Though to be fair I think that may not be true anymore.

Calli has a lithograph of Onondaga Lake done sometime in the early 1900s hanging on her kitchen wall. In the picture the shore of the lake is dotted with amusement parks and restaurants and hotels. People came to vacation there then. She told me that the fish from the lake used to be served in the restaurants in New York City. But that was then. Eating the fish from the lake has been deemed inadvisable since the

187

1970s due to the mercury and the PCPs on the lake's bottom, from the waste dumped there by local industry. It's getting better, but in the summer the lake still smells bad. It took a court order to get the county to stop dumping its raw sewage into the creek that feeds the lake. Now they're finally building a sewage-treatment plant. Heaven knows, it's taken long enough.

I kept on thinking about the lake as I slowly made my way through the village of Liverpool. After several wrong turns I finally conceded defeat and stopped at a gas station to ask directions. The Indian woman behind the counter told me that the Spindle was located in a dying strip mall a little ways out of town. At one time, she informed me, the place had been a sporting goods store. But that was before the owner had gone bankrupt.

Well the woman was right about the dying part I decided when I finally found the place. Of the ten stores that had been there only two were still open, Pierre's Hair Salon and the Spindle. All the rest had For Rent signs in their windows.

The Spindle was at the end on the left. It was a big, square barn of a place. As far as I could see the only thing the owners had done to the outside of the building was to take down the old sign and put up a new one. From the number of cars out front it looked as if the place wasn't doing great business tonight. But then this was a weeknight and the weather was bad. Anyone with any sense was home watching TV.

I stopped for a moment when I got inside and looked around. The place was cavernous. Three of Ian's place could have fit inside here with no problem at all. The area was set up like a dance bar, with a DJ booth over to the left of the entrance. Then there were two dance areas – one to the left and one to the right. The place had been painted a bright, glossy yellow.

The upper part of the wall was decorated with neon beer signs. I counted fifteen of them. Their presence was validation of Ian's theory that the poorer parts of Syracuse were being unofficially redlined by the beer distributors. The lower part of the wall was covered with a hodgepodge of road signs that people had obviously stolen. The total effect was not a happy one.

The bar itself took up a fair amount of space. I figured when things were busy they probably had five people working it. They probably had two shifts – which meant there were a lot of people to ask about Freddy, most of whom I was guessing were going to be here on Friday and Saturday nights. But, as I said, this was hump night and not many people were around. Unless more people were going to come in later, the owner was definitely losing money this evening.

The bouncer was sitting on a bar stool over by the far wall, reading the newspaper and sipping something out of a mug, while the bartender was busy stacking glasses. I counted the patrons. There were fifteen people sitting around, three women and twelve guys, drinking and talking.

They were in their late twenties and early thirties, although there were a couple of younger twenty-somethings sprinkled into the mix. I guessed that most of the patrons were local. It certainly wasn't the kind of place you rode through a snowstorm to get to, unless, of course, like me, you had a reason to.

I walked up to the bar. A neatly dressed man sitting two stools over glanced up at me. A palpable look of disappointment flitted across his face when he saw who I was. He turned away, looked down at his watch, then signaled to the bartender and pointed to his glass.

'Pete. Another shot of Jack.'

Pete nodded. He took the bottle of Jack Daniel's off the call shelf, went over to the man, poured a shot out, put the bottle back, and approached me. He was wearing a long-sleeved white Oxford shirt with the logo of the place embroidered on the breast pocket. His cuffs were rolled up to mid-arm and I could see part of a tribal tattoo peeking out.

'Can I help you?' he asked me in a tone that wasn't exactly friendly, but wasn't unfriendly either.

I ordered a Dos Equis. When he came back with it I asked him how business was.

'Slow,' he said setting the beer down in front of me along with a napkin. 'Glass?'

I shook my head.

'It picks up on the weekend,' he added.

'You must do pretty well then,' I observed. 'One of my nephews comes out here from the city.'

'Yeah.' He absentmindedly adjusted his collar. 'We get a few of those coming up.'

'He really likes the place.'

The bartender nodded politely. 'That's good to hear.'

'He says you have some kick-ass bands.'

The bartender's gaze strayed. I knew he was just pretending to listen, in the same way I did with my customers down at Shamus's. He was probably thinking about what he was going to do when he got off his shift.

'His name is Freddy Sanchez,' I continued.

'Uh-huh.'

'Although I hear sometimes he calls himself Jimmy Slade to piss his mom off.'

'People do lots of strange things,' the bartender commented.

There wasn't a flicker of recognition at my mention of Freddy Sanchez or Jimmy Slade on the bartender's face, just boredom. As I gave him a five for my beer and waited for change I realized that there was always the possibility that Freddy had been using another name, one that I didn't even know about.

For a moment I looked at the snowflakes dancing under the halogen lights. The man sitting next to me looked at his watch again. Then I saw him smiling as a woman came towards him. She was brushing the snow out of her hair and laughing while she apologized for being late. I felt a pang of envy as I watched them kiss.

The bartender brought me my change and drifted back down the bar. I finished my beer and went over and asked the bouncer if a kid named Freddy Sanchez or Jimmy Slade ever came in here. I didn't really expect an answer, but I figured I had to try. Otherwise what was the point of schlepping out here? The bouncer started getting up off his stool.

'I'll take that as a no,' I said.

The bouncer just looked at me. 'Why don't you leave,' he said.

'I was just asking . . .'

He put up a hand palm out. 'I don't want any more trouble.' Now he was standing. He was taller and broader then he'd looked when he was sitting down. He looked meaner, too. I bet he was the owner's solution to the kid that had gotten stabbed in the parking lot in the bar's last incarnation.

'I'm just asking about Freddy Sanchez. I wasn't planning on causing any trouble,' I told him.

'Good. 'Cause you're not going to.' Then he added, 'Cause trouble,' in case I was in doubt about his meaning. He motioned towards the door with his thumb. 'Out.'

'I'm going,' I told him. 'But—'

'Now.'

'I just . . .'

He took a step toward me and I shut up.

He watched me leave. Now that was certainly interesting, I thought, as I stepped outside.

Thirty

It was snowing harder now. I got in my Taurus and started it up. It coughed and sputtered.

'Please,' I said to her. 'Don't do this to me now.'

I didn't want to be stuck out here in weather like this. Finally, on the third try, the engine turned over. Like me she didn't like it when things got too cold.

I patted the dashboard. 'Good girl,' I cooed.

Then I lit a cigarette and rested my head against the seat. All the windows were covered with snow. I couldn't see outside. It was nice and quiet.

I closed my eyes for a few seconds and thought about what had happened inside the Spindle. Nothing much really except for what the bouncer had said about not wanting any more trouble. That implied that there had been trouble fairly recently. The question was, what kind?

The bartender hadn't recognized Freddy's name, but the bouncer obviously had, because he was fine until I brought Freddy up. So what had Freddy been involved in out here? And how could I find out?

Using a phony ID or exhibiting stupid behavior wasn't enough to invoke the kind of response I'd gotten from the bouncer. Maybe Freddy had been delivering stuff out here for someone. That seemed like the simplest explanation. After all, Manuel had said the place was sketchy.

I yawned. I needed to get some coffee on the way home or I'd never make it through the rest of the evening. I took another pull on my cigarette and cracked the window so I could flick the ash into the snow. The more I thought about it, the more the bouncer's attitude intrigued me. But I didn't know how to get him to talk or even if what he had to say would be relevant to what I was doing.

Of course, if I had still been with George it wouldn't have been a problem. I could have called him up and asked him to find out if any reports had been filed with the police out here and after a couple of minutes of bitching he would have rung up one of his buddies who was still on the force, and he would have gotten the info for George, who would have given it to me. But that was not a possibility now. Too bad, but there it was.

Maybe Calli could find out something. I knew she had contacts in the Syracuse Police Department, but I wasn't sure about Liverpool. I decided I'd call her in the morning and ask as I looked at the clock on the dash. It was probably time to get moving. The problem was I didn't want to stand outside and brush off the car.

I decided to take the lazy way out. I hit the button and the window went down a little. Some of the snow fell off, but not enough to be able to see out. Next I turned on my window wipers, but they weren't budging. Probably because they were frozen to the windshield. I was going to have to get out and clear the snow off the car. I finally found the brush buried under some dry cleaning I'd forgotten to take in for the past month or so. I really had to do something about this car, I thought, as I stepped outside.

I zipped my jacket all the way up so my neck was covered, flicked my cigarette into the snow on the ground, and watched as it disappeared into the mass of white. It would resurface in the spring along with all the other trash when the snow melted. The forecasters had said this was going to be an exceptionally long, cold winter and it looked as if they were going to be right. Usually we didn't hit single-digit days until January and February.

I'd just finished scrapping the ice off the rear window and had started working on the side ones when a Ford Explorer swept by me and careened around the counter. Another couple of inches and it would have hit me.

'Hey, watch it,' I yelled.

Where the hell did he think he was going in such a hurry? The more I thought about it the angrier I got. I finished brushing off the Taurus, got inside, and followed the tire tracks around to the back.

The rear lot had been partially plowed. There were nine cars parked next to each other. They were all, unlike the pieces of tin that were parked out front, high end, and all of them were clustered in front of a metal door that obviously served as the rear entrance to the building the Spindle was housed in.

About twenty feet down the brick wall I spotted a loading dock. No cars were parked in front of that. Nor had any been for a long time judging by the amount of snow that had drifted up in front of it. Maybe the metal door was some kind of VIP entrance I hypothesized, although the location ruled against that. Some sort of private club?

I parked next to the Ford Explorer that had almost hit me and got out. I had to turn my head away from the wind that was driving the snow toward the building. As I walked toward the door I had a feeling, given the location, that whomever was inside would be less than pleased to see me.

I'd just taken a couple of steps when my cell rang. It was Ian.

'You wanted to speak to Freddy's brother,' he said. 'He's going to drop by the bar later tonight.'

'That was fast.'

'Yeah. It was.'

'Where was he?'

'He moves around a lot. What are you up to?' Ian asked changing the subject.

I'm not sure why I lied but I told him I was on my way back to the city.

'Good,' he said. 'Because I have some stuff I have to do. Drive safe,' he added and clicked off.

Well, I would be on my way back soon.

I blinked the snow out of my eyes, went up to the door, and took a closer look. It was gray metal. The hinges were on the inside. I didn't see a buzzer. Or an intercom on the wall. There was no way of letting someone inside know that someone outside was there. So obviously this wasn't where stock was delivered. But I did see a numerical lock on it, meaning you had to have the code to get in. I knocked. No one answered. I tried again. I didn't get a response. Interesting. I took another look at the box and it occurred to me that I could probably get in anyway. Three numbers on the keypad were clean, while the others were covered with snow. I assumed that the clean numbers were the three numbers the guy in the Ford Expedition had punched in. It was nice of him to help me out this way.

The numerals were three, four, and five, which meant that, if it was a three-digit number, there would only be six possible combinations. No big deal.

It also occurred to me that I didn't know what I was going to say when I got inside. I'd think of something, though. I usually did.

Three, four, and five didn't work. Five, four, and three didn't work either, but four, three, and five did. As I pushed the door open, I belatedly realized that whoever was running the place probably had a video cam mounted on the wall above the door and I should have looked. I knew I was right about the video cam when a mountain of a guy came towards me after I'd taken five steps.

He filled the hallway. He was wearing black pants and a brown crewneck sweater. Gold chains hung around his neck, or what passed for his neck. In this light it looked as if his head was sitting directly on his shoulders. The fact that his hair was laying in limp strands across his scalp exaggerated the effect.

'How did you get in here and what do you want?' he said.

His tone was not welcoming but then I hadn't expected that it would be.

'Through the door like everyone else.' Then before No Neck could say anything else I added, 'I wanna speak to the guy in the Ford Explorer. He clipped me.'

It was almost true. Another couple of inches and he would have.

'Tough shit,' No Neck said.

'Hey, buddy,' I told him, 'I'm trying to be nice here.'

'Really?' he sneered.

'Yeah. Really. The guy did about two thousand dollars' damage to my car. Given the circumstances I figured I'd spare everyone pain and aggravation and try and settle this privately without the intervention of the authorities. Two thousand dollars is a lot of bucks. Frankly I don't have it. But, hey, if I gotta get my insurance company involved, they're going to need a police report.' I shrugged. 'If you want to play it that way it's okay with me. Maybe, though, you should ask the guy in the Ford Explorer what he wants to do. He might be angry otherwise.'

I could see No Neck was thinking about what I'd said. While he was thinking I took a look around. I was standing in a narrow hallway. The walls were painted a forest green. There were a couple of industrial-style hanging lights strung from the ceiling. That was it in the way of decor. No pictures. No posters. No nothing. I heard voices coming from behind the bouncer. They were male and they were laughing.

'All right,' No Neck said after a minute or so had passed. 'I'll talk to him.'

I smiled. 'Good.'

He pointed at me. 'But you stay here. Don't move.' He ended his sentence with a glare to show he meant business. I wasn't too concerned. If he was going to do something he would have done it already. I nodded to show that I understood what he was saying and dug another cigarette out of my backpack. As I lit up I decided I wasn't doing very well with my five cigarettes a day rule. No Neck gave me another glare on general principle and turned and waddled down the hall.

I took a pull from my cigarette and walked down the hall a little ways after No Neck. From where I was standing I could see six guys sitting around a table playing cards in a room off to the right. Poker, I presumed. High stakes poker from the look of the cars in the lot.

Over to one side I spotted a table set up like a buffet. There were a couple of platters of cold cuts, a basket of rolls, some bags of potato chips, and bottles of soda and beer on ice. Seeing it reminded me that I hadn't eaten anything since breakfast. My gaze shifted. Looking up I could see another set of video cams mounted on either side of the hallway ceiling. I waved at whoever was watching.

I was just about to take another step forward when No Neck came out of the room.

'I thought I told you to stay where you were,' he snarled.

I shrugged. 'Sorry. I was just looking for the bathroom. I have to pee.'

He moved a half a step to the side and I saw the man his bulk had been hiding.

The guy looked familiar, but maybe that was because he looked so much of a type. Middle aged. The beginning of a paunch. Expensive clothes. Master of the Universe stance.

'Now what the hell is this about my clipping your car,' the guy demanded.

'Come outside and take a look,' I said.

The Taurus had been sideswiped a little under a month ago and the door on the passenger side was badly dented.

'I didn't do that,' he said when I pointed the door out to him. 'What are you trying to pull?'

196

'Nothing.'

'Yes you are. This is crap. Your car isn't worth two hundred dollars let alone two thousand. Anyway, I'd have known if I'd hit you. I would have felt it.'

'Not the way you were going, you wouldn't have. Okay,' I told him when he didn't reply. 'Fine. I was trying to do you a favor but I guess I'd better call the cops.'

I reached for my cell. The last thing I wanted to do was make good on my promise, but if I didn't these guys would know I was scamming them and possibly call the cops on me.

'Hold on a minute,' the guy said.

I watched as he dug into his back pocket and came out with a money clip filled with bills.

'Here.' He peeled off eight of them and slapped them in the palm of my hand. I looked down. They were C-notes. 'That's all you're going to get,' he informed me.

'Another two hundred and we'll call it even,' I told him.

He looked at me and I looked at him. I figured if I didn't argue a little he'd get suspicious.

'Fine,' he finally said. He peeled off another two bills and practically threw them at me. 'But I better not see you again.'

'You won't,' I promised him.

He opened his mouth to answer me, thought better of it, and turned to No Neck instead. 'Come on,' he said to him. 'Let's get back inside. I'm freezing my ass off out here.'

'Don't even think about coming around here again,' No Neck growled at me.

'Here? Where's here?' I replied.

No Neck started towards me but the other man stopped him. 'Not worth it,' he said.

'Absolutely not,' I told No Neck as I got into the Taurus.

The realization of what I'd done hit me as I headed back to the city. I'd just scammed a guy out of a thousand bucks. I should give the money to charity, I thought. And then I thought, no. I should use it to fix up my car and pay my taxes. I was beginning to understand Manuel's point of view a little better.

It's much easier to make the right moral decisions when you have a cushion to fall back on.

Thirty-One

After being at the Spindle, Shamus's seemed tiny and dark to me. I counted fifteen people sitting at the bar. Six were regulars, six were once-in-a-whiles, and three I didn't recognize.

'Who are the strangers?' I asked Ian, having managed to dodge Shelley and Bill and Stuttering Sam on my way in.

'Locals.' Ian looked up from the cigarette he was rolling. 'The one on the far left, the bald one, Ron, is a plumber, the other two, are Tino and Mike. Mike's the one with the gimme hat – he's bald too – and Tino is the fat one. Those two are contractors. They come in about two, three times a week, usually in the afternoons, for a couple of Millers, shoot a few games of pool, and leave. Not big spenders.'

I nodded. 'Anything else I should know?'

Ian lit his cigarette.

'Shelley is on a tear about Bill selling her house again. She and Carmen had a fight already and I had to separate them. If they start anything again kick 'em both out. You can do that, can't you?'

'Sure. No problem,' I replied, really hoping it didn't come to that.

'And watch Shelley when she goes to the bathroom,' Ian continued. 'She's already peed all over the floor in there.'

'Wonderful,' I said.

'Well, it could have been worse,' Ian commented. 'She could have pooped on the seat. She did that yesterday.'

I was thinking I hadn't signed on for cleaning that up –

hell, I didn't even like changing my neighbor's kid's diapers
– when Ian nodded in Hector's direction.

'And make sure you call a cab for him. His car keys are
under the bar. Don't give them to him. And that's about it.
I'll be back to help you close.'

I nodded again. 'You know the Spindle,' I said to him.

'Yeah.' Ian reached for his jacket. 'You were just there.'

'It was a rhetorical question.'

'And?'

'It has something in the back.'

Ian put his jacket on. 'A gambling club. It's what they make
most of their money off of.'

'Really?'

'Yup. The place is run by some ethnic fag. He runs the
Spindle, too, and kicks back to the owner of the building.'

'Isn't the security a little tight for something like that?'

'Not really.' Ian scooped his pack of cigarettes off the bar
and deposited it in his jacket pocket. 'Money changes hands there
so the people that own it just want to make sure no one gets in
there and rips anyone off. That would be bad for business.'

'Obviously. How do you know this?'

Ian pushed his glasses up the bridge of his nose with one
of his fingers. 'Now you're questioning my sources of information?'

'More or less.'

'Someone I know DJs there. Anyway, it's not as if it's a
big secret or anything like that.'

'Freddy Sanchez was out there.'

'I know. You told me. Three times. Remember?' Ian tapped
his fingers on the bar. I could see he was getting impatient to
get going.

'I'm just trying to piece things together,' I explained.

Ian snorted. 'There's nothing to piece together,' he said.
'The kid was making a delivery to someone at the bar. The
bouncer saw what was happening and tried to get him out
quietly, but Freddy made a fuss and the bouncer threw him
out. End of story.' Ian picked another piece of tobacco off his
tongue.

'So why was the bouncer so upset with me?'

'Think about it. The kid is dead. You come asking questions. If he tells you anything that'll be like admitting there's a problem at the place. Why should he do that? Then maybe you'll want to speak to the owner. The police. Who the hell knows who? Then maybe he'll get into trouble for having allowed Freddy in his bar, which is not something he needs.'

It made sense.

'One last thing,' I said.

Ian practically rolled his eyes. 'Make it fast.'

'When is Freddy's brother going to get here?'

'Whenever he does.'

'What's his name?'

'Terry.'

'Terry isn't a Hispanic name.'

'I think the father is half Italian.' Ian indicated the customers with his chin. 'You'd better get to work. I see some thirsty folks out there.'

That was nothing new. These people were always thirsty.

'You haven't heard anything from Jose, have you?'

'Nope,' Ian said. 'You?'

'Ditto.'

'Good.'

And he walked out the door. As he left I realized that instead of talking I should have run across the street and gotten some coffee, but it was too late now. The caffeine in hot cocoa would have to do. I filled a glass mug with water and put it in the microwave. I'd just pressed the button when Shelley motioned for me to come over.

'I'm working on your problem,' I told her in an attempt to forestall what I knew she was going to say. 'Can I get you another PRB?' This was my new tactic with her – straight out lying.

Shelley grabbed my wrist as she nodded. 'You'll come to my house tomorrow?' she asked. 'I got something I have to show you.'

'Sure,' I said.

Shelley's short-term memory was so bad she'd forget about

what I told her twenty minutes from now, let alone by tomorrow morning.

Bill pushed his face into hers. 'You don't got nuthin' to show her.'

Shelley stuck her chin out. 'I certainly do.'

This could go on for the rest of the evening. I moved down the line to the three guys I didn't know.

'Are you gentleman good or can I get you something else?'

The three of them nodded. Obviously they'd been spending a lot of time together.

'We'll all have a refill,' Ron, the plumber, said.

I looked to see what they were drinking. PBRs. What else. Then I watched as he reached in his pocket and took a wad of bills out, peeled off a fifty, and slapped it down on the bar. I took it to the cash register, made change, and counted it out before him. Then I went to get the guys their beers. When I got back they were talking about one of the jobs they'd been on.

'I can't believe I found that water heater in the basement,' Ron said. 'It was brand new. I loaded it in my truck and took it up to my son-in-law's house. It's amazing what people will throw away.'

The fat guy shrugged. 'I just got a brand new stove and fridge out of a place before I took it down. The other guy working the job was too lazy to put them in his truck.'

'The problem with people like that is they got too much money,' the plumber said, and he took a gulp of his beer. 'It makes them lazy and careless.'

The guy in the gimme cap raised his beer before he took a swallow. 'Amen to that.'

The fat guy nodded. 'My daughter can't even be bothered taking the empties back to the supermarket. I caught her throwing them out in the trash yesterday. I mean it's all this free stuff people get from the government. If they knew nothing was coming to them they'd be more careful.

'People don't keep nothing up anymore. Look at all the stuff around here that's coming down. Roofs are rotted out. Floors are coming up. No one fixes nuthin' anymore. They're so bad they're worth more torn down. I mean look at that house with all the pigeons in it.'

The two other guys nodded their heads in agreement. They were getting stupid drunk.

'Disgusting,' the guy with the gimme cap said. 'You need a respirator to work in there. Otherwise you breathe that stuff in and get some disease that starts with a P. I seen it on TV.'

The fat guy lifted his can and beckoned for me to come over. I was on my way when I saw Shelley stand up. Her face was red with anger. Before I could stop her she was standing beside the plumber, screaming in his ear.

'You're not touching my place,' she yelled. 'If you come near it again, I'm going to shoot you.'

'Lady, come on,' the plumber said as he leaned back in an attempt to try and get away from her.

'I know what you're planning on,' she continued at the same pitch. Drops of spit sprayed out of her mouth. 'My son will do something about it. You'll see.' She wagged a finger in the plumber's face. 'He'll fix you. He'll fix you good. He won't,' she pointed at Bill, 'because he's in cahoots with you. But my son will. I've seen you outside eyeing my house.'

Now Bill was finally up. I guess he'd been waiting to see if anyone else would step in, but no one had. Why should they if they could avoid it? He had Shelley by the arm and was pulling her back towards her seat.

'Jeez, Bill,' the plumber said to him. 'You got to get control of her.'

'What am I going to do?' Bill replied. 'She's crazy. It's this head trauma thing. Or maybe it's dementia. I talked to the doctor. He said there was nothing they could do. Even her sister won't take her. No one wants her. Not her son, not her brother, not no one.'

'That's for sure,' the guy with the gimme cap said.

'See,' Shelley said, wagging her finger in Bill's face. 'You know their names.'

'Of course I know their names,' Bill said. 'They live around here.'

'You're just with me for my money,' Shelley said.

202

Then she pushed Bill. The force was hard enough to send him reeling back several steps.

'Watch it,' Carmen yelled at him. 'You almost hit me and made me drop my beer.' I could see her hand trembling as she lifted her can up to her lips. 'You know,' she said to Shelley after she'd put her PBR down, 'no one gives a good goddamn about that house of yours. In fact, they should tear it down and put something else there. Like . . . like . . . a Wal-Mart or a development or something. Your house is nothing but a rat trap. And it stinks of cat piss.'

At which point all hell broke loose.

'You cunt,' Shelley cried as she lunged for Carmen.

She had her by the throat by the time I came around the bar. Bill was trying to separate the two women. He managed to drag Shelley away by grabbing her arms and pulling her back. He just had her pinned when Carmen punched her in the shoulder. Shelley slipped out of her jacket leaving Bill holding it, and went straight for Carmen with outstretched arms. She grabbed a hank of Carmen's hair, and pulled. Carmen screamed and grabbed some of Shelley's hair. The women appeared to be evenly matched.

As I looked at them fighting I thought: Why did I ever taken this job? And then I thought: I've got to get control of this. I looked at Bill and he looked at me. I chin nodded at him.

'On the count of three,' I told him. 'One. Two. Three.'

He grabbed Shelley and I grabbed Carmen. She twisted and turned but somehow I managed to hang on to her. I have to say she was strong for someone her size. Then all of a sudden I felt her body collapse. It was as if someone had let the air out of the tire. Oh my God, I thought. What happens if she has a heart attack and dies? And then the police would have to come. And they'd have to file a report. Ian would never forgive me.

But Carmen hadn't died. She'd just lost heart or regained what little sanity she had. Take your pick.

I noticed the same thing had happened to Shelley.

'See,' she croaked. 'I told you something bad was happening to me. That's why I asked you to come over.'

'All right,' I said to Bill. 'Get her out of here.'

'But what about her?' Shelley pointed at Carmen. 'She should go too.'

'Don't worry. She is.'

I found I was panting from the exertion. I really needed to stop smoking and get myself back in shape.

'That's not fair,' Carmen whined. 'She's the one who started it.'

Shelley drew herself up. 'I got a perfect right to defend myself and my man.'

I could see Carmen starting to bristle. This was not going to happen again. I pointed to the door. 'Both of you get your things and get out. Now. Otherwise you're going to be permanently banned from the premises.'

It was the only thing I could think of to say that might get through to them. And it did. Because both women shut up and started for the door.

I turned around to apologize to Hector. He'd been the one closest to the fracas, but sometime in the last two minutes he'd put his head on the bar and passed out. Well this had definitely been an exciting evening, I decided, as I apologized to everyone for what had just happened.

Thirty-Two

When I got behind the bar I looked down at the backs of my hands and noticed that the left one was bleeding. Carmen had scratched me and I hadn't even noticed it. Well it could be worse, I reflected as I washed the cut out in the soak sink and dabbed it dry with a paper towel. At least she hadn't bitten me. Then I would have had to go for a tetanus shot.

And no one had really gotten hurt. And the rest of the patrons didn't seem unduly disturbed. So that was good. In fact, judging from the expressions on Mike's, Ron's, and Tino's faces, they seemed to have enjoyed the whole spectacle, and were now busy discussing who had thrown the first punch, what Shelley had said, etc., etc., etc.

I've learned that the thing with most bar fights is that while the fight is usually over in fifteen seconds or less the discussions centering around them go on and on and on forever.

I was hunting for the tube of Neosporin that I knew Ian kept in one of the drawers when I heard the creak of the inside door opening. I looked up. A kid stood framed in it. He pimp-rolled his way by Hector, who was now snoring, as well as by Stuttering Sam, and two guys who lived in the group home two blocks away. He kept coming until he was standing next to the bar gate. He was all duded up in an oversized orange sweatshirt, big black jeans, and a Tommy Hilfiger black parka.

'Terry Sanchez, I presume,' I said, closing the drawer. The Neosporin would have to wait.

I'd known who he was the moment he'd walked into the place because he looked just like his brother – same eyes, same mouth, same chin shape – only he was about fifty pounds heavier and was wearing a don't-screw-with-me expression on his face. He looked as if he'd been out in the world for a while now and he didn't like what he'd found. He looked like the kind of person Bea Sanchez wouldn't let in her house.

'You wanted to talk about Freddy?' Terry said to me.

'I do.'

I tore off an edge of a piece of paper towel and pressed it down on the scratch, which was still bleeding.

'And why should I be doin' that?'

'Aren't you interested in what happened to your baby brother?'

Terry waved his hand impatiently. 'I been out of the house a long time now. I'm here because I want to know what's all this got to do with you.'

I lifted the piece of paper up. The bleeding had stopped.

'Your mom asked me to gather some information,' I told

Terry as I threw the bloody piece of paper in the trash. I didn't feel it was necessary to mention Jose right now.

'I knew it,' Terry said. 'It's got something to do with money, doesn't it?'

'It might,' I allowed.

'I bet she's going to sue someone. She's always suing someone.'

'She must not be very successful,' I observed.

'You mean because of where she's living?' Terry asked me. I nodded.

'She's cheap, that's all. She's got lots of property in the Dominican Republic. She payin you a lot?' Terry asked.

'She's not paying me anything,' I told him.

Terry snorted. 'You dumb to be doin' anything for her at all.'

'You're right. I think I am.'

'Anyway, the police know who did it,' Terry shot back.

'That's what they say,' I replied.

'And you don't believe 'em?' Terry asked.

I surveyed the customers to make sure everyone was all right before answering. 'Let's just say I subscribe to the dog-catcher theory,' I told Terry. 'I think it's always easier to take the poodle sunning herself in the front yard than go after a pit or a dobe running free. In other words, I think Jose could use a break.'

Terry broke into a smile. 'You the lady he's been talkin' about?'

'Probably.'

'He needs someone on his side. That's for sure.'

'Which is why I was hoping you could tell me a little bit about Freddy. I spoke to your mom, but she really doesn't seem to know much about your brother.'

'That's a laugh.' Terry snapped his fingers again. He didn't seem to be aware that he was doing it. 'But I don't know that much about him,' Terry said. 'You understand what I'm sayin'.'

I nodded. 'I think I do.'

'I was always my daddy's boy. Freddy was my mama's. So we didn't have much to say to each other.'

I offered to make Terry a cup of hot cocoa. He accepted and I reheated my water at the same time that I popped a glass filled with hot water in the microwave for him. When the machine beeped I took the glasses out and spooned two tablespoons of hot cocoa mix into each of them and stirred.

'Here.' I handed one of the glasses to Terry.

He took a sip and made a face. I'm guessing he'd burned his tongue.

'She was always putting Freddy in this thing and that. She never wanted him near me. Said I was a bad influence. Said I was street.' Terry took another, more cautious sip of his drink. 'Well, Freddy, he ended up street anyway. Maybe if she'd let him go some he woulda learned how to handle hisself out there and not be everyone's bitch.'

I took a sip of my cocoa, thought about lighting a cigarette, and decided against it. Ron walked up to the jukebox and put a dollar in the machine. The sound of Glen Campbell filled the room. Terry shook his head at Ron's selection. 'You should do something about the tunes in that thing,' Terry told me.

'It's not my decision to make,' I replied. 'It's Ian's.'

'Well then Ian should be doing something about it.' Terry looked around the bar. 'That way he'd be getting in a livelier crowd.'

'I don't think he wants a livelier crowd.'

I took another sip of my cocoa. It tasted like flavored water. I should have added another teaspoon of mix.

'Yeah,' Terry said. 'I can see his point. All those fights and everything.'

'Freddy was in here the night he died trying to sell stuff. He was totally cracked out.'

'Ain't my doing,' Terry said with a quickness that made me think his mother had told him that it had been.

'I'm not saying it was. I just wondered if you knew what started him off.'

Terry shook his head. 'Could have been anything. Ain't like the stuff ain't easy to come by around here.'

'Maybe a girl?'

Terry snorted. 'Freddy didn't have no girl. Leastwise none that I knew about.'

'Friends could have turned him on to it.'

'Freddy didn't have none of those neither. My moma,' Terry gave the word a sarcastic twist, 'wouldn't let him have none. No one good enough for her baby boy. If my daddy were around you can bet things wouldn't be happen' like they do.' Terry snapped his fingers three times. 'What you care what started him off, anyhow? It don't make no difference.'

'Maybe you're right,' I conceded.

'Damned fuckin' right I am.'

'You and Freddy get together a lot?'

'I already done told you we didn't.' Terry frowned. 'I'm a travelin' man,' he said. 'Goin' here, goin' there.' And he snapped his fingers for emphasis.

'So when did you see him?'

'I'd drop by when my mother was working.'

Meaning, I was willing to wager, that his mother wouldn't let him in the house. Sad. I took another sip of my hot cocoa and scanned the bar again. One of the guys from the group home lifted up his beer can and smiled at me. He was missing his two front teeth.

I got him another PBR and walked back to where Terry was sitting. 'Do you know where your brother got his dog?' I asked him.

Terry shrugged. 'Told me some guy gave it to him same as the laptop.'

Which was what Bea Sanchez had said Freddy told her, too.

'Was this the guy who was going to produce a CD for him and send him to Syracuse University?'

'It was all pipe dreams,' Terry said. 'You understand what I'm sayin'?'

'So you don't think there was a guy?'

Terry thought over his answer for a moment or so before replying. Then he said, 'Well, not like the way Freddy say it was.'

'How do you mean?'

208

'My mom signed Freddy up for one those mentor-things. You know where this guy takes you to baseball games and shit like that. Pretends to be your daddy. Like we don't got one. Freddy didn't want to go. Not at first and definitely not after the first meetin'. He said the guy was an ass-wipe.' Terry smiled. 'Freddy done tole me he said that to my moma's face. But she made him go anyway. That wouldn't have happened if my dad was around. I can tell you that.' Terry snapped his fingers again.

'I bet.'

Terry nodded emphatically and kept on nodding. 'You can take that to the bank.'

Suddenly it occurred to me as I looked at him that Terry was on something. Either that or he had a mild form of Tourette's Syndrome.

'So where do you think the dog and the laptop came from?' I asked him.

Terry looked around and lowered his voice, not that anyone could hear him. 'Freddy was mulin' some stuff. Maybe he decided to go into business for himself.'

'Any idea who the person he was working for was?'

'Don't have a clue,' Terry said.

Which I didn't believe. 'You think the person he was working for killed him?' I asked.

Terry took another sip of his cocoa and put it down. Then he wiped his upper lip with the back of his hand. 'Maybe.'

'But he got his laptop and his dog over six months ago,' I pointed out.

'So?'

'So this person he'd ripped off waited for six months to kill him?'

That made no sense at all.

Terry shrugged. 'Maybe he had to find him.'

I thought about Freddy the night he'd come in the bar. He'd been so cracked out he could barely talk. I didn't see him evading someone who was looking for him for half an hour let alone half a year. At this point I was pretty sure that Terry was just talking to hear himself talk.

'So Freddy never told you anything about what he was doing?' I asked Terry. If you ask the same question over and over I've learned that sometimes you get a different answer.

Terry snapped his fingers again. 'Mostly he talked about the future. About getting a degree and living in Florida or someplace like that.'

'He ever talk to your sister?'

Terry shook his head. His fingers went snap, snap, snap. 'They didn't like each other much. Not at all. They be fighting every chance they get.'

'Did Freddy talk to anyone?'

'Naw. He mostly stayed in his room listening to music on the Internet or playing that dumb-ass game of his.'

'Chess,' I said.

'He kept telling me that game was supposed to make him smarter, increase his concentration, shit like that. Well it sure didn't work with him.'

'No,' I agreed. 'It certainly didn't.'

Thirty-Three

It was one thirty in the morning. I was wiping down the bar and listening to the weather forecaster on TV telling me that tomorrow was going to be as crummy weather-wise as today had been. I reached for the remote and changed the channel to the Home Shopping Network. I didn't care what they were selling, but at least they weren't talking about collapsing roofs, wind chill factors on the minus side, and portending blizzards.

Shamus's had emptied out around twelve thirty. I'd called a cab for Hector around twelve and the cab driver and I had loaded him into the back seat. After the cab had taken off Ron and his friends had called it a night, followed by the guys from the group home. Terry had left as well, and everyone else had followed within ten minutes.

As soon as the last person was gone, I'd microwaved the chicken wings from yesterday that were in the fridge and sat down on the stool to eat them. Zsa Zsa had come out from her place in the back room and sat by my feet.

I'd picked some of the chicken meat off the wings and given it to her while I ate the rest off the bones. When I was a kid my grandmother used to feed chicken to our dog, bones and all, and the dog had been fine. Now of course that was a big no-no. People in this neighborhood probably still did it.

Zsa Zsa and I'd eaten all the wings that there were – fifteen of them. Then I'd gotten a paper towel off the roll and wiped the barbecue sauce off my hands and mouth and thrown the towel and the Styrofoam carton in the trash, after which I'd lit the last cigarette in the pack and sat down on the stool and smoked it. While I did I thought about what I'd learned from Terry – not much.

He and Freddy had a cruddy home life. What else was new? The conversation we'd had just confirmed what I already knew – that Freddy was a runner. Jose or the two kids I'd spoken to across the street from Freddy's house seemed the most likely prospects for Freddy to have worked for. But I couldn't see them killing Freddy or Tony. Of course, I'd been known to be wrong before. But still. I rubbed my eyes. I felt as if I had grit underneath my eyelashes. I needed to get some sleep in the worst possible way.

I tried to blow a smoke ring and failed. I was too tired to even do that. The question was . . . I tapped my fingers on the bar . . . the question was: Was there someone else Freddy was working for? Was it the man Freddy was talking about? Was this man even real? If he existed, he was probably the man Freddy had mentioned to his brother that he didn't like. How accurate was his brother anyway? It made no sense. Well, there was one way to find out. Talk to Bea Sanchez again. I exhaled and watched the smoke drift towards the ceiling. Now there was a conversation I didn't relish the thought of.

But I didn't want to think about that now. I was just too tired. I checked my watch. A half-hour before I could go home. I hoped Ian would come back soon so I could get out of here, because I couldn't leave before he came back. I didn't have a key.

I'd finished stacking the glasses and was wiping down the bar when I heard the outside door open. I looked up just as George came in. My heart sank. I couldn't think of anyone I'd rather not talk to.

'What do you want?' I asked him.

'I already told you. I want to talk to you.'

'And I already told you we have nothing to talk about.'

'Not true. Not true at all.'

George came up to where I was standing and leaned across the bar. He'd been drinking. I could smell the liquor on him. Ian kept a lacrosse stick in back of the bar for situations like these. Although I wasn't sure that would really help if George went nuts. George was a big guy and my aim was never good under the best of circumstances and the more upset I was the worse it got. Hitting George and hurting him would just piss him off more than he already was, which would be a bad thing. Hitting him and knocking him out wouldn't be good either. I really didn't want to explain what had happened to the cops. Or Ian. This was what you called a no-win situation.

'George, go back to Natalie's and sleep it off,' I told him. 'We'll talk tomorrow.'

He slammed his hand on the counter. 'I want a beer and we'll talk now.'

Great.

'I can't serve you, you know that. You're already drunk.'

'You'd better.'

'Don't make me call the cops,' I told him.

George leered. 'Go right ahead. I don't care. One of my buddies is going to answer anyway.'

'Fine. Then they'll take you home.'

'And write up your friend. New rules. Three citations and they close this shit-hole down.'

I'd forgotten about the city's new Certificate of Use ordinance. It was one of those well-intentioned but fundamentally stupid laws the Common Council had passed in the wake of a stabbing outside a bar on New Year's Eve.

Cops got called to a bar three times and it got closed down. First time the bar got a summons. The second time they got a fine. The third time they got their license yanked. On the surface it sounded good. Keeping order. Getting rid of the troublemakers. Blah. Blah. Blah. In reality the law set the scene for vendettas and payoffs. What does one of my lawyer friends always say? Something about hard cases made bad laws. What George was saying certainly bore out his theory.

'Leave the bar out of this,' I told him. 'It has nothing to do with anything, least of all you.'

'You're not leaving Natalie out of it,' George pointed out. 'So why should I leave the bar alone?'

By the bar I was pretty sure he meant Ian.

'Because it has nothing to do with anything.'

'If you weren't here I wouldn't have to be at Natalie's.'

What an incredible load of crap. I could feel my cheeks begin to flush. I was beginning to get really angry, even though I knew it would be way smarter to keep my temper and mouth in check. Which I didn't do.

'Hey bud,' I said instead. 'You're at Natalie's because you have a baby with her and you keep going over there. And just for the record, you were running over there and lying about it before I took this job. And as for why I'm here. Why I'm doing this? We've gone through that multiple times. I need the extra money to keep the store open.'

'And I've already told you that's a dumb reason.'

'Not to me.'

George pushed his face in mine. 'So you say.'

'I do. You don't own me. And you know what I think? I think you should marry Natalie. I think you two deserve each other.'

'I already told you, leave Natalie out of this.'

213

That seemed ridiculous considering she was what we were fighting about, but given the circumstances I acquiesced. I just wanted George out of here before Ian walked through the door.

'Fine. I'll leave Natalie out. Okay? Satisfied?'

George didn't say anything.

'Well?'

'It's not over,' George said. 'It's not over till I get back in the house.'

My cheeks got hotter. I was sure I had two dots of color on them by now.

'First of all,' I told him, 'it's not your house. It's my house. You moved in with me. Secondly, I'm tired of being treated the way I am by you. I'm tired of being cheated on. I'm tired of being lied to. Thirdly, odds are you're getting a job somewhere else so you're going to be moving anyway.'

'Nope,' George said.

'Nope what?'

'I'm going to be staying here. I just got a teaching job at Le Moyne.'

'Swell.'

George ran his hand over his head. 'You'll see. I'll do better.'

I should have said something like, 'Sure you will.' But I couldn't get those words out of my mouth. Instead I said to him, 'You won't do better. You always say that, but you don't. It's the same thing over and over and over and I'm tired of it. My friends are tired of hearing about it. If you don't want to pack your stuff up, I'll do it for you and leave it all in the garage.'

'Don't even think about touching my stuff,' George growled. Then he reached over, grabbed my wrist, and squeezed. I could feel lines of pain radiating up my arm.

'Stop it,' I said trying to pull away, which made him press down even harder. I took a deep breath and relaxed my arm. His grip relaxed too and I managed to pull away from him.

'Sorry,' he said.

I rubbed my arm. 'I don't feel anything for you anymore,

George. Nothing. I want you out. I can't make it any clearer then that. You have a baby and a girlfriend. Go take care of them. Stop being such an asshole. Don't make me get an order of protection against you.'

'Like that would matter,' George sneered.

'What would matter?'

George and I both whipped our heads around. Ian was standing by the door. Neither George nor I had heard him come in. Ian took a cigarette out of the front pocket of his denim jacket and lit it. He put his lighter back in his pocket and patted it.

'So this is George,' he said as he moved forward.

George turned to face him.

'Nice to meet you, George,' Ian said. 'My name is Ian. Ian Yates. I'm the owner of this place. We like to keep everything nice and friendly around here.'

'I don't care what the fuck you like,' George said. 'Or how you like to keep it.'

'Really.' Ian's expression remained the same. Polite. Interested. 'Can I call you a cab?' he asked George. 'You look a little under the weather for driving.'

'Fuck you,' George said.

Ian's eyebrows went up a fraction of an inch. 'I don't see the need for language like that in here.'

'Who gives a fuck?'

'The police might.' And Ian pointed to the security cameras mounted above the door and the one on the wall near the bathroom. 'Those two are running. If there's any more trouble I'll call the police, give them the tapes, and lodge a complaint against you. And if that doesn't work I'll go to the newspapers with the story. I'm sure your new employer will love that.'

'Those don't work,' George said.

'Are you sure?' Ian asked.

'Yes,' George replied, but he sounded less confident now.

I heard the jukebox turn over. Then Ian said, 'Why don't you walk your friend outside, Robin.'

It wasn't a suggestion; it was an order. I really didn't

want to, but I put on my jacket and started towards the door. I didn't expect George to follow me, but he did. Out of the corner of my eye I saw Ian had followed us out as well and was standing by the door watching what was going on.

George didn't say anything else. He didn't even look at me. Maybe the cold had sobered him up a little. At least I hoped it had. His vehicle was parked in front of the bar. He had to walk around the snow bank to get into it. Then he started it up and pulled away from the curb.

When the Explorer had turned the corner on to West Fayette I went back inside. Ian was waiting for me. He'd taken off his jacket, hung it on the bar gate, and was busy firing up another cigarette.

'Remember what I told you about no personal business in the bar?' he said.

'I was trying to get him out.'

'Try harder next time or I'm going to have to let you go. I can't have this kind of stuff going on in here.'

'I know.' I took my jacket off too, and draped it over one of the bar stools. Then I ran my fingers through my hair to try and detangle it. 'I think he blames you for what's happening between him and me.'

Ian shrugged. 'That's fairly standard. I'm always the bad one. Where's this Natalie live?'

'Over in Eastwood on Collingwood Street.'

'Where on Collingwood?'

I gave him the number. 'Why?' I asked.

'No particular reason.' Ian picked up the remote and turned the TV back to the news station. 'Information is always good to have.'

I looked at Ian, trying to read his face, but I couldn't. It was deadpan.

I indicated the wall. 'I didn't know those video cameras worked.'

Ian mouth turned up fractionally. 'They don't. I bought them off of a friend of mine for three bucks each. He got them in trade for a couple of metal beer signs that he got from me.

Nice friend you have,' he continued. His cigarette was still balanced on his lower lip.

'He's an ex-cop.'

'I remember. That's especially why I don't want anything starting with him in here.'

'It's just not fair,' I blurted out.

Ian didn't say anything to that and I was glad he didn't because it was such a stupid comment to make. It was the kind of thing a fifteen-year-old-kid would say. I rubbed my wrist. It was still hurting from George.

'I don't know what to do,' I said.

'You want him back?' Ian said.

'God, no.'

'You sure?'

'I couldn't be more sure.'

'Then if that's the case pack his stuff up and hire someone to take it to his girlfriend's house.'

'He'll go ballistic.'

'So he goes ballistic. Don't talk to him. He'll calm down eventually. It's just his ego talking.' Ian looked around the bar. 'At least he didn't break anything in here.'

'I'm sorry,' I told him.

Ian shrugged. 'Shit happens. You deal with it and move on.'

I wished that I could be as confident of that in respect to George as Ian was.

'What happens if George comes after me?' I asked him.

'He won't.'

'How do you know?'

'Because I do. Now tell me what happened here,' Ian waved his arm indicating Shamus's, 'while I was gone.'

That was Ian. The world could come to an end and he'd want to know how it affected his bar.

Thirty-Four

I was afraid George would be waiting at the house for me when Zsa Zsa and I got back there, but he wasn't. Maybe Ian was right I decided as I turned the key in the door. George was probably at Natalie's house sleeping it off. I almost felt sorry for her. Almost being the operative word. She had no idea what she was getting. George had been living with someone when he started going out with me. He cheated on me with a variety of women. When he moved into Natalie's he'd cheat on her as well. That was what he did. It had just taken a long time for me to realize that his actions had nothing to do with me and that there was nothing I could do to fix them.

I could hear James meowing as I stepped into my hallway. He came running up to me and proceeded to rub against my ankles as Zsa Zsa sniffed at him then went into the kitchen to check out her food dish.

'Poor James,' I crooned as I dumped my backpack on the hall table and squatted down to pet him. 'I've been neglecting you.' He moved the side of his head back and forth against my calves. I took the tips of his ears in my fingers and rubbed them very gently. He began to purr. This went on for fifteen minutes. Then he walked away. I straightened up and went into the kitchen.

I put some more dried food in James's dish and refilled the water dishes for both James and Zsa Zsa. Next I checked my messages. There were two. One was a hang up, probably one of those computerized calls, the other from Calli asking how things had gone with George.

Well, it was too late to call her now. I'd ring her up in the morning. Maybe she'd have some information for me then about the Spindle, not that I really needed any more now. Between my visit there and Ian I'd pretty much found out what I needed to know. I poured a shot of Black Label into a water glass and drank it down. It didn't do much to help the way I was feeling. The second shot didn't either.

I carried the glass and the bottle upstairs. James and Zsa Zsa followed me. My own little retinue. They watched me from the bed as I got undressed, but even as I was doing it I knew I wouldn't be able to fall asleep. Not tonight. I was too pumped up from my scene with George. I poured myself another drink and took a sip.

I put the bottle and glass on the night table and went over to the chest of drawers that contained George's clothes and pulled the top drawer out. For a moment I stared at the contents. Everything was folded with care. That was one thing you could say about George: he was neat.

I went down to the basement and got some cartons and some garbage bags and brought them upstairs. Zsa Zsa and James sat and watched me as I spent the next three hours packing up everything of George's that I could find. I cleared out the dresser and his half of the closet. I packed up his desk and his jackets in the hall closet.

He had lots of stuff, but I got it all. When I was done I dragged the cartons and bags and suitcases out to the garage. I'd call a trucker in the morning, call Natalie to tell her George's stuff was on its way, and hopefully have it delivered to her house by tomorrow evening. Or rather today. Since it was now five o'clock in the morning. I could see the sky beginning to lighten a little in the east. A minute later I heard the rumble of the delivery man's car coming by as he dropped off the morning paper to the home subscribers.

I could go to bed now, but it seemed silly to. It would make it harder to get up when I had to. Sometimes it's just easier to push through. I ran a bath instead, took the book I was reading, and got in it. The water was steamy and I could feel my muscles starting to relax. Suddenly my eyes started to feel heavy. I could feel my grip on my book loosening. I jerked myself awake and rested the book on the edge of the tub. Just five minutes, I told myself. I'd just take a five-minute nap. When I woke up the water was cold and my skin was shriveled.

I toweled myself off, and put on one of my two decent pairs of black pants and a red turtleneck cashmere sweater. Then I did my hair and put on some make-up and went downstairs to the kitchen to make myself breakfast. As I was sharing my scrambled eggs and toast with Zsa Zsa and James, I realized I felt better than I thought I would. Much better.

Manuel came into the store around eleven. I'd spent the time before he'd come in trying to arrange for someone to come and pick up George's things, but so far I hadn't had any luck. It was a busy time of year.

'You want me to call some of my buddies up?' Manuel asked me when I told him what I was doing.

I patted him on the shoulder. 'If I can't get anyone I may take you up on that.'

Manuel nodded. 'I'm glad he's out of your life.'

'You never liked him.'

'Could be 'cause he's an asshole,' Manuel said.

'I guess even you're right once in a while,' I conceded before I sent him off to feed Matilda.

I made a couple more phone calls. Then I left Manuel and Zsa Zsa at the store and took off to do some errands and make some deliveries. There are approximately ten elderly people that I deliver dog food, parrot feed, and kitty litter to on a weekly and bi-weekly basis. The arrangement works well for both sides. I get the business and they get the supplies and someone to talk to. Today, though, the whole thing put me in a bad mood. It wasn't just because I was tired, either. It was because I couldn't help thinking that I was going to be alone like these people were when I got older. But then I thought that if I continued to smoke the way I was this probably wouldn't be a problem and I cheered up.

I had just finished my fourth delivery, to a seventy-nine-year-old woman who had five cats and a pug, when I felt a hand on my arm. I spun around. Shelley was standing there, wearing her oversized tweed coat. She had a bright blue woolen scarf wrapped around her head three times.

'I want you to come to my house,' she told me.

What else could I say except yes? After all, I'd promised her last night I'd go over – mostly because I was positive she wouldn't remember – and here she was. Karma strikes again.

'Just for a minute,' I told her.

Shelley nodded eagerly.

I noticed she was clutching a Burger King bag. I pointed to it. 'Did you have breakfast there?'

Shelley looked confused. 'Where?'

'Burger King.'

She nodded, but I could tell she was doing it out of politeness. I don't think she remembered.

'How'd you get home?'

'I walked.'

The nearest Burger King was a little over two miles away.

'I got tired of sitting there,' Shelley added. She smiled. 'Someone started yelling at me and I left.'

'That wasn't nice of them,' I observed.

Shelley formed her chapped lips into a pout. 'No it wasn't, was it?'

'What do you have in the bag?'

She opened it up and peered in. 'Fries. Want one?'

'That's okay. Where's Bill?'

Shelley waved her hand in the general direction of the street. 'Out.'

'Do you know where?'

She shook her head.

According to Ian, Bill had told him that either he or his sister watched Shelley. Well they sure as hell weren't watching her now. I took my cell out of my backpack and called up Ian as I followed her down the street. I'd dropped back behind her because I didn't want her to hear me talking about her. But even if she had heard I'm not sure she would have cared.

'Do you know where Bill is?' I asked him.

'He said something about fixing Hector's sink today. Why?'

'Because I'm with Shelley.'

'She'll be fine,' Ian said after I explained how I'd met her.

'How will she be fine when she can't remember what happened twenty minutes ago?'

'Listen, they've been doing this for years now. Shelley's still around.'

'That doesn't make it right.'

'It isn't your business.'

'It is when I run into her. Does Hector have a phone?'

'No.'

'Where does he live?'

'At the moment he's living with some cousin on the north side.'

'You wouldn't happen to know where, would you?'

'Nope. Not a clue. You want me to have Bill call you when he shows up?' Ian asked me. For some reason I pictured him lighting a cigarette.

'Please do.'

'Later,' Ian said and hung up.

'This is it,' Shelley told me as I put my cell away. 'This is my house,' she said with a great deal of pride.

The place looked as if no one had done anything to it for a long time. The word dilapidated came to mind. So did the word hovel.

'Come.' Shelley beckoned for me to follow her.

I carefully stepped over the rotted wood on the steps and the porch and went inside. There was a leak on the far side of the wall. Plaster had fallen down and the wood lathing was exposed. Bales of newspapers were piled along the hallway walls.

'Helps keep the heat in,' Shelley explained as she stepped around a puddle.

I did likewise and followed her into what had once been a living room. Bales of paper were stacked along the walls. Some of the bales had gotten sodden and were now wavy and discolored. The couch had lost one of its legs and was listing over to one side, while the top of the piano sitting over by the window was delaminating.

222

Shelley went over and pressed down a key. No sound came out.

'I keep telling Bill to have it fixed,' she told me. 'But he just won't.'

I didn't say anything. We moved through the living room and went by what I presumed to be a bedroom. A sheet printed with Spider Man figures had been tacked on to the window frame in place of blinds. Shelley pointed to it.

'That was my son's,' she told me proudly. 'I got it for him when he was six.'

'How nice,' I said mechanically as I looked around.

The bedroom smelled of the mildewed clothes that were piled everywhere except on the mattress on the floor, which was where I assumed Bill and Shelley slept. The kitchen wasn't much better in the housekeeping department. The table and the kitchen countertops were covered with Chinese take-out containers full of half-eaten food and empty cans of PBR. If it had been summer the place would have been crawling with flies. For once I was glad it was as cold as it was.

'Bill keeps on telling me he's going to take out the garbage but he always forgets,' Shelley said looking around. 'I'm thinking of kicking him out. I mean he should do something, right? Especially since he's living here for free.'

'Absolutely,' I agreed, humoring her. 'Now, what was it you wanted to show me?' I asked her, realizing as I did that she'd probably already forgotten.

'Oh. Was there something I had to get you?'

'No. No.' I assured her.

'There was, wasn't there?'

Shelley slapped her forehead with the flat of her hand. Her face assumed a panicked expression. 'I'm such a moron.'

'I'm the one that has it wrong,' I said, trying to soothe her.

Shelley's eyes misted over. 'It's me.' Two seconds later she straightened up. She smiled. 'I was going to give you a tea set,' she told me, and she bounded out of the room into the back hallway.

'Shelley, where are you going?' I called after her.

I could hear things being moved about.

'Do you need any help?' I asked.

'No. Stay where you are,' she yelled. 'There's no room out here.'

It was probably better that I didn't see what was out there, I reflected, as I lit a cigarette. I flicked the match into the sink – it would be really easy to start a fire here; this place was a fire inspector's nightmare – and cleared off one of the chairs that was stacked high with mail and old newspapers so I could sit down.

As I did I caught sight of a letter addressed to Shelley. It was from Enterprise Industries. I was scanning it as she walked back through the door.

'See what Bill is doing to me,' she told me. And she waved a plastic bird in my face. 'He's trying to drive me crazy, so he can have my house. He knows I have a thing about birds. I want you to do something about it for me.'

'Shelley,' I said, taking the bird out of her hand, 'have you seen this?'

And I showed her the letter I was holding, although even if she had she obviously wouldn't remember its contents.

'That's from the head of the symphony,' she told me.

'May I take it?' I asked her.

'You're going to do something about the bird, right?' she replied. 'You're going to go to the police with it, right?'

'Right,' I said.

'Good.' Shelley clapped her hands. 'Then they're going to put Bill in jail. He deserves it. Trying to sell my house.'

I said goodbye and went downstairs. I needed to think. I remembered there was a coffee shop two blocks down. I reclaimed my car, drove over there, and parked a little ways away. Mama Gege's was empty. I sat in one of the booths, ordered a coffee and some toast from the waitress, and tried to decide what to do about Shelley. The smart thing would have been to call the cops and dump the whole mess in their hands. I know that's what Calli would advise and she'd be right, but before I did that I wanted some more information.

The name and address of Shelley's son, Egon Jefferies, was listed on the bottom of the Enterprise Industries letter. I noted that he lived in an expensive Maryland suburb. He'd obviously

224

done a lot better for himself than his mother, I couldn't help thinking.

I called up information and got his number. Since it was a weekday he was probably at work, but I was hoping someone would be home. I lucked out and got his housekeeper, Hispanic from her accent. When I told her why I was calling she gave me Egon Jefferies' work number.

I took a bite of toast while I dialed. I got put on hold. Two sips of coffee later, the receptionist came on. She sounded as if the place was very high-end.

'Doreset and Barber. To whom do you wish to speak?'

I told her.

'May I tell him what this is about?' she inquired.

'His mother,' I said.

'Just a moment, please.'

I'd finished my toast by the time she got back to me.

'Mr. Jefferies will be with you momentarily,' she informed me as I wiped my mouth with a napkin.

I signaled the waitress for some more coffee while I reread the letter in front of me. It informed Shelley that, pursuant to the agreement with her son, her house had been sold, and she would need to vacate it by March 1st. I smoothed the letter down with the edge of my thumb. Crazy as Shelley was it looked as if her fears had been correct, even if her facts hadn't been. Odd how that goes.

'Yes,' Egon Jefferies said. He sounded impatient.

I introduced myself.

'I'm sorry but we're going to have to make this short. I have a conference call with Chicago scheduled in fifteen minutes.'

I explained about his mother. 'I don't know what you want me to do,' I told him. 'I feel funny leaving her by herself, and I can't locate Bill.'

I heard an impatient snort at the end of the line. 'I pay that man to look after her.'

'Well he's not doing a very good job.'

'She should be in a home anyway.'

'So what do you want me to do?'

'Call the police. Let social services handle it. That's what we're paying tax dollars for.'

'But the house—'

He cut me off. 'I know.'

'She's not quite—'

'Believe me, I know what she is,' her son snapped. 'The whole family does. She's been like this for years and years. Ever since she hit her head. I really don't have time for this,' he said and hung up.

Nice kid, I thought.

I lit a cigarette and went back to trying to decide what to do. Basically there were two choices: call the cops, in which case Shelley would probably be put in some sort of facility, or let it go. In the end I took Ian's advice and let it go. Shelley had been getting along so far. Let her enjoy the time she had left. I had an idea that when they tore her house down it would send her right over the edge.

Thirty-Five

P oor Shelley, I thought as I put up the hood of my parka. But then I thought, no. Maybe not. She had her Bill and her PBRs and when that got boring she had Carmen to fight with, and perhaps that was enough for her, that was all she needed.

I crossed the street, got into the Taurus, and cranked the heat up as high as it would go – which wasn't high enough. I rubbed my hands together to get my circulation going after which I dug my cell out of my jacket pocket and called Ian for the second time in an hour and asked him if Bill had shown up yet.

'He just walked in the door,' Ian said.

'Can I speak to him?'

'I'll ask him.'

'Just put him on.'

I heard Ian say, 'You want to speak to her?'

I heard some murmurings and a moment later Bill was on the phone.

'You found Shelley?' he said.

'She was on the street. She was walking home from Burger King.'

'Normally I drop her at my sister's while I work but she had to go to the doctor's. And Shelley likes it at Burger King. She likes watching the kids,' Bill added.

I thought of the Spider Man sheet Shelley was using as a window blind. Why did I think that her son didn't have treasured belongings of hers hanging in his house?

'Be that as it may,' I told Bill, 'you get money for watching her and that's what you should be doing.'

'I see you've been talking to her son, the little prick, selling the house like that. Didn't consult with me or nuthin',' Bill raged. 'Just get the letter in the mail. When I call him and try and talk to him he tells me he don't got to talk to me. Those people coming around. Me having to lie to Shelley and keep her calm. Having to pretend nothing is happening.' I heard a thump. I knew that would be Bill slamming his palm down on the counter. 'She knows, though. Somehow she knows. '

I agreed with him. 'Yes, she does.'

'Her son thinks she's stupid. But she sees lots of things. She just don't process them like you and me. He wants to stick her in some home. That's a horrible thing to do to a person, especially your own mother. With his money he could afford to get her a new house, not sell the one that she's living in out from under her. Just because he has that power of attorney thing don't give him the right to do what he's doing.'

'Unfortunately it does,' I told Bill.

'Well I'm going to go to court and fight it.'

There was another thump. Bill hitting the bar again.

'You do that,' I told him. 'But in the meantime you'd better improve on your performance regarding watching her or I'm going to call social services and they're going to take her away and then you're not going to get any money at all.'

'Hey,' Bill squawked.

'Don't hey me,' I shot back. 'She could freeze to death outside. What if she can't remember how to get home?'

'She always does. She's like some damn homing pigeon.'

I wasn't so sure about that, but there was one thing I was sure about. 'At least clean up the place,' I told him. 'It's disgusting.'

'You should try doing what I do,' Bill protested. 'And see how much energy you have left at the end of the day. See how you like it.'

'I wouldn't, but then I haven't taken on that responsibility.' And I clicked off.

I lit another cigarette and got out the letter I'd taken off of the chair in Shelley's kitchen and reread it. By now the heater was blowing out warm air. I could feel the blood returning to my fingers. As I clenched and unclenched my fists I thought about what I knew about Enterprise Industries.

There had been an article about them recently in the local paper, but I didn't remember what it said. I was going to call Calli and see if she could look it up for me when Manuel rang. The moment I heard his voice I knew he was calling me about George. And I was right. Evidently Manuel was now the middleman in the message department, which suited me just fine.

'George said to tell you he's coming to get his stuff out of the garage tonight.'

'Good.' Because I hadn't been able to get a mover.

'He also said to tell you to call your guard dog off.'

'Excuse me?'

'Hey, I'm just repeating what he said.' And Manuel clicked off.

I rested my head against the back of the seat and tapped my teeth with the phone. Ian had been very certain that George wasn't going to bother me. Extremely certain. I punched in his number.

'Did you talk to George?' I asked him when he came on.

'Why?'

'Because I just got a message from him about my calling off my guard dog. Would that be you?'

There was a short pause. Then Ian said, 'We ran into each other and we exchanged pleasantries.'

'What did you say?'

'I didn't say anything.'

'Okay. What did you do?'

'George was interested in pressure points and I just shared my expertise with him. He was impressed.'

'I bet he was.'

'And Robin.'

'Yes?'

'Try to keep your personal business out of the bar in the future.'

'You already told me that.'

'Well, I'm telling you that again.' And he hung up.

Interesting. Very interesting. If you'd asked me I wouldn't have thought Ian would have done something like that, but then I wouldn't have thought that George would have acted the way he had, either. I'd have to think about that – but not now. Now I had to call Calli. When I explained what I needed, she transferred me to Patricia Benton, the reporter who covered the real estate beat for the paper. Patricia explained how I could find out what I wanted to know. Turned out it was going to be simpler than I'd thought it would be. It's nice that something about this was simple.

After she hung up I drove back to the store. On the way over I stopped at Dunkin' Donuts and got a coffee with cream and sugar and four strawberry glazed donuts. I'd finished two by the time I got to Noah's Ark.

Zsa Zsa came running up to greet me when I walked in the door. I wiped a small spot of tomato sauce off her nose, petted her, and walked up to the counter.

'We had five sales while you were gone,' Manuel said. 'One of them was for almost three hundred dollars. A woman who lives down the block from you came in and bought a pair of lovebirds, the cage, and everything else.'

That had to be Rosalie Parks. She'd said she was going to buy them as a present for her fifteen-year-old daughter, but lots of people say things like that and don't follow through. I'd have to call her up this evening and thank her and see if everything was going okay.

'Here. These are for you and Bethany,' I told Manuel as I handed him the bag with the donuts in it.

He pushed a pizza box towards me. 'There are a couple of slices left if you want one.'

'Maybe later.'

Zsa Zsa trailed behind me as I went into my office. I gave her a basted beef rawhide bone and she settled down on her bed with it. I could hear her gnawing on it as I plugged my cell into my adapter to recharge it. Then I logged on to my computer. It used to be in the not too distant past you had to go down to the county courthouse to get records of who owned what, but not anymore. Now you could do most of the research you needed to online.

The first thing I did after I got onto ongov.net was look up the owners of the properties that Freddy Sanchez and Tony Shepard had been found in. Both of them came back as Enterprise Industries. That was three abandoned buildings that these people owned in a two-block radius of each other. Then, just for kicks I typed in the address of the building Jose had been staying in. Enterprise Industries owned that, too. I called Patricia back.

'Quick question,' I said.

'Calli told me you were a pain in the ass.' But Patricia laughed when she said it, which I took as a good sign. 'What do you want to know?'

'Why would a company be acquiring abandoned properties on the west side?'

Patricia told me to wait a second. 'Sorry about that,' she said when she got on line again. 'I can think of several reasons offhand.'

'Yes?' I doodled an 'E' and an 'I' and drew a circle around them.

'The most likely one would a Housing Improvement Grant. That's federal money,' Patricia said. 'Receiving the funds

230

hinges on the developer acquiring so many units that they can turn into apartments.'

'Units as in houses?' I asked.

'Exactly. For example, you can convert a house into three, possibly four apartments depending on the size.'

I doodled a question mark on the side of today's morning paper.

'I'm sorry but I don't get it.'

'Okay. How can I explain this?' Patricia stopped for a moment while she thought. Then she said, 'Let's say you, the developer, decide to go after this grant. So you'll go down to . . . oh . . . Ash Street and count the number of vacant houses there, houses that you can turn into apartments.'

'Okay.'

'Now if there aren't enough of them, because you need a certain number within a certain geographical radius to qualify for this grant, you go to the city and get them to cite the hell out of some of the more rundown houses. The houses they pick are usually eyesores that are lowering the value of the neighborhood or are known crack houses. That sort of thing. Thus no one feels too badly when the owners of the houses lose them, because they usually can't afford to make the called-for improvements.

'At that point you, the developer, pick these houses up for pretty much nothing and then go apply to the federal government to fix them up, after which you rent them out. Now you're collecting money on twenty apartments instead of five houses. See how it works?'

'So everyone's happy except for the people that lose their houses,' I said.

'You got it,' Patricia replied.

I doodled a dollar sign. 'Any other reasons for acquiring property on the west side that you can think of?'

'Well there was a rumor about a new strip mall going up on that side of town. And of course there was all that talk a while ago about putting a sewage-treatment facility on the west side. Lots and lots of talk, but most of it doesn't come to anything.'

'What have you heard about Enterprise Industries?'

'Not too much,' Patricia said. 'They've recently started

operating on the west side. Before that they were into bars and video stores. Actually, I think they still are, although I've heard that they're trying to sell those off.'

'Anything else?' I asked.

'They're supposed to be big on giving back to the community,' Patricia continued. 'They donate money to fund after-school activities, that kind of thing.'

'But you don't sound convinced.'

'It's not that.'

'Then what is it?'

'Most of these kind of donations are more about appearing to do good then about actually doing good.'

'That's a rather cynical view of things.'

Patricia laughed. 'Believe me, if you're in this job for a while that's the way you become.'

I thanked her and hung up. Then I turned back to my computer and Googled Enterprise Industries. Lots of information, some of which was even relevant to me. I looked at my watch. It was a little before six. If I was lucky Bea Sanchez would be home by now. I wanted to catch her before she went out again. I had an idea I wanted to check out.

But before I left I made two phone calls. Hopefully the people I called would get back to me with what I needed in a timely manner.

Thirty-Six

It turned out I was lucky. Bea Sanchez was home. But she wasn't happy to see me. At least that was the impression I got from the furrow on her brow and her downturned mouth when she answered the door and saw me standing there. Her tone didn't disabuse me of my notion.

232

'What do you want?' she snapped.

Nice welcome.

I put on my best customer smile and said, 'Can I come in for a minute? I need to clear something up.'

Bea Sanchez consulted her watch.

'Please,' I said.

'One minute. No more,' she told me grudgingly. 'I have a meeting to go to.'

'I know. SNAC. I saw the announcement in the paper.'

She stepped aside so I could enter. I kept my coat on. I wasn't planning on staying long.

'Where's True?' I asked.

'In his crate. By the way,' she told me, 'next week my lawyer is filing papers on the city for intent to sue for defamation of character of my son's name.' And she named someone I'd seen on television promising 'to get you every penny coming to you' as her attorney.

'That's what Terry said you'd do,' I told her.

She frowned. 'When did you speak to him?'

'Last night.' And I started down the hall.

'Where are you going?' she squawked, following behind me. 'I told you I have to leave.'

I kept going. 'I'm sorry. I need a drink of water.' By now I was at the kitchen sink. Bea didn't know what to do. I'd been counting on that. I pointed to one of the mugs I'd seen in the sink the last time I'd been here. Now it was on the counter. 'Enterprise Industries, right?' I asked.

That was me. Miss Sweetness and Light. Bea Sanchez looked confused.

'I recognized the logo,' I explained as I picked up the mug and turned on the tap. 'I've been reading about them in the newspaper. They're a good company, aren't they?' I added as I filled the mug up and took a sip.

Bea didn't say anything. I chattered on.

'My friend on the north side is interested in doing something with them. They're offering to do some sort of after-school activity program.'

'Mentoring,' Bea said.

233

I nodded. 'Is it a good program?' I asked. 'Terry said Freddy didn't like it much.'

Bea scowled at the mention of her older son's name. 'Terry says lots of things that aren't true. He likes to make trouble for me.'

'So, he liked it when he started?'

Bea hesitated for a moment. Then she said, 'It took him a while.'

I took a sip of water and put the mug down. 'He was in it for a year,' I guessed. That was around the time Freddy had started using crack.

Bea nodded. The lines around her mouth softened. 'Mitch said he needed a good role model and he was trying to provide it for him, to teach him some discipline. He certainly wasn't going to get one from his dad or his brother.'

'Mitch?'

'Mitch O'Meara. He's the president of the company. You saw him.'

'I did?' O'Meara. As in Constance O'Meara's husband?

'He was at the SNAC meeting you attended.'

I was about to tell her I hadn't seen him but I realized Bea was right. I'd caught a glimpse of him before I'd had to leave.

I tried to summon up a memory of him, but I couldn't. All I remembered was that he was a moderately big guy and that he was wearing a trench coat. But I did remember other things. I remembered that he'd been the man Bea had rushed up to greet at the meeting. He'd been the one she'd been so impatiently waiting for. I remembered the look on her face when he'd walked into the room. At the time I recalled thinking that she was just pleased to have someone like that at her meeting, but now, studying the expression on her face, I wondered if there was something more involved.

'The president mentoring your son, wow. How nice that he takes time out to do something like that. He must be a very busy man.'

'Yes, he is,' Bea agreed. She began fingering the small diamond drop hanging from her neck. 'But he believes in giving back to the community. He believes in helping people out.'

'That's so rare these days. Freddy was really lucky to have a man like that in his life.'

Bea colored slightly. And that's when I was certain about Mitch O'Meara and Bea Sanchez.

'You two are an item, aren't you?' I said.

Bea froze.

'I don't care.' I pointed to the diamond drop. 'Nice present.'

Bea's face got even redder. Her eyes widened fractionally. She swallowed. Then she pointed to the street. 'Get out of my house.'

'Fine.' And I left. There was no reason to stay. I'd found out what I needed to know. I heard a loud thud as the door slammed behind me. That seemed to be happening to me a lot lately.

Mitch O'Meara. Things started clicking. Something told me he was the man that Freddy was making up stories about. Who else could it be? And really it made sense if you thought about it. So did Freddy's behavior, especially if he knew about his mother's relationship with Mitch. He must have been incredibly conflicted. Here was someone who was being nice to him, but accepting that meant rejecting his father. So he'd rejected Mitch in the real world, but made him out to be his savior in his fantasy life.

Was that conflict the thing that started him using crack? Some adolescents are so fragile. Freddy's mother had had such high expectations of him. But to meet them meant he'd be betraying his father and older brother. And then in his eyes his mother had betrayed him by going out with another man. Maybe that would be enough. Especially if you could go down to the corner and get crack as easily as you could buy a pack of smokes. And it was cheaper too.

As I was walking down Bea Sanchez's porch steps my cell rang. It was Ian.

'He'll talk to you,' he said.

'Great.'

Ian had been one of the calls I'd made before I'd left Noah's

235

Ark. I'd asked him to get in touch with his friend who DJ'd at the Spindle and see if he would speak with me.

'But Paul's only doing it because I told him you'd give him the money I owed him,' Ian continued.

Which, something told me, I wasn't going to be getting back. 'Which is what? Twenty?'

'More like a C-note.'

'A hundred bucks? What are you, nuts? Come on Ian. You know I don't have that kind of cash.'

'Yes you do.'

'Why are you saying that?' I asked him, wondering how he could possibly know about the thousand dollars I'd taken from the guy outside the Spindle. I mean Ian knew lots of stuff, but he wasn't psychic.

'I'm saying that because Ray told me you were talking to him about getting the doors on your car fixed. And you agreed upon one hundred bucks and one hundred in trade. Ergo you have an extra C-note on you.'

'I need to get those doors fixed. They freeze shut from the inside. I can't get out until the car warms up.'

'Use some of the anti-freeze stuff.'

'I've already tried it. It doesn't work.'

'Then get on your cell and call one of your friends. They'll come and let you out.'

'Very funny.'

'I'm not being funny.'

'Hey. I'm doing you a favor, remember?'

Ian chuckled. 'And I'm doing you one.'

'No. You're not.'

'So are you going to take it or leave it?' he asked, totally not responding to my statement.

'Don't you care about what happens to Jose? Don't you care that he might not have committed the murders the cops are after him for?'

'Of course I care,' Ian said. 'He owes me money. If he's in jail he can't pay up. And even worse his pregnant wife will start calling me up and asking me to help her out.'

'You're . . .'

'Satanic,' Ian said.

'You're giving yourself too much credit. I was going to say cheap.'

'How about broke.'

'So am I.'

'Paul's waiting on me. What do you want me to tell him?'

I thought it over. I needed to speak to Paul and I was positive that he wouldn't speak to me without Ian's okay. It looked as if a C-note was the price of admission to this particular game.

'You're on,' I told Ian.

'Good. He'll be at Murphy's Ale House waiting for you.'

'How will I recognize him?'

'He'll be the really, really white guy.'

Thirty-Seven

When I got to Murphy's I saw what Ian had meant. Paul looked as if he hadn't been outside in the sun in the last eighteen of his twenty-five years. Either that or he was doing a stand-in for Count Dracula. His skin was parchment white and his eyes were rimmed with red along the lower lids. He had on a Yankee baseball cap, an expensive looking black leather jacket, and jeans.

The bar was almost empty. Paul was perched on a stool by one of the tables by the window studying the view while he sipped a beer and ate a roast beef sandwich. I got the same thing he was having and joined him. He took a bite of his sandwich and nodded at me.

'Robin?' he asked.

'That would be me.'

'Ian said you have something for me.'

'I do.' I lifted up my backpack. 'In here.'

He took a sip of his beer and looked me over. 'Fine,' he said. 'What do you want to know?'

'I want to know what happened with Freddy Sanchez at the Spindle.'

'Not a lot.'

'Then why did the bouncer act the way he did and throw me out?'

Paul took another sip of his beer and shrugged. 'He's got emotional problems. Maybe he had his period when you were talking to him.'

'They have pills for that now.'

'He takes them,' Paul said. 'Far too many of them.'

I could see this was going to take a little time. I tried to get the conversation back on track. 'Was Freddy dealing drugs?'

'Nothing major. The occasional pill of E or Percodet. Nothing large.'

'Then what?'

Paul took another bite of his sandwich, chewed, and swallowed. I did likewise. I'd forgotten how much I liked Murphy's roast beef.

'Crummy day,' Paul observed.

'Crummy month,' I replied. I settled into my seat. If Paul wanted to chat for a while it was okay by me. 'How long have you been working at the Spindle?'

'Too long.'

'Were you there for the stabbings?'

'I was working that night.' Paul shook his head. 'It never should have happened. Too many people. Too little security. They lost control.' He resettled his cap on his head. 'I should have got out of the business then.'

'Why didn't you?'

'Female reasons. She was an expensive habit. But I'm getting out now. Too much bad blood in there.' Paul took another sip of his beer. 'I'm going to be doing a whole new thing. Goodbye, Syracuse, hello, Philly. My cousin is opening up an Electronics Boutique down there and I'm going to help him run it. In fact,' he gestured to the floor with his chin. I looked under the seat and saw a duffel bag under his chair, 'I'm takin' the bus there tonight.'

'Congratulations.'

He cracked a smile and went back to working his way through his sandwich.

'About Freddy,' he said once he'd demolished it. 'The kid was a real pain in the ass.' He wiped his mouth with his napkin, crumpled it up, and threw it on the plate. 'He started coming around and hittin' on people.'

'You just said he wasn't selling drugs.'

'It was more like he was selling hisself in the men's room.' Paul leaned forward. 'You get my meaning.'

'Yes, I do.' I remembered his brother and the kids across the street calling Freddy a fag because he played chess. I thought that had been ignorance talking, but maybe they hadn't been so ignorant after all. Maybe they knew what was happening but didn't want to say it straight up. Didn't want to say what I should have known: that crack heads do anything they can for money.

Paul took another sip of his beer. 'The landlord found out. He got really mad and told my boss he wasn't having that kind of thing going on in his place and that he'd better take care of it. So my boss told Freddy he couldn't come in there no more. But Freddy did anyway. Got the Big B' – Paul saw my look and explained – 'the bouncer – that's what he likes to call himself – in a shit load of trouble.

'The boss told the Big B that he didn't want to see Freddy's sorry skinny ass in there no more and if he did he was going to cut the Big B a new asshole. Told the Big B not to talk about Freddy and what he was doin', either. Said he didn't want his business being known as a place where things like that happened. Said it would drive all his customers away.' A smile crept across Paul's face. 'Man, he was pissed.'

Which I guess explained why the bouncer had reacted to my questions the way he had. Ian had gotten it right. I retrieved my cigarettes out of my backpack, realized that I couldn't smoke in here, and put them away.

'Did Freddy have a driver's license?' I mused.

'Wouldn't know,' Paul said.

I studied him. He was staring out the window again. I noticed one of his eyes was tearing.

'I was wondering if someone drove him out here? It's a haul out to Liverpool by bus,' I said.

'Yeah. It is,' Paul agreed. 'But I think that's how he got out there.'

'Then how did he get home?'

Paul continued looking out the window. 'Wouldn't know. He must have got a ride or called a taxi. Something like that.'

I wondered what Paul was staring at. There was nothing but the dark, the wall of a building across the street, some parked cars, and the occasional pedestrian scurrying along.

'And that's it? There isn't any more?' I asked Paul.

'If there was I didn't hear about it.' Paul held out his hand palm upward.

'Guess you're trying to tell me something,' I said to him.

He didn't smile.

I got my wallet out of my backpack, counted out five twenties and gave them to him. He recounted them, folded the money up, and slipped it into his pants pocket. Then he stood up, touched his hand to his forehead in a salute, and said, 'Tell Ian thanks.'

'Will do.'

I wished Paul luck. He nodded and headed for the door. I stayed to finish my beer then I left, too. As I was walking to my car my cell phone rang. It was a response to the second call I'd put through before I left the shop.

Thirty-Eight

After I hung up I sat in my car for a moment and thought about what I'd just found out and what it suggested. I should have asked the Labradoodle breeder I'd contacted how many dogs she'd sold in the area when I'd originally spoken to her. But I hadn't. Instead I'd asked her whom she'd sold them to. Which was different. I'd made the assumption she'd sold one dog to each person. But she hadn't. She'd sold two dogs to Mitch O'Meara and one dog to the guy out in Manlius.

The O'Meara family had one. I was willing to bet that True was the other pup. According to the breeder, Mitch O'Meara hadn't bought the puppies at the same time. And they'd been from different litters. Which is why I hadn't made the connection between the two dogs. Since the breed doesn't run true, puppies from the same litter don't have to have the same appearance, much less puppies from different litters.

And if Mitch had bought Freddy the dog, I was willing to bet he'd gotten him the laptop as well. Why would he do that? Because he felt sorry for the kid? Because he was wealthy enough so that spending five thousand dollars on presents for a hood rat wasn't a big deal? Because he was trying to look like a big man for the mother? Hell, she would have been satisfied if he'd taken Freddy to a Syracuse Crunch or a Chiefs game.

Someone else might have left the question alone. But I couldn't. It wasn't in my nature, as the tagline to the old joke about the scorpion crossing the river goes. The scorpion asks a beaver to take him across the river and the beaver says, 'No. You'll sting me.' The scorpion convinces him that he won't and so they start across the river. In the middle of the river the scorpion stings the beaver. As they both drown, the beaver looks at the scorpion and says, 'Why? Now, we're both going to die.' And the scorpion replies, 'Because it's my nature.'

Which is why I called up the O'Meara house. I needed to know. When one of the kids answered I asked to speak to their dad. They went to get him, but by the time he'd gotten to the phone I'd already hung up. Now that I knew he was at home I drove over.

The plows had been out so I made good time. The O'Mearas had added more Christmas decorations since I'd been out there last, and a white wire Santa and sleigh piled high with presents and dotted with lights stood on the snow in front of their house, welcoming me in.

I parked the Taurus in the driveway, rang the bell, and waited. A man dressed in a jogging suit, tee-shirt, and shearling slippers answered the door.

'Mitch O'Meara?' I said.

I couldn't believe what I was seeing. Judging from the expression on his face neither could he. It was the guy from the Spindle. The one who'd almost hit me with his car the other night. And that's when I remembered something Patricia Benton had said about Enterprise Industries owning bars. I'd bet anything O'Meara owned the Spindle. He was the guy Paul had just been talking about.

'What the hell are you doing here?' he demanded when he saw me.

He looked scared. I could feel the heat of the house pouring out into the frigid night air.

'Who is it, dear?' I heard his wife calling out from somewhere in back of him.

'It's someone selling candy,' he called back. 'I'll take care of it.' Despite the temperature he stepped outside and closed the door behind him. 'What the hell do you want?' he said.

I said the first thing that came into my head. 'I bet your wife doesn't know you're going out with Bea Sanchez, does she?'

His fear turned to anger. 'You were following me that night, weren't you?' he demanded.

242

'Yes, I was.'

'Bea hired you, didn't she?'

'Very good.'

'I can't believe you have the nerve to show up here at my house like this.'

I tried for casual. 'Bea thought the point she wanted to make would be more effective this way.'

I could see O'Meara's jaw muscles working. Plus he was clenching and unclenching his fists. 'Tell me,' he said, taking a step towards me. 'Was it for you, that thousand dollars I gave you?'

I didn't answer.

'Bea doesn't know about it, right? You were working some private scam.'

'From the looks of it you can afford it.'

'It's not about what I can afford.' O'Meara practically spit the words at me. 'I don't want you showing up at my house again. Ever.'

I shrugged. 'That depends on you.'

'Well, go back and tell Bea I'm not giving her anything. Tell her that if I see you or her around the premises I'm going to have both of you arrested for extortion.'

'I'm not sure she's going to agree,' I told him just to keep things going.

He gritted his teeth. 'She's just as greedy as her goddamned son was.'

'Yeah. Between the laptop and the dog and the IPod and the electronic chess set, he must have set you back a pretty penny.'

I saw an expression of fear cross O'Meara's face. And that's when I knew. I'd gotten it all wrong. Totally and completely wrong. I'd thought Mitch was treating Freddy well so he could get into Bea Sanchez's pants, but it was the reverse. He was treating Bea Sanchez well so he could into Freddy's pants. I could feel a knot forming in my stomach and working its way up to my throat.

Freddy's conduct. His going out to the Spindle. He'd been doing it to get back at Mitch. Those promises he'd told everyone about. They'd been real. Mitch had filled his head with them and then he hadn't followed through.

Going to the Spindle and making a spectacle of himself was how Freddy got even. How he warned Mitch. Look what I can do, he was saying. When they wouldn't let him in the Spindle anymore he did other things, and one of those other things had gotten him killed.

I began to say something when the door swung open. His wife was standing there. She was dressed in pink. Pink suede pants, pink angora zip-up sweatshirt. She looked beautiful.

'Why, Robin,' she said. 'Come in.' Her brow furrowed ever so slightly. 'You're selling candy?'

'Robin?' Mitch said to his wife. 'You know her?'

Constance did that exaggerated sigh wives do to show that their husbands don't listen to them. 'This is the woman I told you about. The one that wanted to talk about Labradoodles.'

'Really,' Mitch said. He turned around and looked at me. He'd recovered himself in the interval. His glance was cold and speculative. I repressed a shiver.

Constance beckoned to me. 'Come in,' she said. 'Have some Christmas cookies and a cup of hot cider.'

'Another time,' I told her. I think I managed a smile. I'm not sure. 'I was just dropping something off for Mitch.'

And I turned and walked away, when what I wanted to do was grab Constance and her son, put them in my car, and drive away. I felt so bad for her. I wondered if she had any inkling of what her husband's other side was like. I didn't think so. How could she? She'd never stay if she did.

As the door was closing, I heard Constance saying to her husband, 'How do you know her?'

I would have loved to hear what Mitch was going to say to that.

Thirty-Nine

A s I drove down East Genesee Street I kept on thinking about what O'Meara had said about Bea being as greedy as her son. It was the way he'd said it that told me he'd killed Freddy. But try telling that to the DA. All I had were suppositions and connections. No. Short of a confession, Mitch O'Meara was going to skate and Jose was going to go down for two murders.

And then there was me. He knew I knew what he'd done. He'd already killed two people. Why not a third? But maybe I was being paranoid. I probably was. It's not as if I had any proof, and he knew that. In a way, I almost wished he would make a move on me. Then I could call the cops on him. I was thinking how satisfying that would be as I pulled into my driveway.

After the lights on the O'Mearas' house, mine looked drab. I got out of my car and studied the front of my house for a moment. I'd seen decorative lights in the form of Chinese lanterns in a catalog. They'd look nice wound around the banister and the front porch pillars. Even though I really couldn't afford it, I decided to get them as I peeked in my garage. It appeared that George had been true to his word. He had taken his stuff. One thing off the list.

I went inside my house, fed Zsa Zsa and the cat, poured myself a shot of Johnny Black, went into the living room, and turned on the TV. But I couldn't sit still. The more I thought about O'Meara the angrier I became.

And then I realized that Freddy probably wasn't the first boy O'Meara had tried this with. There had probably been others. But finding them, let alone getting them to talk, would

245

be a major problem. I tapped my fingers on the sofa's armrest. Maybe O'Meara was into other things as well, things like porn. I reached for the phone and dialed Shamus's number.

'Ian,' I said when he picked up.

'What?' He had to raise his voice to be heard over the sound of Merle Haggard.

'You know the guy that runs Dolls, don't you?'

Dolls was a strip club, but the real money maker was the adult book store that was housed in the club's basement. It catered to gay men and those straight men who were interested in seeing how the other side of the world lived, as well as your average pedophile. Or at least that's what Calli said.

'Yeah,' Ian replied. 'I do.'

'Do you think I could speak to him? I have a question I'd like to ask him.'

'Why do you need me for that?'

'Because he won't speak to me on his own. As you well know.'

'Pet shop folding? Going into the porno business instead?'

'I wish.' And I explained the situation.

Ian whistled. 'Okay. Hold on. Let me see what I can do.' He called me back fifteen minutes later. 'Howie says he'll meet with you in half an hour at Blue's.' Blue's was a diner tucked away off Erie Boulevard. 'He'll be waiting up in front.'

I hung up, fed Zsa Zsa and James each a treat, and turned the TV onto the nature channel for them, told them to guard the house, and left. I got to Blue's about five minutes early, but Howie was already there.

'Howie.' He stood up as I approached. 'Howie Kaplan.' He put out his hand and we shook.

Howie Kaplan was one of those guys who you would pass on the street and never give a glance to. He was on the slight side, maybe 5'5" tall, slightly balding, with an aquiline nose, brown eyes, and a small mouth. He'd already hung his jacket up on the pegs by the far wall and I could see that he was wearing a blue Oxford button down shirt, a wool vest, and a pair of khaki pants. If you'd asked me what he did, I'd have guessed a college professor or a psychologist.

246

'I know,' Howie said as we followed the waitress to a booth. 'Everyone expects some big guy with lots of chest hair and gold chains.'

I laughed as the waitress handed us our menus. Then she came back with cups and a coffee pot.

'Coffee?' she asked.

Both Howie and I said, 'Please,' simultaneously.

He ordered a hamburger with fries and I got a piece of apple pie. 'And warm it up,' I told the waitress. I knew the pie wasn't going to be very good, but I wanted something sweet.

'You want a scoop of vanilla ice cream on it?'

'Sure,' I said. What is it they say about you only live once?

'So,' Howie said after the waitress had left. 'What do you want to know?'

'Mitch O'Meara.'

Howie ripped open up a pack of sugar, put it in his coffee and stirred. 'What about him?'

'You know him?'

'He owns the building Dolls is in.'

I should have guessed. I took a sip of my coffee. It was hot enough to burn my tongue. 'The Spindle too?'

'Yeah.' Howie made a face. 'He's a sack of shit.'

'That's a fairly strong statement.'

'I caught him coming on to the son of the guy who cleans my building for me.'

'Nice. What did you do?'

'Nothing. Nothing had happened. But I've heard stuff. Gossip.'

'Like what?'

'Like he likes Hispanic kids.'

I thought of Freddy. 'You think it's true?'

'My cleaning guy is Hispanic. So is his kid.'

'Wonderful,' I said as another connection hit me. Juan Sanchez. Juan Sanchez had worked for O'Meara's company as a janitor. I wondered if Sanchez had ever taken Freddy to work with him? I wondered if that's how O'Meara had caught sight of him.

'It's not a nice world out there,' Howie observed. 'A lot of wackos. And I should know,' he added, 'because in my business you get to see them all.'

'I'm sure you do.'

A minute later the waitress arrived with our food. It turned out that Howie had a hyacinth macaw, so we spent the rest of the meal discussing the care, feeding, and entertaining of parrots.

'You know,' Howie said as I finished my pie, 'I shouldn't tell you this.'

'But you're going to.' I swirled the last of the pie crust around in the remaining ice cream and put it in my mouth. The pie had been better than I thought it would be.

'Yes, I am.' Howie picked up a French fry, dipped it into the pool of ketchup he'd made on the side of his plate and ate it. 'Someone should do something about this guy.'

I wanted to say, 'Why haven't you?' But I shut up and listened.

'You have a computer?' Howie asked me.

I nodded.

'You hooked up to the Internet.'

'I've got a cable modem.'

'Good. Check out Twinks Unlimited.'

I went home and did just that.

Twinks Unlimited turned out to be a pedophile site. I felt vaguely nauseous as I scrolled through it. Most of the kids were preteen, although a few were older. I found Freddy in the older section. He looked so vulnerable lying there, posed like some sort of doll. Down at the bottom of the screen were the prices you could pay if you wanted to acquire his picture as well as the web address to contact.

Why did I think that one way or another the address was going to be traceable to Mitch O'Meara?

I called Ian up and told him what I'd come up with.

'Check it out,' I told him.

'I can't,' he said. 'My hard disk crashed yesterday.'

'Then come over here and take a look.'

'I'm running a business in case you've forgotten.'

'I meant after you close. Please,' I said. 'Come and take a look.'

He agreed.

Ian must have closed early, because he was knocking on my door at a quarter to two. 'Slow night,' he explained.

I motioned towards his jacket. 'You want to give me that so I can hang it up?'

'It's okay. I'll keep it on. Now what is it you want me to see?'

I took him into the office and showed him.

'That's disgusting,' he said as he browsed through the pictures. 'Howie Kaplan told you about this?'

I nodded. 'Guess he just got tired of O'Meara. I give these to the DA and Mitch O'Meara goes down.'

'This still doesn't connect him to the two murders,' Ian pointed out.

'How could it not? And even if by some remote possibility it doesn't, he'd still be in a lot of trouble. This would be a hard one to talk your way out of. No one is going to look the other way on this. Killing two hood rats is one thing. This is another.'

'If it's his website.'

'I don't think Howie would have told me if it wasn't.'

'I can check and make sure,' Ian said.

'How?'

'I have a friend in the business.' And Ian got his cell out and walked into the other room. He came back a moment later. 'I should know by tomorrow morning.' He looked at what was on my screen. He studied it for a long time. Finally he said, 'I think I'd like to speak to this guy.'

'Let's just give this to the DA.'

'After I talk to him.'

'If you kill him Jose will get tagged with those murders.'

Ian gave me an amused look. 'What kind of person do you think I am?'

'A person capable of a lot of different things.'

'I'm just going to clarify some issues.'

'Can I come?'

'No.'

'Why not?'

'Because I don't want you there.'

At which point Ian turned around and walked out of the house. I didn't follow him. I didn't argue with him. As far as I was concerned O'Meara deserved whatever he got. He'd turned Freddy into a crack whore before he'd killed him. He'd killed Tony. Jose was on the run. Three people's lives had been destroyed by this man. No. More. Because I hadn't counted in Freddy's mother and Tony's family and Mitch's wife and children.

But things are never that simple.

Forty

I could feel my blood pounding in my forehead. My hands were gripping the wheel so tightly they hurt as I followed O'Meara's car. It was 2:30 in the morning and the sky was moonless. There was no overhead lighting on the road we were on, but the snow on either side provided some light to see by so I had to stay well back of O'Meara. Even though I didn't have my lights on I didn't want him to spot me in his rearview mirror as he went to meet Ian.

Somewhere around one o'clock sanity had returned and I'd realized that it would be better to let the DA's office handle this. But by then it was too late, so I'd decided to do the next best thing. I'd decided to play guardian angel to Mitch O'Meara.

The idea made me want to throw up. Like I said, whatever he got he had coming. But I cared about what happened to Jose and Ian. I didn't want Ian arrested and I didn't want Jose to shoulder the weight of O'Meara's crimes. I believed Ian when he'd said he had no intention of killing O'Meara, but accidents happen. People lose control. Press too hard on the wrong spot in the wrong way and someone can die.

Not that Ian was going to thank me for this. Far from it. I was trying to work out what I was going to say to him when I saw something moving across the road out of the corner of my eye. I tried to brake but it was too late. The next thing I knew a deer was bounding over my car. The deer kept going, but I spun out and the Taurus slid off the road into the snow. When I looked around the deer was gone. So was O'Meara's car.

Damn deer. As I lit a cigarette I realized my hands were shaking. I took a puff and got out to survey the damage. The Taurus's hood was dented in pretty well, but the major problem was the front end of my car was buried in the snow. I was completely off the road. It was going to take more than a little bit of shoveling to get the Taurus out. It was going to take someone to pull it out, and the only person I could think of to do that at this hour of the night, unfortunately, was Ian.

Basically I was screwed whichever way I went. That being the case I figured I might as well go ahead and try and find O'Meara. I was pretty sure I knew where he was going. If I was right, the place wasn't that far from here. Maybe a mile, maybe a little bit more. And if I was wrong I could hike back to the car and call Ian and try to think of a really good story to explain why I was out here at 2:30 in the morning.

I took my backpack and flashlight out of the front seat. I put on the wool hat I keep in the car for emergencies, after which I put up the hood on my parka and zipped it up till only my nose and my eyes showed. I started walking, careful to keep to the side of the road. Not that I needed to; it took me a little over twenty minutes to reach the quarry and during that time not a single car passed by me.

I almost missed the sign for the quarry, a small placard with an arrow with the name of the place hand-lettered above it. Fortunately I didn't because by now my toes had begun to burn from the cold. The road to the quarry had been plowed, so it was fairly easy going.

251

I ducked under the fence and skirted a tractor and a crane. They looked prehistoric in the dark. The quarry was huge, comprising several acres, and it suddenly occurred to me that finding Ian and O'Meara was going to present a problem. I didn't see any cars and the only noise I heard was the sound of my own footsteps as they crunched on the layer of ice that had formed on top of the snow.

I was beginning to think that I'd made a mistake, when I felt myself being shoved to the ground. I landed face first in the snow. Before I could get my breath back to yell someone had grabbed me by the back of my jacket, yanked me up, and pulled the zipper of my parka down. I smelled tobacco and hot cocoa.

'I might have known,' Ian said, letting me go. I brushed the snow out of my eyes. 'Always pushing in where you have no business going.'

'I think you're wrong,' I pointed out as I cleaned the snow out of my ears and shook it out of the inside of my jacket.

'Then why didn't you call the DA?'

'Because by the time I decided it was too late.'

'Bummer,' Ian said. 'Where's your car?'

I told Ian about the deer.

'So on top of everything else you want me to pull you out?'

'Something like that.'

Ian shook his head. 'How did you figure where we'd be?'

'Once I thought about it I figured that as soon as you heard from your friend you'd call O'Meara and arrange for a meeting after the bar closed.'

'Very logical.'

'I think so. I parked my car near O'Meara's house and waited to see if he came out. He did. So I followed him. Simple.'

'Why didn't you follow me?' Ian asked. 'It would have been easier.'

'Because you're too paranoid and you would have been checking behind you the whole way.' My eyes swept the space in back of Ian. 'Where is O'Meara?'

'Robin, go home,' Ian said.

'I see him,' I said.

O'Meara was leaning against a rock. The rock was sheltered from the wind, because there wasn't much snow on it. Once I got closer I could see that O'Meara's arms were duct-taped to his sides. His legs were bound together as well.

'What did you say to make him come?' I asked Ian.

'I told him I'd found the pictures of Freddy and I wanted money or I was going to the cops with them.'

And naturally O'Meara had responded. He couldn't afford not to.

'Who is that?' I pointed to the figure that had just come out from behind the rock.

'That's Terry,' Ian said quietly. 'I figured he had a right to be here.'

'It isn't too late to call the cops,' I said.

'And what? Have them arrest us for kidnapping?' Ian said. 'No. I don't think so. I didn't want you here. That was for your sake, not mine. But you came anyway. Fine. Now you're not leaving till it's over, understand?'

I nodded.

'Good. You keep out of my way and let Terry and me do what we have to do and I'll let you alone. But you start anything, anything at all, and I'll duct-tape you up. Are we clear on that?'

'Like crystal.'

'And don't think I won't,' Ian warned. 'Because I will.'

'I know you will.'

As I drew nearer I could hear O'Meara saying, 'I didn't do anything. You're crazy. I don't know what you're talking about.'

'You do, too,' Terry yelled in his face. I could hear the catch in his voice. He was crying while he was talking. 'You do, too, you fuckin' piece of shit.'

'I swear I don't.'

'Then why did you come out here?'

'I didn't take those photographs,' O'Meara explained. He was the voice of reason. 'Someone else did. I just wanted to clear up the misunderstanding.'

'But you didn't go to the cops and you brought your gun,' Ian said.

'Of course I brought my gun,' O'Meara replied. He could have been talking to a slightly dim-witted company employee. 'You would have done the same thing in my position.'

'I'd never be in your position,' Ian told him.

If Terry was crying, Ian was calm and almost disinterested. Somehow that was scarier. I watched Ian and Terry exchange looks. I felt slightly light headed and oddly detached. As if I was watching something unfold on a movie screen.

'Are you sure you don't want to tell us what happened to Freddy and Tony?' Ian said to O'Meara.

'Nothing happened,' O'Meara cried.

Ian nodded and Terry went around the rock and came back with something in his hand. He gave it to Ian, who took it and showed it to O'Meara.

'This,' he said, 'is a stick of dynamite. It doesn't have a real long fuse. Sixty seconds to be exact. I'm going to duct-tape it in your mouth and light the fuse if you don't start talking. What do you think?'

'I think you won't do it,' O'Meara said.

'Really?' Ian said. 'Let's see, shall we?' And he took the stick of dynamite, jammed it in O'Meara's mouth, and wrapped duct tape around it. Then he slapped O'Meara on the upper shoulder. 'Still think I'm kidding?' And he took out his cigarette lighter. My stomach jumped. 'What do you say?' Ian asked. 'Want to talk? No? I think I actually prefer this.' And he lit the fuse.

O'Meara started making moaning noises. Ian went up and ripped the duct tape off his mouth. O'Meara spit the dynamite out.

'Well?' Ian said.

'Please,' O'Meara sobbed. 'Please.' Steam from where O'Meara had peed rose off the ground.

Ian scooped the stick of dynamite up and used the tips of his fingers to extinguish the flame. O'Meara was still sobbing.

'You'd better start talking,' Ian told him. 'Because I can relight the fuse, only this time I won't put it out again. In fact, there won't be time.'

'I will, I will.'

As he started babbling, I noticed Ian reaching his hand inside the breast pocket of his flannel shirt. Then I stopped watching him and started watching O'Meara.

Everything came pouring out of him. The first time he'd seen Freddy. How his cousin had brought him to work. How he'd said hello to him. How he'd found out whose son he was. How he'd maneuvered Freddy's mother into letting him spend time with her son. How he'd introduced him to crack. 'To loosen him up,' he said.

Ian put a hand out to restrain Terry then. I don't think O'Meara even noticed.

He went on about how he'd given Freddy the dog and the laptop and the electronic chess set and how he'd tried to be a good influence on Freddy, but Freddy had just kept wanting more.

'He was never satisfied,' O'Meara said.

It seems that Freddy wanted to go to Syracuse University, he wanted to record a CD, and he just couldn't or wouldn't understand that those things weren't in O'Meara's power to give him. So he'd started acting out. Doing things like going to the Spindle when he knew O'Meara was going to be there and giving blow jobs in the bathroom. And when O'Meara threw him out of there, he told him he was going to talk to his wife.

'I couldn't have that,' O'Meara said. 'I just couldn't.'

I thought about O'Meara's home. About his wife. About how gracious she'd been, how pretty she was. I thought about his son and his dog and I could understand why O'Meara felt the way he did.

His life with Freddy intruding onto his other life was unthinkable. So he'd done the only thing he could. He'd set up a meeting with Freddy in one of the abandoned houses he was rehabbing and shot him. He hadn't expected Jose to be tagged for the killing. He even felt bad about it, but what was he going to do? It wasn't as if he could go and confess or anything.

He was just breathing a sigh of relief, thinking that he'd gotten out from under everything, when he heard from Tony Shepard. Freddy had talked to Tony. It wasn't like he'd said what they'd been doing, but he had told him about the dog and the recording contract. Worse yet, Tony had the phony recording contract O'Meara had given Freddy.

'What could I do?' O'Meara blubbered.

What he did do was arrange to meet Tony outside the building Jose was staying in and shoot him. O'Meara's reasoning was that as long as Jose was being tagged for one hit, he might as well take the heat on two. Then O'Meara had called in an anonymous tip about a body; but it was too late. Jose had already moved Tony by the time the police arrived. Moved him and disappeared. So the Ni Mo guy found him instead.

'Satisfied?' Ian said to Terry when O'Meara had stopped talking.

Terry nodded. I don't think he trusted himself to speak.

'Fine.' At which point Ian reached into the breast pocket of his flannel shirt again and pressed something. I was about to ask him what he was doing when he went over and stuck his finger up high on O'Meara's shoulder and pressed.

O'Meara screamed. 'My arm,' he cried as he staggered and fell sideways.

Ian jerked him up. 'I'll do worse if you don't shut up. Terry's going to take you to the PSB. And then,' Ian continued, 'you're going to go in and tell the nice policeman at the desk that you wish to confess to a double homicide, and then you're going to tell the people at the DA's office exactly what you told us.'

O'Meara nodded his head.

'And just to make sure you do, just to make sure that you don't get to the DA's office and change your mind and say that we coerced a confession out of you and you want us arrested, I have this.'

256

Ian reached over and pulled what looked like a piece of duct tape off O'Meara's jacket collar and held it up for him to see. 'This is a microphone. Nice, huh? I slapped it on your jacket right after I put the dynamite in your mouth. Everything is recorded. This recorder is something Freddy sold me. Sold it to me for a buck at the bar. Guess it's kind of ironic.' Ian poked O'Meara in the shoulder. O'Meara screamed. 'You don't think it's ironic?' Ian asked him.

'I do,' O'Meara whispered. 'I do.'

'Good man.' And Ian patted O'Meara on the back hard enough to make him lurch forward. 'I'm sending this recording along with you. Now I know you think that when you get into that room with the police you'll say the confession was coerced. That would be a bad idea, because if you walk out of there I'll be waiting and before I kill you I will hurt you very, very badly. And even if you think you can protect yourself from me, you can't.'

O'Meara nodded and Ian turned to Terry. 'You think you can drive him downtown on your own?'

'You're not coming?'

Ian gestured in my direction. 'I need to pull her car out of the snow bank. I'll call Mike and tell him you're on your way. He'll be waiting for you.'

'I could kill him now,' Terry said.

'No,' O'Meara shouted.

'You could,' Ian agreed ignoring O'Meara. 'But then I'll never get my money back from Jose and I'll have to come after you for it and that would annoy me.'

'Good point,' Terry said.

I watched as he and Ian loaded O'Meara into the car. It took a while because O'Meara had to hop, and given that the ground was slippery he kept falling.

'Terry will cut the tape off when they get there,' Ian told me.

'Did you mean what you said?' I asked.

'Some people deserve to be thrown out with the trash.'

'I think he's going to recant.'

'We'll see,' Ian said. 'And there are the pictures. He can't expain those away.'

257

'That's true.' I watched my breath smoke up the air as we walked towards Ian's car. 'Were you really going to blow him up?' I asked. I found my voice was high. I was having trouble speaking.

'No,' Ian said. 'If a stick of dynamite like that went off it has a blast radius of at least 800 yards. Terry and I and you would have been dead. I just wanted to scare him.'

'But what if you hadn't gotten the fuse out in time?'

Ian shrugged. 'The stick was a dummy. I took the blasting powder out.'

'Really?'

'Of course.'

I studied Ian's face. I couldn't tell if he was lying or not. In fact, I had a very strong suspicion that the stick of dynamite was live, but it made me feel better to think that it wasn't, and that was the view I was going to hold on to.

We didn't say anything to each other on the ride back to my car, probably because there was nothing else to say.

Forty-One

Three weeks later things had pretty much returned to normal. Christmas had come and gone. Noah's Ark was still standing. I'd even turned a profit. Not a big one, but big enough to stave the tax collector from the door for a little longer. And I hadn't heard anything from George, which was a good thing. I wasn't even interested in how he and Natalie were doing.

When I wasn't working at Shamus's I was spending most of my free time repainting my house. Manuel and Bethany were helping. For free. I think it was Manuel's way of apologizing for what he'd gotten mixed up in, though I don't know for sure, because we'd never discussed it. Ian and I hadn't talked about the night in the quarry, either. I guess neither of us wanted to.

As it turned out, I'd been wrong about O'Meara. He hadn't recanted his confession. In fact, he'd stood by it and waved a jury trial. He was due to be sentenced in another month.

'He won't live very long on the inside,' Ian had predicted when I'd read the article to him. 'People like that never do.'

'They'll put him in solitary confinement,' I'd said.

'There are ways around that,' Ian said.

I tapped a little fish food into the tank I'd set up at Shamus's as I thought about O'Meara. When the DA had announced the arrest, the media frenzy had been comparable to the way the fish in the tank were feeding. There'd been an article in the front section above the fold every day for a solid week.

They'd interviewed his wife, his sister, and his mother, as well as his high school and college friends. The only people they hadn't talked to were his son and his dog. Now the story was off the front page, but I was sure it would be back on when he was sentenced.

As I looked around the bar I realized that the people in there now were the same people who'd been there when Freddy had wandered in off the street. There were Shelley and Bill, Carmen, Hector, and Stuttering Sam, as well as two kids, Mohawks by the look of them, who were shooting pool.

Shelley grabbed my arm as I put down another PBR. She pointed to Bill. 'He's my honey, you know.'

'I know, Shelley,' I replied.

'And you can't have him.' She patted Bill's shoulder with her free hand.

Bill lifted up his can of PBR and took a swallow.

'How's the cleaning coming along?' I asked him.

'It's coming,' he said.

In what universe, I thought. But at least they still had a roof over their heads. Enterprise Industries had turned out to be on the verge of bankruptcy and O'Meara's indictment had pushed the company over the edge. They were out of the housing market, which meant Shelley's house had reverted to her son.

I was sure it was only a matter of time before the son found another buyer for it or the city cited it and tore the place down, but for now they were safe.

'Buy you a beer?' Hector asked me as I went by him.

'No thanks.'

'Leave her alone,' Carmen snapped at him. 'She's working, for cripes' sake.'

'That doesn't mean I can't buy her something,' Hector said.

He was trying hard to speak each word clearly, the way that people that are really drunk do. He'd come in drunk and he hadn't gotten any better in the two hours since he'd been here. But I had his car keys and I'd already deducted money for a cab so I figured I was covered in that department.

Bill lifted his head. 'Let him buy you a hot cocoa,' he said to me.

I agreed because it was easier.

'You know,' Bill said to me as I collected the money from Hector, 'you did good. She did,' he said to Carmen. 'I told you she could figure things out.'

'What did she figure out?' Carmen cried. 'That O'Hara turned himself in. It wasn't because of anything she did.'

Bill corrected her. 'It's not O'Hara. It's O'Meara.'

Carmen shrugged. 'All those Mick names sound the same to me.'

'Let's keep it nice in here,' I told everyone.

'What Carmen said, it's not true, is it, Robin?' Bill asked me.

'Yeah. I'm afraid it is.'

'Someone just turns himself in like that?' Bill said. 'Doesn't make any sense to me.'

'He had a guilty conscience,' Hector said. 'Some people have them.'

Bill glared at him. 'You saying I don't have a conscience?'

'He w ... w ... was ... wasn't ... saying that at all,' Stuttering Sam said.

'Yes, he was,' Bill said. His voice rose.

The two kids shooting pool stopped and waited to see what

was going to happen. I moved in and I told everyone to calm down.

'I don't know,' Hector said. 'On the news, O'Meara's wife said something about going somewhere else.'

'Of course, she wants to get out of town,' Bill said. 'Too many bad memories. Look at Bea Sanchez. She's gone. Moved out to California last week.'

'The whole thing was her fault,' Shelley said.

'No it wasn't,' Carmen said. 'How do you get that?'

'Because she liked the O'Deara guy. It said it in the paper.'

'O'Meara,' Bill said.

'Who cares,' Carmen told him before turning back to Shelley. 'Everything with you is sex,' she told her.

Shelley started off her bar stool. 'That's better than not getting any, you dried up old—'

'Excuse me,' I said. Both women looked at me. I took a dollar from the register. 'Anyone want to listen to some music?'

Sometimes distraction works.

Carmen and Bill and Hector were busy arguing about which song to pick when Jose and Manuel walked through the door. Jose was carrying a cake box while Manuel was holding a plastic bag from P&C, the grocery store a couple of blocks away.

'What are you guys doing?' I asked as Jose put the box on the bar.

'Celebrating your birthday,' he said as he lifted the top of the box up. He'd gotten a new piercing on his eyebrow to replace the one he'd taken out. 'But I can't stay long. Frieda's in the back of my car.'

I peered in the box. There was a layer cake with vanilla frosting and pink roses and an inscription that read *Happy Birthday, Mary.*'

'They got the name wrong,' Jose explained.

'It's fine,' I reassured him. And somehow it was.

Manuel opened the bag he was carrying and set out knife and forks and plates and napkins. 'We were going to get you a card, but by the time we remembered the store had closed,' he told me. 'But we got you a present.'

261

'Yeah,' Jose said. 'We set it up for you at your house. You're going to like it. It's got a seventeen-inch screen, a CD burner, DVD player. Everything.'

Only the best in hot merchandise for me. But that was okay, too. I leaned across the bar and hugged Manuel and Jose.

'Thanks guys,' I told them. 'I can't tell you how much this means to me.'

'No,' Jose said. 'We should be thanking you.'

Then Manuel put thirteen candles in the cake and lit them and everyone sang 'Happy Birthday' to me, after which we got down to eating the cake. Zsa Zsa got the first piece. I washed mine down with two mugs of hot cocoa and everyone else washed theirs down with beer.

People had pretty much gone by the time Ian came back to Shamus's to help me close.

'What's with the cake,' he asked.

I was wrapping it up to take it home. I explained.

'Today's your birthday?' he said.

'No. It was three weeks ago.'

Ian did a calculation in his head. 'Hey, that's the same date as mine.'

I reached for the box. 'Here,' I told him. 'Have a piece of cake.'

He took a bite and spit it out 'This is stale,' he said.

'I know.'

'So why are you taking it home?'

'Have you ever heard the saying, "It's the thought that counts"?'

'Not where I come from,' Ian said as he threw his piece into the garbage.

Then he turned off the TV. He cleared out the register and stuffed the money in his inside pocket while I cleaned out the tip jar. I'd made fifty bucks tonight. Not great, but not horrible either. Ian was going to give me Saturday nights soon, in which case I'd make considerably more.

'Everything worked out okay,' Ian said as we walked out the door.

I knew he was referring to the quarry.

'Except for O'Meara's family,' I said.

'Well, as good as it could given the circumstances,' he amended as he locked the outside door. 'I knew it would.'

'Did you, really?' I asked.

Ian laughed. 'No.'

'Neither did I,' I said. 'Did you ever get your money?'

Ian shook his head. 'Probably won't either,' he said.

'Probably not,' I agreed.

'Hey, shit happens,' he said.

'I know. And then you move on.'

'Exactly,' Ian replied as we headed towards our cars.